The Outside Man

A Novel

by

Ran Register

Book Design - Jim Henry
Editing - Ann Henry
Cover Concept - Lauren M Duffy

ISBN 978-1-7347476-4-5

Library of Congress Control Number: 2020923417

Moonglade Publishing
303B Anastasia Blvd
St. Augustine FL 32080

The Outside Man

Babble

We like to think of ourselves as unique, special, and we are, but our collective circumstances and experiences most often parallel one another. How we deal with them is what individualizes us. I'm afraid I haven't dealt responsibly with some of them for a long time. I'm good at rationalizing my wants and desires to suit me, and though I think I'm a good person, I have serious flaws. Then, we all do, I rationalize once more.

I guess my main flaw has most often centered on the male-female thing, that being much of what life is about. I blame it on Mom. She was strong and independent, one of the first married moms to work full time, probably the curse and model of my future attractions.

I had my first sexual experience at an early age after watching the movie *Solomon and Sheba*, starring Gina Lollobrigida. I awoke in the middle of the night sweaty, wet, and confused. Frightened by acutely pleasurable sensations and images, I was to discover my erogenous shaping had only just begun.

The next day I noticed our young German housekeeper in a different way, and that night I was off again, waking several times amid erotic images of Ursula interspersed with Gina's Sheba. I had moved on, in a sense. Ursula was real.

I'm only attracted to women possessed of some special femininity, a combination of qualities, I suppose, pulling me with some force of their essence. A strong, independent woman, one who doesn't need me, is powerfully attractive. Or is it just safe for me? Perhaps, on some level, those particular qualities make me less responsible for my actions. I don't know. I'm exploring it and thankful that I've only come across a few whom I've felt drawn to in such a compelling way.

Where to begin is hard. I'd like to say it was my dick's fault, and it had been enough times in the past for that to be a reasonable assumption, but this time there was more. It was the heart all the way. The outside man can't hide from himself any longer.

I've only heard that term once, years ago, upon overhearing a nanny tell her friend that she herself would go crazy if it weren't for her outside man.

"That no 'count scuse for a husban', Rufus, don't do nothin' 'cept drink all day and pass out at night. A girl needs more than that from her man. Now Dillon, my outside man . . . honey, he's my private joy. He makes the world right for me. Oh, what that man do to me! He makes life bearable, he do. And then, God bless him, he goes away."

She wrapped her arms around her friend's shoulders, and they laughed as they held onto each other, unaware of me sitting nearby.

I recall that conversation now, many years later, as I recognize that I have become "the outside man."

Somehow, this is all a beginning, realization attempting to understand self, conscience pushing reality, a growing need to accept responsibility and move on as a better person. Penance has never been my strength. Reflection has always led to rationalization, ultimately justifying my behavior. But something is going on now. Maybe maturity weakens denial, giving way to accountability and more. I don't know. It started so long ago. Now I'm dealing with it.

Damn, I hate responsibility.

Chapter One

She came into view on my right as I flowed through the exercise, punching left to right, right to left, on and on with some kicks thrown in. Every time we moved to the right, she was there. My neck started to hurt as I punched left, glanced right. She commanded my attention, this weird vision of a slender wrestler. My mind fought with it. A skinny sumo wrestler wasn't making sense. But that's what caught my eye and propelled *sumo* into my head: a tall woman with oddly cut short hair. She possessed great poise and grace as she moved through the exercise.

Finally, my brain made the connection. It was the knots. The two knots of short hair, held one above the other with rubber bands. That's what triggered the sumo impression.

My neck ached as I focused on the exercise. I appreciated the attractive vision, making it easier for me to get through the grueling cardio routine. My breath came hard, but I knew I'd settle in shortly and move to automatic as I progressed through the early stages of the kickboxing workout. I hadn't been to one in a couple of months though I'd maintained my cardio regimen by jogging at every opportunity. What a wonderful alternative this was to the monotony of placing one foot in front of the other, again and again.

I jogged when there was no other choice for cardio, but I'd never achieved the high of jogging, never had a so-called "endorphin kick." Runners rave about the kick. Hell, I don't even know what an endorphin is. I just know when I've had a good cardio workout, and I need it since crummy heart problems run in my family. After all, I'm not getting any younger as my brother pointed out to me a couple of years ago. We were struggling with some heavy equipment when I reminded him I wasn't thirty anymore. "You're not fifty anymore, Michael." Younger brothers! They have a way. Maybe I dunked him in the river too many times growing up.

The gym was new, built since my last visit to Jacksonville a few months before. It was also closer by several miles, so more convenient than the one I'd previously used. It was going to be a good fit for the time I anticipated being in town, probably several months.

The short, busty instructor was about twenty years my junior. Probably more as she couldn't be more than thirty. She kept up a good pace, pumping us up with motivational dialogue like my drill sergeant back in the Army. Her voice took on a quality belying her petite size.

"Move it! Get those legs up! Kick, punch, kick, punch. That's it. Left, right . . ." on and on. It was inspiring to release myself to her guidance. The music, the instructor, and the sumo—damn, she was graceful— all were invigorating, and I was getting a great workout.

As the class ended, I gathered my towel amid the "thanks," "good class," and like comments offered to the instructor and moved towards the door. I got there just behind Sumo. She headed through the door, holding it for the next person. Me.

"*Domo,*" I said in the only Japanese I knew other than *sumo.*

"What?" She turned towards me. God, her eyes were gorgeous. Her femininity coupled with her sweating body and

4

labored breathing jolted me for a moment. Something about her connected with something in me. It happens, but not often.

"Thank you, sumo lady," I said with a short bow and low, deep voice. Heat rushed to my face at my poor imitation of Japanese-English.

She laughed as she turned away and strode down the hall. *Nice butt.*

I stepped aside, wiping the sweat from my face, allowing the crowd behind me to pass. Last was the instructor. She hadn't even broken a good sweat. *We'll see how you do at fifty-three.*

As I drove away from the gym, I took inventory, examining myself, Michael Donovan. Just a quick look because I know me. But it was good for me to reflect. And upon reflection, I realized I'd been away too long and needed to get back to Stephanie.

I'm a regular guy, attracted to other women, but I normally wouldn't act on it as I'd just done with Sumo. Stephanie's my girlfriend, my complicated relationship. Complicated, but she deserved better than me flirting with Sumo.

Guilt reached out and grabbed me, and crazily, Stephanie suddenly looked back at me from the windshield. Her smile, surrounded by auburn hair, taunted me as her blue eyes sent promises to my core. I blinked, and the swollen nipple she offered was too real. I closed my eyes and shook her out of my head, afraid of what another blink might bring.

I concentrated on the road as I approached the Publix supermarket. Too crowded. The parking lot was packed. I decided I only needed ice, and I could get that at a convenience store rather than face the crowd. I generally did my shopping when everyone else was at work. Today was bad planning on my part, but I still needed to eat.

A free meal with Nan and Nathan, friends of mine who lived on my property in Jacksonville, flashed through my mind, immediately followed by the realization that they were still visiting family out of town. But Hannah might be around. Hannah is not only a friend and a neighbor, but more. The four of us are close, more like an extended family. Hannah works for me and also does the books for Nathan's lawn business. She and Nan are best friends.

I called Hannah. One beep and she was on, always the efficient one.

"Hey, Michael. What's up?"

"I just remembered Nathan and Nan are gone for a few more days."

"So, you're hungry? Is that why you're calling me?"

I could see her, eyebrows arched, head bent to the phone, and her foot, the one on the good leg, tapping. She could be so superior, so knowing at times it could be irritating. But not to me. I had to laugh. "Yes, but I wanted to ask you out for dinner."

"Can't wait till the last minute to ask a girl out. I already have plans. You're gonna have to order a pizza or something."

"Okay, how about tomorrow night?"

"I'm not cooking," she said. "Pick me up at seven." The phone clicked as she hung up.

I gassed up at the convenience store, threw a bag of ice in the cooler in the back of my old pickup, and headed home. It was a short drive, and as I approached, I hit the remote. Twin gates glided inwards, opening smoothly. I never tired of the view and coasted through the gates, slowing even more before stopping. I sat a minute looking over the property. The click of the gates latching behind me brought me back, and I eased forward to park.

Home was a fully equipped thirty-foot travel trailer. It sat on a three-acre piece of land on the St. Johns River in the San Marco district of Jacksonville, Florida. The property included a two-story house and a detached three-car garage with a large two-bedroom apartment above. The main house was a 1950s version of an old southern mansion. Complete with four bedrooms, three bathrooms, wrap-around porches, and a circular driveway, it was nestled under a magnificent canopy of oak branches. A wall of bamboo shielded the property from the street and neighbors. Four hundred feet of waterfront provided a panoramic view of Jacksonville's developing skyline, and the remnants of an old dock jutted a hundred feet out from the shore to deeper water.

I took the ice out of the truck's cooler to another one sitting outside the trailer. If I ever took the one cooler out of the truck, I'd probably get distracted and never put it back. I grabbed a beer out of the fridge and put a couple more into the ice-filled cooler. Pizza sounded good. I called and ordered one. Then I walked the grounds towards the house, thinking of how fortunate I was to have discovered it.

I'd bought the property a few years before when the place and neighborhood were run down, property values were low, and everything else was high. I loved it immediately and could easily afford it, but I didn't like to pay top dollar for anything. Goes back to my upbringing, I guess. Mom taught us how to shop early on. Of course, name brands or clothing styles were not her main concern. I'd learned to find my own balance over the years to manage best value, especially on the simple needs, like buying my clothes post season at good stores to get the best price. It's nice to be rich, but core values still prevail. Best value doesn't mean cheap.

With a significant down payment, the squabbling heirs

were willing to hold the mortgage at a low interest rate with a balloon note for the remainder due in twelve years. They had inherited the property with an existing mortgage and done little to maintain it over the years. Their inheritance was costing them monthly and my offer was reasonable, presenting them with a way out of the mortgage payments plus a monthly income.

Nathan and Nan had agreed to look after the place for me in exchange for rent-free use of the apartment above the garage. I think I got the better end of the deal, or at least Nan insists so. Nathan has a landscaping business and has worked wonders on the property. It was a good deal for both of us if you didn't count Nan's opinion, which, unfortunately, I did. She tried to renegotiate every time I saw them, but a deal's a deal. I had a stunning though raw property that needed care, and Nathan was able to live closer to the upscale clientele he served. He had put the grounds in good order but not so manicured that you would think you were in a resort or subdivision. I could always close my eyes and feel it, the solitude and privacy, the natural simplicity of it just a few blocks from the bustle of the city. The whisper and creak of bamboo swaying in the breeze and the splendor of the St. Johns River provided an ever-changing mural of life.

With the exception of the main house and dock, the place was immaculate. The house was livable if you were willing to camp out in a mass of tools, stacks of lumber, wallboard, wiring, and such. I wasn't. Hence, the trailer.

The house itself was a work in progress, still in need of significant renovation and upgrading. The dock needed replacing. The pilings that provided the base for everything were probably rotten below the waterline. I made a mental note to check them at low tide or ask Nathan to do so. The faded gray walking boards were either missing, rotted, or hardened to the point of turning up on end, curling back on the few remaining nails.

I'd spent considerable effort working on the place, especially over long weekends during the past three years. It wasn't enough, not if I was going to fetch the price I had in mind, which was why I was here—that and not having anything else to do. Jacksonville was growing, cleaning itself up, and attracting new industry. Property values were skyrocketing, and interest rates were low. Even so, I loved the place. So why sell it?

The honk of a horn brought me back. Pizza, and I didn't have to share it. The only upside to eating alone.

***

The next morning I was up early and worked steadily throughout the day. Even so, I added more to my to-do list than I accomplished. Late afternoon, after a shower, I fished a beer out of the cooler. I needed more ice.

There was still an hour before I was to pick up Hannah. I wondered where we should go. Being Friday, I might be able to talk her into a drink at one of the clubs later. No, by the time we had dinner, Hannah would be ready to go home. Maybe Saturday or Sunday I could get in some live music.

It was relaxing there under the awning of the trailer as I sank back into a lawn chair, thinking of Hannah and all that had passed over the years. We'd had some bumps, but we'd come through, and now we were part of a complex, extended family. Somehow, I attracted odd relationships, characters and circumstances that entered my life and became a part of it.

In the first few months after buying the property, I

moved into the travel trailer and routinely jogged the streets in the area. Most of the houses were well maintained while others were a bit rundown and some abandoned for the new, self-contained developments with water parks, golf courses, jogging paths, and the like. This was an old neighborhood but one of great location and value, especially if the downtown area were ever to come back. Location and the water, plus the sense of privacy and remoteness, were why I bought the property. I fell in love with it the first time I saw it.

One day, I saw an elderly woman with a cane sitting amidst serious overgrowth and a couple of bags of mulch. Behind her, a house, definitely in need of new paint and more, hovered like a forgotten lover, adored and admired then cast aside when age had moved in. In the detached one-car garage, I caught a glimpse of what looked like an old white Karmann Ghia. Whatever it was, it was in need of a lot more than cleaning and paint.

I slowed down and called out good morning to her as I passed.

"Good morning," she replied. "I'll trade you. You take care of this yard, and I'll throw away this cane and jog."

"Okay, you're on. Give me the cane," I said, turning around and walking back to her. She was sitting on the ground, surrounded by the growing pile of weeds she'd scraped up in preparation for the mulch.

She cocked her head, looking at me a moment before speaking. "You were supposed to say something like, no way would you trade places with me."

I smiled. "I know, but I had to call your bluff. Let me help and you can keep the cane."

"Don't need any help, thank you," she said. "Go on with your run."

I started to jog off but turned back to her instead. "No way are you getting this done by yourself. I suppose you're going to restore that old car, too. How much do you want for it?"

I'd known too many proud people who felt pitied if you were simply nice sometimes.

She laughed. "You're an insensitive young man with no respect for the elderly."

"Yeah, I know, but you're slacking. I hate yard work, but I'd do it for the car. Think about it." I jogged backwards a few yards, smiling at the look on her face before turning and picking up the pace.

My cheeks rose with a smile as I remembered that look. It was good to be back. I looked forward to seeing Hannah.

The phone rang, and I almost fell out of the lawn chair as I scrambled to get up. I ignored the steady ringing and jumped into the truck. It had to be Hannah. Good thing she only lived around the corner. I pulled into her driveway to find her leaning against her cane. She didn't look happy. Such an actress. She loved to make me squirm, so I did. A little.

"Sorry, Hannah, I got distracted," I said, looking at my watch. *Five minutes? May as well have been half an hour.*

"Guess you forgot how I hate this truck, too," she said.

No, she hadn't changed much. I got her situated and buckled in before I said anything.

"Hungry?" I asked as I got behind the wheel.

"Starving since you're so late."

I sneaked a peek at her. She was smiling.

"So, what distracted you?" she asked.

"You. You and me, actually, and how we first met."

She laughed. "You were the rudest person I'd ever met."

I ignored the comment and pulled into the Thai restaurant she loved.

I had asked Nathan about her. Turned out she was too stubborn and proud to accept his help. "Why are you interested in that old woman?" he asked.

Just seemed odd, I told him. Most of the run-down places in the neighborhood were abandoned, yet there she was, working in a yard she had no hope of restoring by herself.

"So, what are we going to do?" Nathan asked with that great grin of his.

Hannah knew the menu well and ordered some kind of meat-and-vegetable plate with curry. Double asterisks annotated her selection. I took a drink of ice water and held out my glass for more.

Hannah looked over at me with a smile.

I smiled back. "I'll have the same thing," I said, "without any asterisks." This wasn't my first time here with Hannah.

"Wimp," she said. "It's not that hot. You could have gone with one asterisk."

"I'm fine, but I'll have that ice water now," I told the waitress.

It was a nice evening, and we had a good time catching up even though we talked weekly when I wasn't there.

"Powder room," she said, and I stood up and pulled back her chair.

"I'd order some ice cream for dessert," I told her, "but it would probably melt before you get back."

I got the haughty look, the one straight down her nose as she looked into my eyes.

"Sherbet," she said but couldn't leave it there, of course, and so ended with a muttered "butthead" as she turned towards the ladies' room.

I maintained my dignity with a smile. No, she hadn't changed much since our first meeting, and I loved it.

I had surprised myself at our second meeting. I'd found her there on the scraggly lawn the next morning, slowly toiling away with little progress.

She must have heard me coming. As soon as I got close, she looked up. "You're a little late this morning. I've already put in an hour on the yard."

I slowed to a walk, stopping as I came back to her. "It looks like you're getting farther behind to me."

She gave me the evil eye I expected and a sharp tongue. "I'm getting there. This yard will be right by spring."

"Right," I said, "and I'm the Mad Hatter come to lead you through Wonderland, Alice."

She looked at me, started to say something, and laughed instead.

"You are a total butt. No way am I taking your crap every day unless we're introduced."

"Okay. I'm Michael Donovan, and you're ruining my chance at some big bucks."

"I'm Hannah . . . Hannah Eilson. I know the estate you jog out of, rich boy, and I know that black man who works for you has been dropping off supplies, hinting that I should get this lawn in shape."

"Is that what you think? That doesn't sound like Nathan. Don't you remember his coming by and offering his services free?"

"Sure, I do. I'm not senile, and I don't need your pity sending him down here with some token offer to do my lawn."

I could barely hold in a belly laugh. The grin escaped. "Wait till Nathan hears you think he's my boy or something."

"I didn't . . . I didn't say he was your boy," she stammered. "I respect that man. He's hard working and quite a gentleman.

"Unlike you," she added, squinting up at me with that

pointy chin out as the early sun rose a little higher behind her.

I began to laugh. "Well, you're right about that. He is a hard-working man and a gentleman. Guess you think I'm some softy rich boy who never did anything but jog and look good, huh?"

"Kind of full of yourself, aren't you? And you are soft. You can go to the gym and jog in those fancy . . ." Looking at my old sneakers and raggedy shirt and shorts brought her up short.

Oh, she got to me that day, but I was having fun.

"Look at this," I said, holding out my hands. "These are calluses." I pointed to each one as I spoke. "I work for a living, and Nathan doesn't work for me at all. He and I have an arrangement. We trade goods and services to our mutual benefit."

"Slow down, boy. My head is spinning. I appreciate the calluses, but tell me why I have to know all this."

"Hey, I'm thirsty. Do you have some water?"

"Water? You want water now?"

"Yes, please. And by the way, what can you do?"

"What do you mean, what can I do? That's none of your business." She took a breath as I waited. "The water hose is over there. I don't have any bottled water for guests."

I wandered over to the hose. "You know, what did you do for a living? Any skills?"

"You little shit. Yes, I have skills. I did accounting both before and after my husband died. Now, if I work, they want to take away some of my social security."

I finished taking a drink from the hose and started to shut it off again.

"Don't shut it off yet. I need a drink," she said.

I hesitated, and she smiled. "Going to tell me to get it myself, are you?"

I couldn't hold back the laugh. "Well, not now. It wouldn't be a surprise."

I brought her the hose, fantasizing as I did. Reaching for it, she hesitated.

"I can see it in your eyes," she said. "You want to spray me with it. You want to, don't you?"

What could I say? "Yeah."

"Least you're honest about it." She took a drink and made a face. "Bottled water would be better than drinking from this hose."

"So, do you mind being a little criminal about it?"

"About what?"

"About working under the table."

"For you?" she asked.

"Hell, no. For Nathan. I'm too soft to keep a mean old woman busy."

"I really have become a mean old woman, haven't I?" She laughed and kept laughing until I joined in.

"Actually, what I have in mind," I told her, "now that I know something about you, is for you to do some things for Nathan and me. Now, about that old car . . ."

"No."

Flickering shadows from countless restaurant candles took on new life, bringing me back to the present as I became aware of Hannah standing over me.

"That's an awfully naughty smile, Michael. What's going on?" she asked.

I stood and took her arm, pacing myself with her imperial exit as she maneuvered with her cane towards the restaurant door.

"I was just remembering the time you begged me for a job," I told her.

Thankfully, my arm was longer than her cane, but it still got my shin. Good thing she didn't notice I forgot the sherbet.

Chapter Two

A few days later, while in the grocery store, I noticed several people dressed up and realized it was Sunday. No doubt they were shopping on the way home from church. At one point in my life, I spent a lot of time going to church, then different churches, but that's another story. Now, I just go for things like weddings and funerals or for special penance. Special penances alone could require a couple of times a month. I save them up.

Other shoppers looked at me and nodded politely as though I had a light over my head that confused them with a halo. No halo, I just didn't fit. I was out of place. I wore faded khaki shorts, a pullover with a couple of holes in it, and boat shoes that cried out for the trash can. I was comfortable, wearing my normal attire when it was too warm for jeans. My many years of grown-up clothes and shoes were behind me. Only one tie left, just enough for those special occasions, and I wasn't sure where it was. Come on, I'm rich. I love the theater, symphonies, ballet, and all the other great stuff like rock and roll concerts, so yes, I had the dress-up wear, too. It just happened to be in Orlando with my other life.

I'd taken a slow run this morning after a late night out exploring the Jacksonville nightlife and listening to live music. After a shower, I decided I'd better get some groceries. I'd be in town a while and knew better than to wear out my welcome with Nan when she came home.

I had felt good, enjoying the day, loose and carefree, in a playful mood. Then, I'd found myself in the middle of the after-church crowd, the only sinner who hadn't done proper penance that morning. I had to laugh at myself even as I resolved not to be in this situation again. Go early or dress better. *Go to church* rang like bells in my head. Mom had chosen to speak to me in odd ways since she passed.

Pushing my cart down the entry aisle, I started making a mental list of what to buy, knowing I'd forget something. Of course, I would. The grocery list I'd written while drinking coffee this morning was still sitting in the trailer. I was just happy to be on a roll though. Nothing could mess up this day.

Still, I was admonishing myself for not bringing the list when I noticed a lovely woman to my right. At least she was lovely from the back. I stopped flailing the one arm I was berating myself with and took another glance just as she reached for something on a shelf. She wore a simple green dress and strappy low heels with no hose. *Yes!* Her tawny hair fell slightly above shoulder length, allowing me to admire her bare shoulders, and gave the appearance of being in between cuts. I took pleasure in the sight of her slender, fit body, especially her petite but shapely derrière and long legs.

Mind you, this was all in a glance, an instant of time. I'm always amazed at the gift of a glance we males have been equipped, its power. But what really caught my eye was her overall presence, her poise. She possessed a simple elegance. That's what drew my attention.

The glint of something on her left hand saved me. It had to be a wedding ring. Damn. *Run, Grasshopper, run,* screamed through my head. I quickened my pace, moving down the aisle. I loaded the cart mindlessly while fantasizing I had redeemed myself by this virtuous shutting out of a married woman.

I was too preoccupied with women for some reason, but I was also amused. I really was having fun. I'd been in a rut lately, between things for a while. Now I had purpose again, and I was on an adventure of sorts. Though I had been to Jacksonville many times and spent many weekends and a few weeks there each year, this was different. I was there to finish the project that kept me coming back. I was living there now, starting a new life, at least until I completed the project. But for now—new town, new things to see and do, new energy. There was a definite reason to get up in the morning. Yes, I was reenergized, having fun with life.

As I moved quickly down the aisles, I almost bumped into an elderly woman rounding a corner.

"Whoops. Excuse me," I said, backing up to let her by and smiling at her.

Elderly, yes, and plump, but not overly so. Attractive, actually. She smiled at me.

"Good thing I'm still quick," she said. "What's the hurry?"

I laughed as I moved alongside her.

"I'm starving," I said. "Never come shopping hungry. I need to get out of here and get something to eat. Are you hungry? I'll buy lunch."

She giggled. "I would, but my husband will be home for lunch soon."

"Just my luck. I was hoping you'd want to go a little crazy."

She laughed as I grinned my wicked grin at her. "Rain check," she said, raising an eyebrow and still laughing.

"Of course," I said as she continued on her way.

That was harmless fun. I like fun days.

As I knelt before the canned seafood, studying two cans of tuna—one in spring water, the other packed in oil—I became aware of someone else waiting. There were two feet with pink toes peeking out from strappy heels. Damn nice toes, too. Another fetish to overcome, I thought, smiling to myself and really enjoying this day. I glanced up, excusing myself as I stood to move out of the way. I looked again. It was Green Dress.

"Sorry, I didn't mean to block you," I said, looking into amused green eyes, eyes set in sharp angular features that enveloped and drew me in, lips and cheeks presenting just a hint of a smile. I wanted to taste those lips, feel those hips and small breasts against me. Damn it, I wanted to devour this woman.

"Spring water," she said, reaching beyond me to take a couple of cans. "It's better for you."

I stupidly looked at the two cans I held and mumbled thanks as she continued down the aisle.

I looked after her. "Excuse me, do I know you?"

Looking back over her shoulder with a smile, she said, "Sumo."

It took a moment to sink in. "No way," I said.

She stopped and came back with her hand extended. "Melanie. We had a kickboxing class together."

The name startled me, but I snapped out of it. I hadn't heard that name in a long time. "I'm Michael," I managed to say, remembering her outstretched hand just as she dropped it.

"Are you okay, Michael?" She looked at me oddly.

"Yes, yes. I'm fine, Melanie." The name sounded even stranger coming from my lips. It had been a long time. "Your name surprised me, and you floored me with the sumo thing." I felt like an idiot.

"Yeah, I didn't get the sumo thing at all," she said. There was that wicked little hint of a smile again as she stood there.

I couldn't disappear, and it seemed as if she was waiting for an answer. The moment felt like forever, but finally my mouth moved again. "The knots you had in your hair, they somehow reminded me of a sumo wrestler. It was the hair."

She closed her eyes for a moment. "I can see that, I guess. I'm trying to keep it out of my face while it grows out. Sumo knots, huh? I like it."

A real smile this time, spontaneous and uninhibited. Ahh . . . and those eyes. But there was more. That simple elegance was powerful, and the nose, a little large and just a bit crooked to the left. Perfect. *Run, Michael, run!* My feet were rooted, so I just stood there dumbly.

"And my name?" she asked. "Why would my name surprise you?"

"No reason, really, just a name from the past."

She nodded as her eyes took in my comfortable clothes. I mumbled something about not realizing it was Sunday.

"Oh, do you normally dress up on Sunday?" she asked in an amused voice, still eyeing my shirt.

"Well, yes. I mean if I'm going to church, I do."

"What church do you go to?"

"Different ones. I change denominations whenever I go, but I haven't been in a while."

What's wrong? Why is she eyeing my shirt that way? Then it hit me, and I backed away. "You want to stick a finger in one of these holes and rip it, don't you?"

She laughed, bringing her hands to her face, and leaned forward at the waist. Her head tilted as she looked up at me with those enchanting eyes, her cheeks glowing and alive. "Yes! How did you know that's exactly the impulse I had?"

I laughed with her. "Because you're a woman. My mother used to do that to my clothes if I wasn't careful." I put my hands up in self-defense. "Just stand back and leave my shirt alone. I worked hard to get it this comfortable."

She backed away from the mock reproach, eyes wide, head shaking, "Okay, okay, but sooner or later, it's going to happen. One of us girls will get it."

Then she stepped forward, holding out her hand again. I took it this time and felt the charge of it. Why is beyond me, but her touch pulsed with some urgency, an uplifting, exciting energy.

"It's good to meet you, Michael. Thanks for a good start to my afternoon. See you in class," she said, and walked away.

I pushed my cart in the other direction but couldn't help looking back. God was good with temptation but stingy with reward for me. Just once, you'd think I'd find the right woman without one of those rings or something taunting me. I liked her, enjoyed talking to her. It was more than the cute rump. Whatever happened to fate, soul mates, destiny, and all that other romantic stuff?

I was surprised Green Dress and Sumo were the same woman, but I was shocked by her name. The name belonged to a fabrication, a slowly evolved manifestation of a girlfriend invented to cover my illicit affair with a married woman. Melanie, the name synonymous with my ideal woman, was now taking on a physical presence. She had a face, a body, a being I was attracted to. I couldn't have wished for anyone lovelier to have that name. My mythical Melanie, now personified in this woman. This *married* woman.

I was past the "all the good ones are taken" stage. I was resentful that this woman I found so desirable was beyond the realm of maybe being the right one. I brushed it off. She was probably a hollow, high-maintenance pain-in-the-butt in private.

No, that wasn't fair. None of that fit. I remembered the dress. On her it was elegant, a simple A-line dress like my mother used to make. No, I'm sure she was a sweet woman, an excellent mother, and her husband was a lucky man. I hoped he appreciated her.

"So long, Mel," I whispered, determined to stay away from her. I couldn't get her out of my mind that easily though. I felt I'd been there before somehow.

As I walked away, an image of Stephanie overtook me. Her poise, her presence, her simple elegance. I blinked and saw Melanie. My mind was a camera, clicking between alternating pictures of them as I walked.

I should have seen it before. My lover, Stephanie, and the real Melanie were so alike in the way they carried themselves, the way they presented themselves with such ease, innocently unaware of the effect they had. It came naturally to them, but their grace appeared as aloofness to many. A few minutes in conversation would prove otherwise and leave an entirely different impression.

Stephanie was my complicated relationship and more—the reason my pretend Melanie was born in a moment of needed discretion to an innocent inquiry. Sure, Stephanie could have been the right one, but like I said, it was complicated. She was married.

Now I'd met the real Melanie, and she personified the made-up one. I didn't want to live in the shadow of make-believe anymore.

***

That evening, Nathan turned his Lexus into the open gates of the property and eased past the wall of bamboo to park next to my pickup truck. I could see a great smile grow upon his face as I jogged over. His eyes disappeared for a moment with the rise of his cheeks. I glanced left to see the same look of welcome on Nan's face.

"Well, look who's here," she called out when Nathan opened his car door. "Looking for a decent meal, or did you actually come up to work?"

Nathan just laughed. "Don't be so glad to see him. He might stay longer."

I ignored him and scrambled around to open Nan's door.

"Missed me, didn't you?" Nathan reached a hand out to me as I took the tall, slender woman in my arms. I took it and pulled him to us. Nathan was a big, broad-shouldered, older man, well over six feet tall and still slim.

"I am not cooking," Nan retorted, snuggling into me.

"You must be psychic. I'm just putting the finishing touches on some spaghetti and a large salad. Plenty for us all, but it'll cost you later."

"No doubt it'll cost me five times over, but I'm famished, and Nathan won't stop for anything but gas on the road. Any meatballs, or is this one of your vegetarian meals?"

I laughed. "Yes, real meatballs. You know I'm a pagan meat eater."

"Real meatballs? Let's eat!"

Nan led us both towards the picnic table outside the travel trailer. I got them settled and brought out a pitcher of iced tea, glasses, and tableware. Dish by dish, I piled it on: a large bowl of salad, a heaping mound of pasta, a bowl of meatballs and sauce, and a platter of garlic bread.

"Whoa," Nan said. "You could feed an army with all this food."

"You know spaghetti is better the second time around.

We'll do it again tomorrow night," I said. "Besides, Hannah was supposed to come over, but she remembered she had one of those woman-thing meetings or something."

Nan's eyes locked on me. "Some 'woman-thing' meeting?"

Uh oh. I glanced over at her as I chewed. She shook her head. I looked to Nathan for support, but he ignored me and kept eating. "What?" I said.

"Nothing, Michael," Nan said. "It's just always interesting listening to you." She smiled at me. *Uh oh. Here it comes.* "These are some fine meatballs. How did you do it?"

"Thanks, Nan. It was easy. Once I found your freezer key, I just warmed them up."

Nathan burst into laughter, watching for Nan's reaction.

I laughed, too, but Nan simply said, "I thought so."

We ate and discussed their weeklong trip to see the grandkids and what I'd been up to. Then we unloaded the car, and Nan said her goodnight, leaving Nathan and me alone.

"Didn't you have a Cadillac last time I was here?" I asked Nathan.

He sputtered, "You . . . you know I've had that Lexus for years now, Michael, and it didn't cost near what your little Porsche did."

"Touchy about those high-end cars, aren't we, and what Porsche? All I have is that old truck. Besides, I was just checking. You keep that car in such good shape, I never know."

"Darn right, I keep it in good shape. It's got to last Nan and me another ten years at least. Now, let's open up that last garage door and take a look at the Porsche."

"Okay, okay, it's there, but it's an old one, remember. Much older than the Lexus."

"And worth ten times more," Nathan grumbled.

***

For the next couple of days, I continued to survey the property, determining what needed doing, arranging for a carpenter, plumber, and electrician for when I needed help or more expertise to get the job done. As many skills as we all develop over the years, we still need the pros to bail us out more times than we like to admit. I could easily see myself getting overwhelmed as I had a tendency to go too deep into things.

Tuesday, I got down to planning how to bring the kitchen up to speed. It definitely needed new appliances; maybe upgrade the cabinets and lighting. After three hours, I'd sketched out a complete remodeling plan with a list of materials.

I was stunned at the magnitude of the work and potential expense I was taking on. Then I rationalized that the kitchen is a major selling area of a house and this would give prospective buyers a sense of potential. Besides, I like a functional kitchen. But no way would I redo the whole house. After all, I'd only come up from Orlando to paint the house, complete some minor repairs, and sell it. I had no intention of a whole-house renovation. Whoever bought it could do the rest themselves.

Some days, I attended an early morning or afternoon kickboxing class, varying my routine and getting some weight training in. I didn't see Mel, as I'd come to think of her, during those times, but the one class I'd had with her had been in the evening. She probably worked days.

Good, I didn't need any distractions. She just happened to bear the name that had come to represent my lifeline, my sanctuary, a place to go when needed to cover my relationship with Stephanie. Yet, at the time, my make-believe Melanie had become both real and necessary to me. But no longer. I didn't need a Melanie in my life anymore. I was away from the environment that had fostered that bit of smoke and mirrors.

I pictured the sumo lady, then put her out of my head and moved through my work. I had established six months as reasonable time to accomplish my goal and put the property on the market. Nathan and Nan knew of my plans, and Nathan kept insisting I'd change my mind.

When I asked why I'd do that, he just smiled and said, "We'll see."

Nan gave a little laugh and said, "You're going to put us poor folks on the street, Michael."

"Now what can I say to that, Nan? Why are you trying to make me feel bad? You know that poor-folk thing isn't going to work on me."

"I know, but a girl's got to use what she can." She laughed again. "Everything will work out. You'll see." Then she asked if I was coming to dinner that evening.

Nan is an excellent cook, and being a bachelor, I get the occasional invite to dinner. Or maybe, as Nan says, I tend to be around their place at the right time. I was becoming selfish, or maybe I'd always been so. But now, thinking about selling the place, I wondered for the first time what would happen to Nathan and Nan. I could really be oblivious of others at times. I knew they had come to love the place, and I did, too, so why was I looking to sell it? I didn't need the money, and if it weren't for Steph, I'd probably move here and bring the boat up.

Nan fished regularly from the shore, refusing to go out in Nathan's old johnboat even though he kept it in good shape on a trailer behind the garage. He and I generally took it out for a day at least once during my annual two weeks a year here or the odd long weekends I could get up, more when I stayed over, periodically catching bluegill, catfish, and trout, even netting some shrimp during the season.

Nathan was retired from the US Navy and drew a nice pension; plus, he was coming up on Social Security age, so they'd be all right financially. They'd already sent their two children through college, one of them becoming a successful accountant and the other a naval officer commanding a missile frigate out of Norfolk, Virginia.

There were grandkids, but day to day, it was just the two of them now and they were secure in life and each other. Nan and Nathan chose to live on the property because they loved it. Besides, it was convenient, and Nathan loved the work he was doing. He'd served his country for thirty years as a chief boatswain's mate aboard aircraft carriers. That translated into a lot of time at sea. I could understand he'd had enough of the sea and the harsh gray behemoth of a US warship to last a lifetime.

Nathan told me there was a simple, satisfying beauty in bringing order to something. He always laughed when he said, "When you cut grass, you can look back and see progress immediately."

It was more than that, much more than the beauty of the colors and order he brought to the world every day, and I could understand why he enjoyed what he did.

He employed several young people who loved working for him, all good kids, and some young adults as well. All of them were trying to move on in life, going to school, some taking courses at night, and all of them reliable. That said something about them and about Nathan. If they weren't in school, he would tell them to come back when they were and he'd have a place for them. Word got around. Nathan never lacked for employees, and he was making a difference in the world. The subtle influence, the impact Nathan was making on the lives he touched, was significant. I was aware of it and used his goodness and judgment whenever I could.

I'd been fortunate the day I talked to Nathan about buying the property, fortunate to have Nathan and Nan as friends. Life bound us. This was home, for them and for me. I wasn't ready to admit it, but they seemed to know.

Chapter Three

"*I* like martinis. I like them a lot."

I looked to my right, noticing Jigger for the first time since starting my jog on the treadmill. I'd been lost in thought and hadn't noticed her take the machine next to me.

She was an attractive woman, lovely in all ways. But she had that bright ring on her left hand. A ridiculous thought maybe, but important regarding my past. If I was attracted to a woman, I automatically looked for the ring. Really, I should just look first. Married women are taboo. Somehow, I had rationalized my involvement with Stephanie as different. It wasn't. I knew better. But no more! I tended to act differently around married women now.

Jigger and her husband owned a local bar, the watering hole I'd favored over the years. She seemed to be there at the infrequent times I stopped by. They named the bar Harvey's after a pink, or maybe it was a white, pooka, a benevolent but mischievous creature from Celtic mythology. Whatever its color, it was a giant but invisible—well, invisible to all but the Jimmy Stewart character—rabbit if I remember the movie correctly.

Harvey's was classy, a cocktail lounge with a roomy bar area and a small dance floor surrounded by tables. Well-dressed university students worked part time there serving light lunch and evening fare. A popular bar, you had to pick your nights and times if you wanted a quiet drink.

I was surprised I'd never met her husband. I didn't know Jigger well, but we'd talked a few times at the bar during my recent and earlier visits. I'm sure if her husband had been there, she would have introduced him.

I glanced at her as she walked briskly and stared straight ahead. With the best legs in the gym, she was attractive in an understated way, never appearing to wear makeup beyond a hint of crimson on her lips, even in her bar. Blond hair, cut just above her slim shoulders, curled softly around a pretty face. She always wore a sun visor in the gym. Kept her hair out of her face, I guess. She had one for each outfit, color coordinated. Today's color was green. All my life I've been taught green is good, the "go" color. All five feet and about four inches of her looked good. She had an odd gait to her walk that fascinated me. I was careful not to stare, but damn it, sometimes it was tough. Thankfully, her walk smoothed out as she picked up the pace. It was sensuous, and I'm convinced she was unaware of it.

I'd noticed her in the gym before, but our communication was generally along the lines of a nod. Now, *I like martinis.* Where in the hell did that come from? She stared straight ahead as she walked. Had she even been talking to me?

"How do you like them?" I asked. "On the rocks or straight up?"

"Straight up. Vodka ice cold. Right out of the freezer where I keep it," she said, smiling for the first time. "And now that I think about it, that's bad."

Intrigued, I slowed my machine to a walk, matching her speed. "Why is it bad?"

"Because it's next to the ice cream." She laughed as she glanced at me.

I was enjoying the conversation, growing comfortable with

her, amused. But now, the glance. Something about the glance made me nervous. I struggled with the ice cream—and the glance. Was it a shy look or provocative? Shy. It had to be.

Okay, she's married. I could be attracted to her and still respect that. "Get rid of the ice cream," I said.

She laughed and glanced at me again. "I did. I ate it."

Damn it, this was fun! I laughed with her. "Olives?"

"Yes, blue-cheese olives."

"I didn't know they had them with blue cheese."

She seemed coy, seldom looking at me. "They do at some of the gourmet shops. I love them."

"Vermouth?"

"Just vodka and the olives. That's all."

"I'm thankful for the olives, then."

"Me, too," she said, "they really make the drink."

"No, I mean the olives are the only thing that keeps you from being an alcoholic."

Laughing, she looked at me. "No, Michael, I'm not an alcoholic. I just like my martinis."

"Good. I was worried for a minute. I've never seen you take a drink. You're not drinking alone, are you?"

"I don't drink at the bar," she said. "Too much like drinking on the job, I guess. I have one at home—after work. Sometimes two."

"Then, how you drink it becomes even more important. It's very elegant, the martini. Like dragonflies. Simple, yet powerful and complex at the same time. How do you drink yours?"

"Just straight up with olives like I said." She giggled. "I really do like them."

"I mean, do you do them justice? Do you have your martinis while wearing flip-flops or bunny slippers? Or do you wear heels?"

"No heels, just slippers."

"You really need to try one with the heels," I said. "High ones. Maybe dangle one off your foot."

The glance, but this time her face glowed—red, and I could feel the heat of her. Had I embarrassed her? What the hell was I doing?

Enough! Jigger is married. Leave it alone. You're beginning to flirt with her, you idiot. Stop.

My mind wouldn't stop . . . It flirted with visions—Jigger drinking martinis in bunny slippers. Then heels. Jigger in slippers, her hair in curlers, wearing a tattered pink robe, smoking a cigarette. Not pretty.

Jigger in heels. Yeah, Jigger in heels. She wore a short black dress and long white gloves. A string of pearls hung from her delicate neck. She sat on one of the high stools at her bar. One leg draped over the other, a black, shiny, leather stiletto dangling from her toes, precariously so. I held my breath waiting for it to fall. It didn't. The vision held me. Then her foot moved to the music, fully accentuating the muscles of her thighs and calves. Damn! A large black orb of a ring and complementing bracelet adorned one glove. She was the perfect picture of elegance and poise. Except for the cigarette. I blinked, but it wouldn't go away. Damn it, I couldn't picture her without it. Maybe it was the martini. Maybe I couldn't imagine one without the other.

I brought my treadmill to a stop and turned towards her. "You don't smoke, do you?"

She slowed her machine. "No way. Never have."

"Good. Want to hear my theory about all this?"

She looked at me steadily now, seeming to enjoy the conversation. Her ease concerned me. No, *I* concerned me.

"Sure," she said, "let's hear it."

"Well, drinking a martini wearing bunny slippers makes it about the martini. With heels, it's about you, how you feel about yourself. Either way, when you go home tonight, put on those heels and have your husband make you a martini. Maybe light some candles. See how you like it."

She looked at me oddly, turned off the treadmill, and stepped to the floor. Smiling, but a bit misty-eyed, she turned back to me. "Thanks, Michael, I'll do that."

What happened? A moment ago, we were having a fun exchange.

"Promise to tell me how it goes," I said softly, baffled by the abrupt change.

She looked back and, with a brief nod, put her water bottle and towel in her gym bag. With a little wave of her hand, she walked away.

Something was wrong. Was it something I said? My mind fought to replay our conversation, but it wouldn't come. I guess I just didn't understand women.

I glanced over at her and smiled as she walked away. I didn't need to understand women. I liked them. Even loved some. That was enough.

But was it? I looked at her again and knew it was more than those lovely legs and bounce to her rump that held me. In some way, I was tied to her. It wasn't attraction that pulled me, it was . . . it was . . . damn it, it was concern. Concern for the odd twist our conversation had taken. What were her words all about? *I like martinis.* I felt I had failed her somehow.

So much more to life than casual acquaintance allowed. Normally, you just moved on. But sometimes, like now, doors opened. We'd always been casually friendly. But now, were we friends? I could go through that door and be a friend. Or not.

An important choice in life. Her sadness drew me.

I looked her way again. She had reached the sign-in desk.

Damn, I hated responsibility. I had to do something.
I needed her to be okay, wanted to be her friend, help take
away her sadness. What was it that brought her to me? Was I
making too much of this?

I didn't know, but something about her compelled me.
Something brought her to me. Life didn't just happen this way.
I wanted to share something with her. Stupid things came to
mind. How I loved peanut butter, had to have my sandwiches
cut diagonally, dumb stuff. And, besides, I hadn't asked her
about the white gloves.

I looked for her again and saw her going out the front door
as I stood helplessly on the treadmill. I had failed her.

Damn!

I resolved to go by Harvey's again soon.

***

As I was leaving the gym, I called Stephanie. I missed her,
and though we talked almost daily, I had already been away a
couple of weeks.

"When are you coming home?" she asked. "I miss you."

"It may be a few weeks. Maybe we could meet in Daytona
for a day or two. It's about halfway."

"Michael, you know it's not that easy. Why don't you come
down here and spend some time at your condo? You must have
things you need to do in Orlando, too. I can meet you about
four o'clock, any day."

I did have some things to do in Orlando. Mainly, get away
from local attractions. I realized that over the past year, my
relationship with Stephanie had taken a turn, but I had no

business being interested in Melanie or Jigger. The change was in me, evidenced by my growing awareness of other women. Even married women, damn it, and I had vowed never to go there again. I needed to see Steph, get my balance back.

"All right, can we try for the middle of the week? I'm set up to have workers here on weekends during their time off from their regular jobs."

She was quiet for a moment. "Come down Tuesday. We can have that evening together and I'll take off Wednesday."

"Hey, I like that. I need some quality us time."

She laughed, "Me, too."

Two years I'd been seeing Stephanie, two great years. I was happy with her, happy with the relationship. Unorthodox as it was, it worked. As long as she didn't spend too much time away and we were discreet. We were.

Stephanie is a vibrant woman, elegant and extremely sensuous to me. I remember the first time I saw her walking across a restaurant floor, gliding to the table next to mine where we were both attending a retirement function. We were introduced and ended up talking together for some time. She was a few years older than I was. I reflected on that later, wondering at the immediate attraction, the sexual pull I'd felt when we met. *Shouldn't I be drawn to young, ditzy, sexy things at my age?* I wondered at the time. Then I laughed at the thought and put her out of my mind but later ran into her again, and then again. I finally recognized that we were both arranging the opportunities and scared myself with the realization. Soon we were having frequent coffees together. At some point, we just happened.

Chapter Four

*F*riday night, around eight, I drove the truck to Orlando's, a small club on San Jose Boulevard that I'd discovered on previous visits. I knew things wouldn't heat up until later when the real partiers came out to play after their combat naps, but the happy-hour crowd should be long gone by now. I just wanted to have a couple of drinks and lose the week. Tomorrow was another workday; I still had to get up early and finish a few things. No late night tonight. I thought about hitting the gym in the morning but decided against it. I'd seen Mel in a class earlier in the week. She'd given me a smile and nod of recognition.

There was more of a crowd than I'd expected this early. I was able to find a place at the bar though and ordered a scotch and water. Gradually the music sifted through me, and soon I was lost to those around me. Oblivion. Such a wonderful place at times. Sometimes it was good to be unaware of—or at least unaffected by—politics, personality, and especially, bullshit. It had been a good week. I'd accomplished much and established a routine.

I was barely aware of the small band setting up. I was in the nowhere zone, or close to it, when I became aware of the abrupt shift in music. Somebody unplugged the jukebox. I looked up to find the band just starting to play. I ordered another drink, listening to the first few songs. They were good, '80s and '90s music with a little of today thrown in. The crowd responded, dancing and shedding the workweek, making new acquaintances or renewing the old, enjoying the atmosphere. I released myself to the music, chasing it with scotch, my body responding to both. I felt myself gently swaying to the moment, my mind wandering aimlessly, only dimly aware of my surroundings. I was just where I wanted to be, and then, from my left, a soft, soulful voice called, "Help." I fought it but finally turned to find the woman on my left declining a dance.

She turned toward me, smiling. "Help," she said softly again before turning back to the guy. Finally, it sank in, pulling me back to the moment, a place I didn't want to be. I stood and turned to her, "Honey, I'm sorry to tear you away from your friend, but you promised me the next slow dance."

"Oh, that's right. Please excuse us, Fred. I did promise my boyfriend. I'll see you later."

"I . . . I, ah . . . I thought you were married," he said.

We moved together through the crowd on the dance floor. I held her away from me and had my first real look at my new friend as we danced.

She smiled back at me. "I didn't know if you would respond or not. You seemed kind of tuned out."

"Just absorbed in the booze and music," I said. I took a moment to appreciate a very attractive face, surrounded by nicely styled long brown hair. Then we were forced closer together on the crowded dance floor.

"Well, it took you long enough to rescue me. Thank you if I didn't say so before."

I laughed, enjoying this diversion, the attraction. It was different from the magnetism of Sumo or Jigger. The attraction was more as a friend or acquaintance. "Somehow I think you'd have done all right," I said.

"Yes, but it was more interesting this way, and now I have

a new friend. I'm Valerie."

"Michael. I'm pleased to meet you, Valerie, even if you did spoil my mindless reverie. Are you married?"

"You talk funny, Michael. I like it." She released her left hand from my shoulder and showed me the rings. "Yes, I'm married, and I dance with Fred. Just dance." She emphasized with a look. "Sorry about the boyfriend remark."

"So, he's just an acquaintance that you dance with at times, but you're married to someone else."

I led her through a turn, and her eyes left mine as she nodded. "Yes."

Then she started laughing. Her eyes focused on me again. "I'm so sorry, Michael. You must think I'm a real tramp. Please don't think badly of me. Fred just wouldn't leave me alone. I'll tell him you're an old friend."

"So, he's just an acquaintance you see here occasionally?"

She looked at me oddly as I moved us into a turn. She was a good dancer. She started laughing again, uncontrollably this time. We stopped dancing in the middle of the floor, surrounded by people as her forehead bounced against my chest. I just stood there like an idiot and held her as couples danced around us, staring. I felt her tremble with the laugher as her hands squeezed my hand and shoulder, grasping me for support. After a moment, she gained control of herself, took a deep breath, and led me off the dance floor.

"I'm a ballroom dancer," she explained. "A lot of us meet here, including Fred. We're good entertainment for the early crowd, so the management gives us a couple of hours to practice."

I nodded. "I see. I just . . ."

"Oh, no," she said. "There's more. I have a great husband, and I'm a good wife. My husband insists he has two left feet, but he's very supportive of my dancing."

It could be the way of ballroom dancers or just part of her vibrant personality, but she ended this explanation by bending into a curtsy with an arm out for emphasis. "So, on Fridays he goes out with the boys and I come here."

Before I could speak, she looked over my shoulder and grabbed my hand. "Come on, quick! Fred's just leaving. I need to save his spot for my girlfriend."

Grabbing my hand, she led me back to the bar. I felt the large stone on her finger. It's funny how I've become so aware of such things over the years.

"Darn," she said when we arrived just too late to save the seat. "She'll be here shortly. I should have been watching." She looked up at me as she took her seat. "Let me buy you a drink for saving me."

"Thanks, but I've had enough for tonight and have a big day tomorrow. It was good to meet you, Valerie."

She turned in her seat and looked over the crowd towards the entrance. "Oh, can't you stay for just a bit? I wanted you to meet my friend. She's really great. You'll love her. Are you married, Michael?"

I laughed. "Are you trying to set me up?"

Her eyes went wide. "No, Michael, I'm trying to set my friend up. You seem like a nice guy. Time she met one."

I answered her playful expression with a firmer one of my own. "No, I'm not married. I can't stay, but if she's anything like you, I'm sure she's great. Maybe I'll see you again."

She reached up and hugged me. "Thank you. Please come back next Friday. I'd like to dance with you some more, and I do want you to meet my friend."

"Sounds like fun. Your husband is a lucky man."

I headed towards the door and stopped in at the men's

room. Coming out, I glanced back to where I'd left Valerie. A slim blonde was moving into my seat. *Nice.* Then Valerie was turning towards me, so I faced the door again and continued walking. Something familiar about the blonde though. My mind immediately leapt to a name—Mel. But it couldn't be. Too much coincidence. Suddenly, I was seeing this new Melanie everywhere.

I chuckled at the ridiculousness of it all. There must be hundreds of slim, blonde women in this town. As I walked to the truck, my mind continued down its crazy path. I needed to put the whole Melanie myth—and this woman I seemed to be obsessed with—behind me. There was no more need for Melanie. Stephanie and I were no longer in the same work environment, and we mostly stayed in Orlando together, away from all but the remotest possibility of running into others she knew. That time of my life was over.

No more need to play pretend for those around me, I thought. At least I wrote it off to that even though I accepted that man had been born to do a little penance ever since the apple thing. Perhaps this woman was my special penance personified, coming to me in the form of this lovely and oh-so-real Melanie. Yes, she could be a reminder of my having taken the wrong relationship path as my norm in the past.

I laughed to myself. I was getting too old to be taking more bites from that apple. But it wasn't a joking matter.

"No more," I said to the night as a deep and real need for absolution weighed heavily within me. "No more."

Chapter Five

I hadn't done any cardio in a couple of days, too busy with an electrician inspecting and planning some work. I decided to get back into my routine starting now. There was an early morning class that I could make. By early, I mean 9:00 a.m. I generally got to class a little early, the first time being an exception. This way I could do a few stretches and pick out a good spot. Not in the back though. I knew how important that place was for a beginner. So, I stationed myself to the far right, away from the entry door and about halfway down the invisible checkerboard arrangement.

The women strolled in, styled in the latest fashion, looking trim and fit and intent on staying that way. I said good morning to a few who occasionally attended the early evening classes. It was common to exchange small talk and loosen up before the instructor began the drill-sergeant barrage, commanding us all to follow her lead.

After I'd moved through a couple of warm-up exercises, she came in. Melanie! Late and trying that invisible thing, maneuvering to get to the only open position available, forward and to the right of me. She steadily made her way there. *Nooo*, screamed through my head. I needed this workout and couldn't take the distraction today. In that moment, I was determined to find another place to work out.

Arriving, she saw me and smiled with a slight nod of her

head, then immediately picked up the timing, executing the moves with grace and perfection. I concentrated on the work I planned to accomplish later in the day.

Lost in my thoughts, I'd missed the cue and was now out of sequence with the rest of the class. I figured only the beginners in the back would notice. I thought wrong. The instructor got into the space in front of me. It served as a notice to all that somebody needed extra direction. Me, one of the few males in the class. Mel looked back. *Great, now she knows I'm totally uncoordinated.*

I think the instructor was picking on me. I knew everyone in the class would notice now. But I recovered well, and to my relief, the instructor moved on. At least she was a nice distraction from Mel.

I had been in this instructor's class before. She was lovely, and she wasn't wearing a ring. She was attractive for sure, but I wasn't attracted to her.

When the class was over, I was ready for it to end. I was drenched in sweat, the front of my tank top imprinted with a damp silhouette of Mickey Mouse's head, ears and all. Some people see the Virgin Mary in a potato; I sweat Mickey Mouse on my shirts when I work out. That was definitely enough of a workout for me.

I slowly made my way to the door, giving everyone, including Mel, time to get out before me. She had to choose that class to go up and talk to the instructor. I moved to the door, letting it close behind me since I was the last one out.

"Ahhh, you only gentleman when convenient."

I turned to apologize and found Mel behind me. "Sorry, Mel, I thought I was the last one out."

"Mel? You don't remember my whole name? Or maybe I'm just one of the boys now." She said it again, her face scrunched up while one hand went to her hip. *"Mel?"*

I laughed at her tone and the terrible face she was making. "All right, Melanie. I apologize."

"It's okay," she said, laughing with me. "I kind of like it. A friend of mine calls me that all the time. I'm just feeling bitchy this morning. But please, I'd rather you call me Melanie."

My hands felt clammy. "Deal."

I tried not to stare at her slim figure, but it was difficult. My eyes shot to her left hand. Her eyes followed mine. She wasn't wearing her wedding ring again. Was it just a workout thing?

"I was surprised to see you. It's been a while," she said.

"I normally come in the early evening. How about you? Are you a soccer mom like the rest of the ladies, working out while the children are at school?"

Her laugh was deep and infectious. I was confused, watching her trying to catch her breath. What was so funny? All the while, Mickey Mouse continued to expand and dissolve on my shirt while my legs turned to rubber. This woman got to me.

Finally, she gained control of herself, looking at me with a great smile, shaking her head. "Flatterer, I'm beyond soccer mom years now, but I was one. Thanks for making my day, putting me in league with these young mothers."

I began to laugh. I hadn't even made the connection though I knew she was older than the majority of the group, in her forties I guessed. I'd made the statement in all innocence, and she knew it.

"I confess I was hoping you were closer to my age," I said. "I'm going for coffee. Will you join me?"

"No," she said. "I'm a married woman." Then she began to laugh again.

I just stood and watched until she looked at me with a sheepish smile on her face. "Sorry, I haven't let loose like this in a long time. It feels good. I needed that. Thanks."

We were quiet for a moment. Her eyes held me for what seemed like forever before she spoke again. "Actually, I was just going to ask if you'd like some coffee. Gail, our instructor, is going to meet me at Starbucks, so we'll be three then, all right?"

"You sure?" I asked.

"Yeahhh." She drug out the word. "See you there in a few minutes."

"Sounds good," I said as she turned to walk off.

I took a deep breath. Where the hell did that come from? *Would you join me for coffee?* he asks the married woman. Stupid, stupid, stupid, I berated myself. And don't read anything into her asking. She told you she's married. Besides, it's just coffee, and Gail will be there, too, so get a grip.

I collected my gym bag, deciding to shower later as it was hot out and I might get in some outside work at the house later. I was comfortable dressed this way but decided to take off the wet Mickey shirt, pulling on a dark T-shirt as I made my way to the parking lot.

As I threw my bag into the back of the pickup, I noticed Melanie getting into an Infinity. Nice ride.

When I arrived at the coffee shop, Melanie and Gail were standing at the register.

Melanie saw me as I approached. "Regular? Decaf? Latte?"

"Half-and-half, tall, black."

Her head cocked to the right, questioning. "Half-and-half?"

"Yes, regular and decaf, half of each."

"Oh, okay."

As she paid, I noticed she was wearing the rings again.

We took our coffees to an outside table and did the formal introductions, thanks to Melanie. I had enjoyed a few of Gail's classes before but had never really met her. Conversation was good, and I came away with a healthy appreciation for the two women although I was a little disturbed when I began to suspect Melanie might be subtly setting me up with Gail, playing the matchmaker. I was beginning to understand her inviting me to coffee. Gail was nice, but that wasn't where my interest lay.

It was Melanie, and I knew I shouldn't be there. I was playing a harmless game, exploring my attraction but accepting it was going nowhere. Hidden behind my sunglasses, I studied her face. Those eyes still compelled me, and again I noticed the slight drift of that angular nose to the left. It added depth to her eyes, and those lips painted a shade of lipstick a bit short of red beckoned me. Her two front teeth, one barely overlapping the other, suited her.

Her hair was down now, no more sumo, gently combed out and a little messy after the workout. Earrings—gold hoops, a pair of them—hung from two holes in each ear. Dimples, when she smiled, stood out in cheeks still flushed with exercise that further narrowed to a lovely chin. A little pointy maybe, but still lovely.

I was mesmerized and realized I had failed to keep up with the conversation only when Gail waved a hand in front of my face asking, "Is anyone home in there?"

Coming out of my stupor, I recovered with a smile. "Sorry, ladies, I just drifted off to a different place for a moment."

"Better than here?" Melanie questioned, her eyebrows arching.

She could be a provocative one.

"No," I said, "not even close. This is wonderful. I'm a lucky guy being here with two lovely ladies. I thank you both for putting up with me."

"Melanie was just saying how she saw you trying to seduce an old lady in the grocery store, said you were asking her out to lunch." I choked on my coffee for a moment. They both laughed as I felt the blood rush to my face in embarrassment.

I turned to Melanie. "You heard that?"

"I think she would have gone if I hadn't come around the corner."

"So, you saved her from me, did you?" I laughed as the scene played through my head once more, this time with Melanie behind me.

"She goes to my church. I was obligated," she said in mock seriousness.

"I knew she wouldn't go with me."

"What if she had?"

"Then I would have taken her to lunch and probably been shot by her husband."

They laughed, and I continued. "I was having a good day. Of course, you didn't see me almost run down the poor lady, did you?"

Small lines creased the skin around Melanie's eyes. "No, I just saw you leaning over your cart towards her, your body language, and words telling her you were interested."

"Hey, I was having fun, and she loved it."

"Oh, she did that. Probably let her husband know she was propositioned, too. Now he'll be looking for you."

"You're right. I'll have to change stores," I said with a serious face. They started laughing again.

We continued our conversation, and I learned that Gail and Melanie were nurses, Gail full time and Melanie part time, both nurse practitioners. Melanie was actually job-sharing, as she called it, whereby two or more people worked one full-time job. It made sense as she explained it.

Gail was a single parent, one child, and Melanie was married to a lawyer and had two children, one in college and the other living on his own trying out his wings before deciding what to do with his life. Then, of course, we talked about me.

"What about you, Michael? What do you do?" Melanie asked. "What brings you to Jacksonville?"

"I'm retired, so I just work out and hang around with the soccer moms when I'm not in grocery stores looking for old ladies to seduce."

We started laughing again before I got serious.

"Actually, I am retired and working on a property here to keep busy for a while. Then I'll figure out what happens next. Maybe go to Europe for a while or sail to the Caribbean."

"You're too young to be retired," Gail said. The look on her face told me she thought only the very old retired.

"Not that young." I laughed. "I've retired a couple of times actually."

"You're never too young to retire," Melanie joined in. "But twice now, that's different. What did you do?"

"I'm an engineer, retired from the government." That's the story I told everyone, and there was some truth in it. At various times, I had worked for government, but never long enough to retire.

"What about the second retirement?" asked Gail.

"Well, after retiring early from the government, I started a small laser-grading business for commercial property development. It became pretty successful, but I had other interests, so I sold it. And here I am."

"Wow, must be nice. It seems most people can't retire

until they're too old to enjoy it."

"Okay, enough of that," Melanie said. "Now that we know you're an old retired guy, you get to buy the coffee from now on. You get a senior discount, don't you?"

I threw my napkin at her, and she ducked, laughing, as I protested, "But I'm retired and on a fixed income. Besides, have a little respect for your elders."

"You two are something," Gail said, laughing along with us. "We need to do this more often."

"Agreed!" Melanie and I said in unison, starting another round of laughter.

"So, do you live around here, close to the gym?" Melanie asked.

"Temporarily. Home is a condo in Orlando. For now, I'm down the road in the San Marco area. This is the closest gym that has more than just weights. I like the cardio classes, thanks to Gail," I said, turning towards her. "You really give a good class."

She smiled at that, blushing, and said, "Thank you. I'm no kick-butt like Anna, but I enjoy it."

I laughed as visions of Anna and her staccato routine ran through my mind. Just like my old drill sergeant in boot camp, I told them.

"Navy?" asked Gail. Jax was a Navy town, three bases at one time during the Vietnam War and afterwards. Now it was down to two.

"Army."

"My ex was in the Navy," Gail said. "That's how I came to be here."

I nodded and raised my coffee cup. "Well, here's to the Navy for bringing such a wonderful instructor to us." Gail giggled as we toasted her.

I gave them each one of my cards and told them I was looking for a couple of good part-time people to do a little labor. "If you know anyone, have them give me a call. And if you want to stop by and see the place sometime, let me know. It's really beautiful out there."

"Who does it belong to?" Gail asked.

"Well ..." I faltered for an awkward moment. "I guess I'm not really at liberty to say. The owner is a very private person."

"Very mysterious," Melanie said. "Someone famous then."

"Now we really have to know," Gail added.

"No, no. You wouldn't even know the name, but you're welcome to come by sometime. I've probably built it up too much though the property really is something. The house, I'm afraid, is in bad shape, but that's why I'm here. My girlfriend still works, so I'm trying to get some things done before she retires next year."

I saw the surprise in their faces. They didn't think I had anyone in my life at the time. It also confirmed that Melanie was playing matchmaker of sorts.

"Oh, will we get to meet your girlfriend?" she asked. "What's her name?"

I suffered a moment of panic as the name Melanie came to my lips. My face must be flushed red, I thought. "It's, ahh, Stephanie. She may come up some weekend. If she does, I'll bring her to the gym."

"Great, we'd love to meet her," Gail said and stood up to leave. I stood, too, and seeing Melanie about to leave also, made a hand motion only she could see and shook my head.

"I'll see you tomorrow, Gail," she said.

I turned to Gail. "It was a pleasure to have coffee with you. I really enjoy your kickboxing class."

"I enjoyed it, too, Michael. Maybe we can do it again

sometime."

As she left, I turned to Melanie and gently shook a finger at her.

Her eyes got larger. "What?"

"Matchmaking is what. She's an attractive woman. I'm flattered you think well enough of me without really knowing me to try and set us up."

"Uh oh, caught. Sorry. You're right. I don't really know you, but how else do you get people to meet?"

"No, you don't know me, and actually, this is a good way to meet someone." I sat again and studied her a moment before continuing. "I'm making more of it than it is, and I am flattered. For the future though, while she's charming, she's not my type."

"So, what is your type? Anyone here close?" she asked, looking around.

I made a small show of lifting out of the chair a little and looking around before I answered. "Yes, there is, and one day I'll point my type out for you. How's that?"

She looked casually at the women around us and said, "Okay. So, is there really a girlfriend, or was that just your way of getting out of it?"

I looked at her a few seconds before replying, thinking, I guess, about how to respond. I should cut it off here.

"Yes, there's a girlfriend, but it's complicated."

She leaned closer. "How do you mean, complicated? All relationships are complicated."

I just smiled at her. She was so inquisitive, nosy actually. "Oh, no, we're not going there, lovely lady. I don't know you well enough to go there. I don't know why I've told you this much."

"So many mysteries," she said. She drew back in her seat,

her face smiling, but those incredible eyes and mouth were a little tense. "Can't you see how mysterious things intrigue me, like who's the owner of the house? And now I have to know about 'complicated' and what your type is as well."

"Good, so we'll have coffee again. I like that, so mystery is good from my side. Let's talk about you a little more."

Melanie laughed and abruptly stood, slinging her handbag over her shoulder. "I'm up for next time. See you in class."

Then she was off, leaving me to admire her backside as she walked away.

Chapter Six

*E*arly Tuesday morning, I took care of a few minor jobs and coordinated some work for the upcoming weekend with a plumber. We agreed to meet Saturday. Then I cleaned up the trailer, packed an overnight bag, stripped the bed, and threw the sheets and rest of the laundry in a bag. I loaded it all into the Porsche I kept in one of the three garage ports under Nathan and Nan's place.

As I pulled out of the garage, Nan was there to greet me. "Leaving without saying goodbye, sneaking out in broad daylight?"

"Of course not," I said, getting out of the car, "just on the way up to say goodbye."

"I think it's a good thing I caught you, or I might have made too much dinner for Nathan and me. Going to be gone long?"

"Three days at the most."

"Stephanie, I hope. When are you going to bring her back to see us?"

"Yes, my sweet, nosy one, I'm going to see Steph, and one of these days maybe she won't be so involved and can come up for a few days again."

Nan stepped up and gave me a hug. "Tell her we asked about her."

Then I was off, enjoying the feel of the Porsche and being

a part of Nathan and Nan's family. It was good.

I was excited to be seeing Stephanie again. It had only been a few weeks, but I missed her and needed to get some things out of my system. I intended to get back on track and leave the diversions behind with this trip. We could talk. She could help me with what I was going through with the house.

Maybe I'd tell her about Melanie and this attraction to her. She might get a laugh out of it. After all, Steph was the original Melanie.

No, I decided, this was not something I should talk to Stephanie about. She might not understand, and besides, I planned to stay away from Melanie. I knew her work schedule now, so it shouldn't be difficult to avoid her.

I decided to stop off for coffee and a paper before getting on the road. It was an easy two, maybe two-and-a-half, hour run to the Orlando condo. All I had to do was drop off the laundry when I got there. Everything else was taken care of except for a stop at the grocery store.

I sat at an outside table sipping coffee, absently watching the few people around me. Somewhere in the midst of mindlessness, my thoughts drifted back to Stephanie. A darker side, the reality side I'd always tried to suppress, clouded everything around me, drawing me to her, perfect in every way—except she was married to another man. She was my lover and more, the latest and longest in a string of safe relationships. Complicated for sure, but it worked. I wasn't married, so she couldn't be my mistress. And I wasn't her gigolo, either. I had looked it up, my penchant for wrong relationships, but there was nothing to define what I was when it came to Stephanie.

The sound of a chair scraping against the floor brought me back, and I looked around. People behind me were leaving, saying their goodbyes. I took a sip of coffee, still hot, so I hadn't been away long. I stretched and reached for the newspaper, but my mind was charged now, compelling me to finish the line of thought.

I hadn't gone beyond Wikipedia and Urban Dictionary, but there was no word to describe a man in my situation. Undefined. That says something. Once again, things didn't fit the norm for me. I was somewhere between the round peg and square hole. How do you describe a relationship with a married woman that goes beyond sex?

That was the least of the complications, yet somehow she was able to balance everything. As long as she wasn't away too long, everything was all right. Nothing kinky, but her husband knew of our relationship. John was twenty-something years her senior, already a man of the world before he'd married Stephanie thirty years ago. A better man than I, for sure.

This was not my normal type of relationship. My norm was not to get involved with married women. Well, separated, truly separated and moving towards divorce, was okay, but that was different. Yet Stephanie was not only married but happily so. She loved her husband and didn't want a divorce. Discretion was an absolute necessity.

Yeah, it was complicated, and I didn't want to dwell on it. I was happy with Steph, but now I wasn't sure the relationship could continue. Doubt had settled on me recently, especially as I was away from her more now. *Doubt*—it sure as hell wasn't guilt. I'd worked through that long ago. I was too old for a family now, but something was missing. Months earlier, standing at the Tower of Pisa of all places, it had come to me. Everyone around me had someone. A life unshared is . . . I guess I just finally realized life is better shared. I'd flown home the next day. The romance of my next stop, Venice, would have been too much.

Motion shifted around me as something blocked the sun. I looked up to see Melanie smiling before me.

I jumped up. "Hey there." My heart was beating like crazy. "I was just looking for you."

Her smile changed to confusion, and I laughed. Whew, I'd needed to break the moment.

"Just kidding, Melanie, but it is kind of a déjà vu. Weren't we just here?"

"Yes, we were actually." It was good to hear her laugh.

"I'm surprised to see you. Do you have time to join me, or are you with others?"

She glanced at her watch. "I have a few minutes if you're sure I'm not imposing."

"Please, sit with me then."

I pulled out a chair for her and returned to my own.

She pulled the lid from her coffee cup and blew some heat away as she looked across at me. "So, what brings you here this early?"

"Going out of town for a few days, but I did get in a little jog earlier. How about you?"

"Well, I got a call asking me to come in. The full-time nurse is sick. I got a good walk in before the call though. So back at ya." Her eyes twinkled. I loved the way she held the coffee in both hands, blowing on it gently.

She peered over the steaming cup at me. "Business?"

"A little, but mainly to see family and the girlfriend I mentioned."

One eyebrow rose as she said, "Ah, *complicated*."

I couldn't help but laugh. "I speak too freely around you, and you seem to remember everything. I have to be more careful."

She had that little smile going all the time, nodding her head as I talked about being careful.

"So, we won't be seeing you for a while then?"

"A couple of days in Orlando, then back to get on with the work. Probably back Thursday and to the gym Friday. It's a good morning class with Gail. I hate to miss it."

"Funny," she said, "I was in Orlando's Friday night."

"Really? It's a small world, isn't it?"

She smiled, her eyes gleaming with mischief.

"Orlando's, not Orlando. It's a nightclub in San Marco."

"Oh," I said, "I've been there. Did you have a good time?" It is a small world.

"It was okay. Met a friend there but didn't stay long."

No way, I thought. I was there that night. My mind went to the slim woman slipping into the seat beside Valerie as I left.

No way!

We sat quietly, sipping our coffees, comfortable in each other's presence. Finally, I took a slow look around, my gaze eventually coming to rest on Melanie again.

"Are you expecting someone, Michael? I don't want to intrude. I can leave now."

"No, please, stay as long as you can. I enjoy your company. I was just looking to see if there was anyone here my type."

"Oh!" She set her cup down and smiled slyly. "Is there? Where?

"Wait, don't answer," she said with a nod to my left. "Hmmm, is it that sexy young brunette over there? No, no, hold on. I'll bet it's the blonde with the big, uh . . . hair."

"No, no, you haven't a clue. She's right there," I said nodding in her direction.

She looked confused and looked around behind her. "Where?"

"Right here, in front of me. It's you. You're my type, lovely woman."

I was laughing again as the realization of what I'd said came to her. Her cheeks flushed, but she said nothing. She was good for me. She was fun and had the right disposition.

"Find me one like you, a single one, and I'll be happy for you to set me up."

I had taken her off balance for a moment, but I wasn't surprised at her poise. Her cheeks glowed red. I couldn't imagine what was going through her mind in the few seconds it took her to respond. She looked at me steadily the whole time, her eyes penetrating mine. Her response was cool and controlled for such an awkward moment.

She cocked her head a little. "I can understand that." She gave me a big, exaggerated smile. "Excellent taste," she said.

My directness must have startled her. I could see she was struggling with more of an answer. When it came, she delivered it in a serious, businesslike manner.

"I'm flattered," she said.

"You should be," I replied in the same serious tone and manner she had.

"Oh?" She cocked her head the other way, her brows arched as if considering an important question.

I needed to lighten things. Waiting another moment as she looked at me expectantly, I leaned forward and whispered, "Well, yes. You're probably a little old for me, you know, a man of my age and all."

It came immediately, another napkin thrown at me, then the laughter, neither of us caring about the attention we'd attracted.

We settled down, quietly looking and smiling at each other. Then she glanced at her watch and jumped up.

"Michael, I have to go. I can just make it in time."

I stood up and put out my hand as she'd done that time at Publix. Instead of taking it, she stepped forward and grabbed both my arms with her hands. She pulled me to her and kissed my cheek.

"We're friends now," she said. Her eyes and smile lingered a moment before she turned away towards her car.

***

So much for resolve, I thought, shaking my head as I drove south. Our relationship had changed in those few moments. The attraction was still overwhelming, but the comfort in each other's company was extraordinary. We had only run into each other a few times, but it was always significant in some way.

I tried to put it aside and gradually did, but not before wondering who my heart would be making love to that night, Stephanie or Melanie.

I shook my head at the thought. "I need to put Melanie behind me," I said, looking into my own eyes in the rearview mirror. No more married women. No more Melanies, I vowed silently. It all ends with Stephanie. *No more married women.*

Thinking of Steph, I became excited. The anticipation of those lovely strong shoulders, her lean body and perfect breasts, that soft, thick red hair and, finally, the scent of her arousal as lithe legs opened to me was too much. I was extremely conscious of the shiver running thorough my body.

Chapter Seven

I walked to the door as I heard her key in the lock and stood there as she came in. She was something to behold, sexy with a beautiful body even now, in her late fifties. She worked at it, like we all should, not from vanity but as part of her daily routine, natural as brushing her teeth each morning.

It wasn't just her long legs, tight butt, or perfect breasts. It was all of her, how she embraced life, reveling in it. She had grown even more compelling as she got older. I was proud to be a part of her life. She was beautiful to me, though probably not by traditional standards. Her nose was just right but probably too large for most guys, and that damn sexy bump on it, high up, right between her closely-set blue eyes, drove me nuts.

"Hi," I said.

It was those eyes that grabbed me now, icy blue and penetrating. They held me captive; nothing else existed until she smiled, and then her eyes warmed to me and her lips drew me in. So much going on that you never got to the nose unless you had a thing for it. I do.

Her head tilted in a small nod as her face became all smile. "Hello, baby."

We understood each other.

I don't know how we became one, but my need was too great. She bucked against me, the heels of her feet urging me on. I was too close, but as I tried to back away, she held me tighter. "No, Michael, no," she moaned in my ear.

Her eyes opened, wild with need as her mass of red hair lifted from the sofa. Every muscle, every tendon, was tensed, her eyes pleading as her fingers gripped my butt, sending pulses of pleasure through me as she took in short breaths of air. Her eyes held me, demanded of me, and then she threw her head back with a groan while pulling me frantically by my shoulder and butt. I felt myself rising at the end, my arms extending, my hips pushing harder as I sought to be more a part of her in that moment.

Slowly, I became aware. My arms were fully extended and my head thrown back as I lifted my chest and stomach from her body. I gasped for air while a vision of having morphed into a wild man flowed around me. Excruciating pulses of pleasure continued to radiate through me. I didn't want to move, afraid it would stop. My head fell forward, overcome with weakness.

Gentle motion caressing my behind and little murmurs brought me back to find Stephanie smiling up at me. Her hands moved to my hips then, and she held me captive with thighs and other muscles that continued to squeeze me.

She held on as I tried to separate, and I collapsed back to her. We must have slept. I awoke slowly, part of me on the sofa with one knee on the carpet straddling a leg as Stephanie held me with the other wrapped around my butt. She slipped from my grasp and covered my face with little kisses before propping herself up on one elbow. I let myself roll onto my back on the carpet and lay there exhausted. I was aware of her moving, and then she ran a hand in small circles over my chest.

"Welcome home," she said. "I think we skipped that part."

I opened my eyes. I was groggy, enjoying the moment. I loved looking at this woman anytime but especially during and just after sex, but my eyes wouldn't stay open. "You're an animal, woman."

"Who attacked who? I'm thinking someone else is arousing my baby. I'm not complaining though, not as long as you continue to come home like this."

I was startled. There was truth in what she said. I did the best thing I could—nothing—and just lay there quietly.

"Be careful when you don't," she continued. "I'm spoiled. No way are you staying away more than two weeks at a time." My mind had jumped to Melanie during her talk, and I was fearful the guilt would show.

I pushed her away playfully and poked my bottom lip out in a pout. "Sex, sex, sex. That's all you want me for."

She laughed. "Is not. I missed you a little, too.

***

Later, we had wine and a salad that she'd brought. We held each other on the balcony, looking out at the city as we talked. Despite the fact that we talked on the phone almost daily, we lived separate and distinct lives.

She asked about my Jacksonville family: Nathan, Nan, and Hannah. She didn't know them well but knew they were important to me. She'd met them a couple of times over the years.

We talked long into the night and then slept, curled up together in my big bed. What a difference from the trailer bunk. That's really what it was, a bunk. Yeah, I'd definitely missed the big bed. And Stephanie, too.

As good as it was with Stephanie, something had changed,

and it nagged at me. Everything seemed so temporary, so fleeting now, but so what? It had been this way for many years, over several affairs, and I'd always liked it this way. I'd always felt fortunate in my relationships, able to look forward to being with my lover even if it were simply time together. How many marriages had that? How many failed even though the partners were together all the time? After receiving a Dear John letter from my wife as I was coming home from a combat tour in Vietnam, I'd vowed never to marry again. My relationships were too valuable, too fulfilling to endanger with marriage. Why was this bothering me now?

It was Melanie. Meeting her had brought it to the surface again, but it went back farther, deeper. I think it started before Italy even. Maybe an age thing, I don't know, but there was a longing to share more than the wonderful fleeting time Stephanie and I had together. It wouldn't be any different with another married woman.

We made love again in the morning, more slowly and tenderly this time, deeply absorbing one another. She stayed with me all day, taking time off from work. A night and day away from John was significant. She didn't do that often, and I understood. We were just having an affair, only much deeper.

A couple of times we were able to be together for a week when John went fishing with some of his old buddies in Georgia. That was the most ever, a week once a year. She took that one week off to be with me, our special time. The neighbors looked after their place, thinking she and John were on vacation together.

My brother David and his wife lived in Orlando, and Stephanie and I had lunch with them that afternoon at a Chili's near the condo. Then Stephanie left at five since she had to work the next day. And John would be waiting.

Chapter Eight

*Y*ou're my type. I turned on the light for the second time
that night. The first time I woke had been much better.
I'd had a vague notion of dreaming about my two Melanies.
Judging by my erection, it must have been good. Not this time
though. Guilt had descended.

My type. The provocative words pestered my sleep,
rudely reminding me of having crossed the boundary into
forbidden territory. Yeah, I was seducing Melanie. Strange how
my mind didn't haunt me while I was sleeping in Stephanie's
arms. I'd been just as guilty last night, more even. I'd been
curled around one and dreaming of the other and had no
problem sleeping. *Maybe if I had them both...* I laughed at the
arrogance of that thought and got up. There would be no more
sleep for a while.

It was just after one in the morning as I walked onto the
balcony. Even on a work night, traffic still moved a few blocks
over on East Colonial Drive. It was warm and comfortable
twenty floors up, no mosquitoes this high. I looked to a dark
space in the sky, to where the sun would come up later in the
morning. No tall buildings there. I closed my eyes and felt for
the beauty and warmth that would fill that space in a few more
hours.

The balcony was more of a terrace wrapping around the

whole penthouse. In the evening, I could move to the opposite side and watch the sunset. This was still a special place, even with the constantly developing Orlando skyline of taller and taller buildings.

I sat back on one of the chaise lounges, closing my eyes, trying to relax. I'd had just enough sleep and too much brain activity for that though. My thoughts jumped around to little bits and pieces of nonsense: Melanie's hands on my shoulders, lips on my cheek, her words *we're friends now* echoing in my head.

My eyes popped open at that. Yeah, we're friends. That sudden kiss on the cheek, spontaneous as it was, had meaning behind it. I was no innocent, playing that game about my type. I had managed to rationalize that it had all come from a weakness in my relationship with Stephanie. And there may be some truth there. But the sense of need I now felt had invaded my soul while I was in Pisa. That need may have started in Italy, in a moment of loneliness, but this was reality, and Melanie was real.

She was the first woman in several years who had drawn my interest. The last had been a single mother named Mary, a very competent and independent young woman working on her master's degree in accounting. Mary and I enjoyed our short time together, but it was never serious for either of us. She helped me find my riverfront property in Jax, and then . . . I guess we just sort of cheerfully drifted apart as I spent more time in Orlando. Then I met Stephanie.

Had I really thought it would ever be any different for Stephanie and me? Something beyond the little time we had together, something more than the one week a year when John went fishing? No, but it wasn't enough anymore, and seducing another married woman wasn't the answer either.

That's what I was doing though. My version of "Hey, little girl, want some candy?" Playing the old game, planting seeds of interest and letting them grow naturally. Planting seeds, just as John had done in slowly giving Stephanie permission to know another man, gently pushing her in that direction, unwilling to watch her vitality be diminished prematurely to mere contentment due to his advancing age. She was too full of life, too vibrant not to taste more of life now. And, as I was to learn later, it was more than his not being able to perform sexually anymore. His letting go of her was one of the most altruistic things I'd ever witnessed.

I was beginning to accept the realities of my epiphany in Italy, a life unshared. Stephanie would never leave John, and I could never ask her to. If she did, she wouldn't be the woman I loved. Life's little paradox.

Maybe I'd just have someone else finish the house, go back to Italy, back to Pisa, and start again. Stay away from women, visit a monastery. Join one!

Enough. I moved from the patio lounger and went back to bed. I had to get some sleep. It was good to lie back and close my eyes. I must have dozed, but Stephanie was waiting for me on the other side of sleep. She wouldn't let me go. It was like she knew my thoughts. Was some womanly intuition breaking through, sharing my dream? It was ironic as some form of guilt took me back to find her and she made everything right again.

It was the beginning of our relationship, our first time together. Her body had responded, overcoming her anxiety at what she was doing. Physically, it had been wonderful, but the guilt she'd suffered greatly affected me. I'd apologized for seducing her, but guilt hadn't stopped me.

"No, no," she said, "it's all right. It'll be all right." Then she wrapped herself around me, bringing me comfort in her touch.

"John knows about us," she told me as we lay there holding each other.

I was shocked. I couldn't understand. My immediate thought was that it was a kinky thing, that maybe she and John had done this before, that they somehow used her sexual involvement with other men to bring excitement to their marriage. I asked her.

"I've never done this," she sputtered. "And it's not kinky," she added, punching me in the ribs. Then she paused a moment. "Or I don't think it is. He had surgery for prostate cancer a few years ago."

It stunned me. "I knew there was a reason I was able to seduce you."

"It's not that simple, Michael. Even before that, John had lost interest in things. Things I enjoy, like traveling, Broadway shows, concerts, the ballet. Even movies. He lost interest in all of that. He loves his golf, entertaining friends at home, and especially our children and grandchildren being around. That's enough for him, and it was for me, but he wouldn't let it go. First, he started talking about my seeing someone else to attend events with, just little inferences at first."

Her deep blue eyes filled with pain as she spoke.

"I didn't know," I said. "I thought it was an age thing."

She blushed. "No, it was the cancer. John led an active sex life in the years before we met. Maybe that's one of the things that attracted me to him. Like you." She rolled over in my arms and smiled that naughty smile of hers, the one that sent my blood surging. "He's a lot like you. Unselfish and wanting me to enjoy life as he had in the years before we met. He didn't like seeing me wasting on the vine, he said."

"So, he wanted you to have an affair?"

She shook that mane of red hair, and I nuzzled into it.

"That's too simplistic an explanation of John. He said he saw opportunities for me to do things I'd always wanted slipping away. He encouraged me to pursue them without him."

"With other girlfriends?"

"Yes, but he wanted me open to having other men as companions, too. It was later that he brought up my having sex with another man." She laughed suddenly and turned away.

"What's so funny?"

She turned back to me, seeming embarrassed. Soft freckles melded together in a blush that was startling. Her skin was exquisite, a shaded, tanned-looking tint that some redheads are blessed with. "It was a little kinky," she said with another laugh.

"That's okay, too," I said.

She sat up in bed and pulled me up with her. Her legs straddled mine as we sat upright facing each other, her eyes watching mine. "He started talking, encouraging me actually to see other men sexually, and it excited him. He couldn't get an erection, but he brought me pleasure as he fantasized with me about it."

Her head bowed to my shoulder, and I held her. "You shouldn't be ashamed about that," I said.

"He wanted me to open myself to a relationship but keep it private, preserve the substance and outward image of our marriage."

She paused and looked up at me again.

"I shouldn't be telling you this, Michael. I see what a toll it's taking on us. I didn't sleep with you for John. I wanted you. But if John hadn't prompted me and opened the door with his approval, it wouldn't have happened."

"I know," I said.

"I love him, Michael. I would never do anything to hurt

him. I hope you realize that."

***

My dick woke me this time. Dream sex, reenacting our lovemaking. There was no longer any guilt though. Stephanie had absolved me of that during the dream talk and left me with this hard-on as a bonus. I loved this woman.

I jumped out of bed and made for the coffeepot. It sat there, nice and black and cold. Normally, I would wake to the aroma of freshly perked coffee in the air. It had been a long, crazy night. I heated a cup in the microwave and took it to the balcony. I'd missed the sunrise, but the morning was glorious with the sun at an angle that didn't make my eyes squint. I sipped hot coffee and finished my night of thoughts and dreams.

While John believed he was ready, he wasn't. Fantasy isn't always as good as reality. He had broken down with her when she was first with me. In the end, he insisted that she continue. I figured John now knew the depth our relationship had grown to. I had only met him once, and that by accident at a cocktail party. We both handled it well though we were obviously taking each other's measure. But unlike two roosters circling, ready to fight for the hen, I felt we were looking at each other through Stephanie's eyes. We talked about a variety of things. In the end, I was pleased somehow and proud for her to have such a man as John. I wondered if someday I could be as giving and loving as he. Could I subordinate my ego and disdain for another with my woman? Could I be that loving, given the same circumstances? I only knew how I felt about her, about us, and how much I respected John.

I tore it all apart again as I sat with my cup of coffee going cold. I set the cup aside and let it all wash over me—guilt, anguish, pleasure—and from some hidden consciousness emerged a kind of salvation. Oh, but we sinners need so little understanding to justify our rationalizations. We're all equipped from birth with the basics of right and wrong. The rest is rationalization and justification coupled with an unconscious willingness to suffer the penance. Ultimately, I was left with the acceptance that I never should have gone where I did in the first place. Stephanie had been too good, too forgiving and enabling in my dream. The three of us shared responsibility for the affair though. That was my salvation. This time.

Steph and I had been together two years now, and we were good for each other, more than lovers but still less than true partners. She and John, on the other hand, were soul mates.

Was mine out there, my soul mate? Did she exist? How would I know, and would I ever find her?

Chapter Nine

I leaned over the fountain for a drink. So lovely here, so different from the first time I saw the place.

"Come on in, Michael. Have a cup of coffee with me," Hannah said.

"Okay, I think I will."

I took her arm as we strolled to the house.

"Hey, when are you going to sell me that old Karmann Ghia?" I asked.

"No way. I love that old car. Especially now that you had it restored."

"You paid for it."

"Oh, I paid for it all right. Sometimes I think that's why you hired me, so I could afford to," she said, then laughed.

"No, I hired you so you could afford to have it hauled off. Nathan was keeping a close watch on it so that when you did, I could pick it up cheap."

"Well, it backfired," she said.

"This place is beautiful, Hannah. You've done an excellent job," I told her as we entered the kitchen.

She looked around and smiled, then ran a hand along one of the granite countertops. "It is, Michael. I love it here. Thanks for taking a chance on me back then."

I had to smile. We'd never had this talk. Our relationship just naturally grew, and now she was intimately involved in everything material in my life.

"Those couple of days we sparred," I said, "with you sitting out there picking at weeds, told me everything I ever needed to know about you. Besides, Nathan liked you."

She wrapped her arms around me in a great hug. "Thank you, Michael. You're much sweeter than I realized back then. Of course, there's the great work I do that you forgot to mention."

"Oh, yeah, there is that, and besides, I trust you."

She continued to hug me with her head on my chest. "And I'm a really nice person who's enjoyable to be around."

I eased her from me and held her at arm's length. "That's stretching it a little, Hannah. Remember when we met, those first few days we talked?"

She giggled. "I mean now, not back then. I'm different now."

I shook my head and took a seat at the kitchen table. Hannah poured us each a cup of coffee before sitting opposite me. She picked up an envelope that had been lying on the table and handed it to me.

"I emailed this to Curt but printed this copy for you since you won't open my emails," she said.

I had to smile at that. She was right.

Curt's my accountant in Orlando. Someone else I should have seen when I was down there. I opened the envelope. It was a spreadsheet of expenses associated with the house refurbishment. I scanned it, then folded it back into the envelope and put it in my pocket.

"Thanks, Hannah. Looks like I need to ease up on the kitchen. It's starting to get expensive."

"I don't know," she said. "The kitchen is important."

"You're right. It is important. Thanks for reminding me." Actually, I was pleased with the way it was coming along. I was pleased with Hannah, too. We'd come a long way together.

"Now, how about some Foundation business," I said. "How are we doing?"

A couple of years back, a friend who knew about my wealth and the source of it cajoled me into forming a foundation to do good things. Dwight was smooth. A couple of drinks, and he had me out there on some philosophical tangent again. This time it was about how deserving people often weren't able to break through and succeed through no fault of their own. He already had me agreeing and wanting to do something when he hit me with his proposal.

Quietly, he said, "We can make a difference, Michael. Our money should stand for something more than this." And he waved his hand in front of us as though indicating his luxurious home, a converted sea-going barge where we lounged under an umbrella among numerous potted palms.

Later, I discovered Dwight was just the messenger. A mutual friend had put him up to luring me in. But we all loaded a lot of money into it, and now we had the beginnings of a good thing.

"Great, we're doing great," Hannah said, "and I love it." There was a lift to her voice, excitement. "There are so many opportunities out there. I love doing the research and helping these people out."

"So, we're still not spending enough Foundation money?"

"No, so expect to hear from Marge soon. She wants to talk to you about that."

I nodded. Marge, the third partner, headed up the Foundation. She was also the wife of a Department of Justice special prosecutor who had stepped into a lawsuit I'd filed against a major Department of Defense contractor. That's where I earned the seed money for the real wealth I earned later. Marge was just born rich but determined to have a meaningful life. Dwight? Well, he's another story, a good one, but no matter for now; he's rich and a lifelong friend of Marge.

Help others help themselves was our basic tenet. No politics or judgments beyond helping deserving people succeed. We needed to work harder to identify more of those people though.

"You've done a wonderful job on this program, Hannah."

She laughed and slapped the table. "I know, I really have, and it's fun helping people. I love it."

Her enthusiasm was catching. I laughed with her. All that she'd brought to the process, all the people she'd helped came to mind. "I know you do, Hannah.

"Speaking of which," I said, "is Christy, that single-mom waitress I sent to you, a good candidate for the program?"

"Oh, God, yes, you know she is. She brought her little boy with her, too. He's so sweet."

"That's great, Hannah."

"And . . ."

"And what?"

She raised an eyebrow and presented me a big smile as she held the silence for a moment longer. "And I understand you keep pretty late nights some weekends."

I laughed. "Early mornings, Hannah. I get up early and eat breakfast where she works."

"Right, very early, it seems. And the other thing—I think she has a crush on you."

That caught my attention. "No, she's just grateful and curious."

"I don't know. She was shy about it, but she asked about you. I just told her you were working on the big house over there and were a nice guy."

I smiled at Hannah. She could be a real mess sometimes. "Good. Thanks, darling. She's a cute thing but way too young for me."

She didn't answer for a moment. "Maybe," she said with a little shrug. "My husband was much older than me and we were wonderful together."

"I'm not that much older," I said and headed towards the door before the conversation got too close. Too many women things were going on in my life already. I didn't need to talk to another woman about the mess I was in. "Your turn to bring in someone we can help. The money's just sitting there going to waste, especially since you're so good with funding outside the Foundation, what with all those grants and scholarships you keep finding for people."

"Me? I don't know many people."

"Well, get out and get more involved. You're only like seventy or so, right? Get with it," he told her.

"Sixty-six, you butt."

Laughing, she followed me out the door. I stayed away from her cane.

"And by the way, at that age, I'm no longer punished by Social Security based on income. So you need to be nice to me."

"Yes, I do, but not because of that. You're a part of this now, and we need you.

"Just one a year, Hannah. We're helping to plant good seeds. At the right time, maybe you can discuss it with Christy or some of the others. They probably have some ideas."

We stopped in the yard, and I said, "Let's go to dinner later and celebrate."

"Okay, but I'm not riding in that truck, you understand."

"Why? I bought a new cushion for you to sit on."

"No."

I laughed. "All right, I'm going to ask Nathan and Nan, too. Maybe get him to drive so we can go in style."

She smiled.

Yeah. She liked that idea.

***

Nathan drove the Lexus that night, and we headed out for seafood at a little place close to Julington Creek.

"Better than the truck?" I asked Hannah.

"Oh, yes, even with the cushion. Better than that tiny Porsche thing, too. The Karmann Ghia has more room. Nathan," she said, with theatrical emphasis on his name, "knows how to pick a nice ride."

Nathan gave thumbs up from the front seat. "You tell him, Hannah. This is the way to ride."

We had done this many times in the past, the four of us. I enjoyed our outings. When I was away, which was most of the time, the three of them went out to dinner or cooked out a few times a month. Generally, it was at Hannah's place since going up the stairs to the garage apartment was difficult for her with the cane. Nathan always said it was because of the odd jobs she seemed to have waiting for him. Said he missed the old days when she wouldn't let him do that raggedy yard.

It took a while, but Hannah finally confided in me that her bad leg was due to an old car accident. Some kind of nerve damage had resulted in a numbness that plagued her. The cane gave her confidence to walk. Another year passed before she told me her husband had died in that accident.

As I opened Nan's door, Nathan opened Hannah's.

"Now just sit right there, Miss Daisy, and I'll get a

wheelchair for you."

"*What?*" she said. "Get out of my way and don't play that stuff with me." She eased out of the car with the help of her cane. Then, she shook it at him.

Nathan backed up laughing, the palms of his hands held out in mock defense. "Just like the movie, huh," he said, winking at Nan and me.

"It is, darn you," Hannah said, laughing as she limped toward him. Nathan back-pedaled gingerly, doing a boxer's shuffle, feinting moves as he stayed out of range of the cane.

"Come on, Michael," Nan said. She took my arm as I admired Nathan's footwork. "Let's go in while these two remake the movie."

"Hey, we're coming. Wait up," Nathan called out. He reached for Hannah's arm in spite of the cane and gently pulled her along.

"We're pretty good," he said. "Maybe we should try out for the movies."

Later, we stopped in at Jigger's place for a nightcap. I hadn't seen Jigger since the martini episode at the gym, so I was a little apprehensive. I'd meant to stop in at the bar sooner, but each time something got in the way. Going into Harvey's, Hannah walked with me, telling me about the times she and her husband went out like this, how he loved to dance. "He was a good man, Michael. He just didn't plan very well."

We held hands as we went in. "Times have changed, girl. Used to be Social Security was enough for most people. Dan was a man of those times. Things changed fast. Besides," I told her, "you're too active and valuable to be retired."

We got a small table in the back, and a waiter came over to serve us. Settling down with drinks, we were engaged in light-hearted discussion when Jigger stopped by the table. Damn, she was easy to look at. She smiled as she saw me glance down at her shoes.

Nathan and I stood as she approached. Nathan, ever the gallant one, took her hand and kissed it. He missed seeing Nan's little tilt and shake of her head as she rolled her eyes, but somehow I thought he knew. Comes from a lifetime together, I guess, being soul mates. I was sad in that moment. Would I ever know such intimacy?

Still holding Jigger's hand, Nathan turned his head to Nan. "Caught you," he said with a laugh.

He released Jigger's hand to mine as he moved to Nan and nuzzled her cheek with his.

She giggled. "Yeah, you did."

I held Jigger's hand and gently pulled her close enough to whisper. "I love the heels, but they should be higher when you have a martini."

"Okay, but I'm working now," she whispered back. We both laughed as we looked down at her shoes.

"Hey, what's going on, you two?" Nan asked.

"It's a martini thing," I told her. "I think I'll let Jigger explain it."

As I took my seat, a familiar face caught my eye.

"Damn," I said softly, but Jigger caught it.

"What is it, Michael?"

"An old friend." I stood, still surprised. "Will you excuse me a moment folks? I need to say hello to someone."

Turning back to Jigger, I whispered, "You're lovely as usual. And I love the heels."

I walked across the empty dance floor to a small table where a very large man was seated.

"Hello, Robert."

He stood, reaching out a hand. "Why, hello, Michael." We

shook hands warmly. "Please have a seat."

He was an old friend and mentor, but he shouldn't have been there. I glanced back at Nathan. I couldn't catch his eye, but I'm sure he knew something. "What are you doing here, Robert?"

"Just having a drink. Please, have one with me."

"It's spooky when you show up. Couldn't you just call and talk instead of all the drama it took to find me here at this particular time?"

He laughed. "Keeps my hand in the game." He held out his hand to the chair. "Please, sit down for a few minutes."

I couldn't resist.

"The reason I didn't call is because I didn't know if you'd see me," he said.

I sat down. "That's baloney. You really need to lighten up on this spook shit."

He went into role then, acted embarrassed and even a little shamefaced after I said that. He was always a drama king.

"Yeah, you're right. I just wanted to know what watering hole you were using these days, so I called Nathan. I didn't know when I'd be in town. Remember, the last time we talked, you told me you were going to be working on the place here."

"I remember," I told him. "I also remember saving you guys at the US Attorney's Office nearly four hundred million dollars over the past few decades with my qui tam suits. So, my question is what brings you here now, Robert?"

"How much have you made so far?" he asked, ignoring my own question. "Thirty million and still driving that old truck?"

I had to smile at the man who'd become a good friend over the years. I still didn't like his little surprises though.

"Good to see you, asshole."

He grinned, "Yeah, you, too. Glad I caught you here. I was

afraid you were out with that lovely slender thing."

I was surprised to hear that. "What lovely slender thing?"

"I don't know. Nathan said he saw you at Starbucks with a sexy lady when he was bidding a job a few days ago."

"He never said a thing to me, the rat."

"Oops. I didn't even know I'd be here, Michael. I called Nathan from Tampa, and he told me all of you were going to dinner. My flight made a stop here because some light flashed on in the cockpit." He glanced at his watch. "I'm stuck here until tomorrow. Soooo, Nathan didn't even know I was going to be in town."

I nodded. "You're right. He wouldn't hold it from me intentionally, but I'm talking about his seeing me with a woman. He never said a word."

I looked over at Nathan. He was all smiles, shrugging his shoulders, palms in the air as he mouthed something.

"Want me to check her out for you?" Robert asked. He had leaned forward as though seeking my approval.

"Stay away from her."

He looked over his shoulder for a waitress. "I was only kidding. You'd have to be really nice to me before I'd do that."

Jigger showed up as we talked. We stood, and I made introductions. Robert shook the hand she held out to him.

"We're going to be joining the other table soon," I told Jigger. "How did the explanation go?"

"Well, Hannah said bunny slippers are better with a drink. Says she does it all the time."

I was laughing as she slipped away. Robert turned back to me with a questioning look.

"No, that's not her, but she's something, isn't she?"

"Sure is. I love the name."

"She's married, Robert, and you definitely are. How is

Marge?"

"She's great. I'd love to bring her down sometime."

"Do it. The condo is available most of the time, and there's always Cay Tam."

"I've always loved that name on the boat, you arrogant bastard. Even though you changed the name, it's still pronounced the same, Cay, Key, or Qui."

"But most people don't know that, so Cay will do." I could only smile. The name was important to both of us. I had made a million dollars in a qui tam lawsuit against a corrupt Department of Defense contractor. It was early in Robert's career, and he was less than enthusiastic when assigned the case. That changed quickly when he understood the circumstances. But it had taken the government a long time before exercising their right of involvement in the prosecution. In the meantime, I'd been pretty much beat up, fired, and blacklisted from other employment by the defense contractor.

My passion still showed regarding corruption. I was still indignant about it all. Robert just laughed. He had long ago accepted that greed and the resulting corruption were a part of this wonderful world. Only a part, he insisted. You had to keep perspective, and he could. He knew how it offended me and had used that to feed my talents to root it out and expose it in the past. Qui tam suits seldom resulted in criminal prosecution of individuals, but they at least served notice to the offenders. Someone was watching and penalizing them where it really hurt, their bank accounts. It was up to the stockholders to finish the job the whistleblower had started.

"How about it?" I asked. "Coming down?"

"Maybe in a few months. We have a few issues going on right now."

"You always have a few issues. Always will."

"Listen, Michael, there's something that's come to our attention. Something in healthcare, insurance stuff. We'd like to get you involved. Same deal as always. We give you the lead, and you go in cold from there. File under qui tam on your own when you have proof. Then we'll come in."

"No, no, I'm out of it now."

"All right, I tried. I told Sam you wouldn't go for it. I'll tell him you've retired, but you know he'll send me back."

I nodded as he reached down and placed a large business envelope in front of me.

"Marge sent this with me when I told her I might be seeing you. There are several actions the board acted on and thought you might want to review."

Michael pushed the envelope back. "Tell her thanks, but I trust them. It's enough just to know they're helping good people succeed."

"You, too, buddy. You're helping, too."

"With Hannah's talent for ferreting out scholarship and grant money, we're spending very little. Tell Marge thanks for me though. We need more people like her and Hannah who do the real work."

Robert raised his glass in a toast. "To being a part of what you, Dwight, and Marge started."

"And to you," I said, raising my own glass, "for selling me out to Marge and Dwight and making me a better person."

His face lit up, and we clinked glasses.

"If I can't talk you into doing one more job," he said, "let's go visit with our friends for a while."

Everyone knew Robert and greeted him enthusiastically.

Nathan started to give me all the excuses of why he hadn't told me about Robert's being in town that night. I just shook my head as he rambled on. He suddenly stopped when I asked him about Starbucks. While he was chewing on that, I caught Jigger's eye and asked her to join us. She did, but no martini.

We all chatted with Robert for a while and then hugged him goodbye as he needed to leave for his early morning flight to Washington.

"Thank you for including me," Jigger whispered as we were leaving. "I like your friends."

I got a kiss on the cheek, and all I could think about was Melanie. *We're friends now.*

Chapter Ten

*T*he next day's weather forecast was for afternoon rain, so I got into the work early. Some of the supplies needed to go inside so they wouldn't get wet. A quick jog around familiar old streets would have to do instead of going to the gym. Hell, I was avoiding Melanie, too. I was determined to keep my distance. I was in a real quandary about my future with Stephanie, and I didn't need the complication of another married woman in my life.

Melanie had gotten to me, and I didn't know what to do except move on and stop arranging to run into her. I'm sure I'd done that occasionally though not consciously. Now, I was aware.

After putting away the supplies, I settled into planning. It sure looked like rain, and the forecast was for seventy percent all day. I never got the jog in. I'd only stopped long enough for a late breakfast on the way back from the local hardware store—two-for-two-bucks hotdogs at a convenience store—and now it was after lunchtime.

My cell phone went off across the room as I got ready to leave for the trailer. For a moment, I was going to let it go to voicemail, but it might have been about a delivery, so I answered.

"Michael?"

My heart jumped to my stomach. I felt nauseated as my knees turned to putty and threatened to buckle under me. *I'm trying to be good here, Lord.*

"Hello? Michael?" she asked again.

"This is Michael."

"Hi, Michael, this is Melanie. Is this a bad time?"

"No, no it's fine. Is everything all right?"

"Yes, everything is fine. Listen, I'm with a friend and just wondered if you were up for company."

What? Damn. Not now!

"Well, sure, sure. It's starting to rain, so nothing here that can't wait. Did you want to come over here?"

"Yes, if it's all right. You said to stop by, and we're in the area."

Oh, shit. Me and my big mouth.

"Sure, where are you? I'll give you directions."

"That's all right. I have your card and a street map. It looks like we're just a few miles away."

The sky opened as we ended the call. *Shit!*

I grabbed an old yellow rain slicker and ran through the downpour just before God decided to let it all out at once. The air crackled, and it was suddenly dark then bright with flashes of lightning. Why didn't it strike me?

I just had time to straighten up a little and check the fridge for something to serve. It didn't look good. Beer and a bit of rum, not even a Coke. Popcorn and beer would have to do.

The gates were open. Lightning flashed as the wind whipped everything, driving the rain hard in all directions. It was difficult to see anything. Protected by my hooded poncho, I stood under the trailer awning that flapped violently against my temporary home and waited for the woman who had made a storm of my life. Questions and misgivings boiled within me and raged against the crazy excitement of her coming to see me.

Car lights illuminated the mailbox as I watched. I dialed the number she'd called me from.

"I see you." Her voice sounded excited. Maybe it was the storm.

"The storm is going to last a while. Park next to the truck. I'll bring your friend in first, okay?"

"Okay."

I carefully opened an umbrella against the wind and moved to the passenger door. A woman climbed out, and we huddled together under the umbrella until we arrived under the awning.

"Go on in. I'll get Melanie," I yelled over the roar of the storm.

I brought Melanie in under the whipping awning and opened the door for her. I was taking off the dripping poncho when she stepped inside. As she cleared the door, her friend called out.

"Michael!"

"Valerie?" It was the dancer from the nightclub.

"You two know each other!" Melanie cried out.

"This is Michael from Club Orlando's," Valerie said. "He's the guy I wanted you to meet."

Melanie bent at the waist, her elbows tucked in, hands clasped. She stamped her feet against the floor as she turned in a little dance. She laughed as the realization struck her. "No way, Val."

For an awkward moment, we all stood there looking back and forth at each other. Then Melanie broke the silence with introductions despite the knowledge that we all knew each other.

The girls laughed and hugged each other while I got some towels so we could dry off.

"Hey!" Val said. Her voice rose well above the chatter of the rain on the metal roof of the trailer. "You were supposed to come back a couple of weeks ago and dance with me. Remember?" The girl had a mouth on her. "I guess you've been too busy seducing my best friend here."

"Michael has always been a gentleman," Melanie told her. "I want to know about you two. Dancing, huh? Slow and close, I bet."

I just stood there, toweling my hair.

Val walked over to me and pulled me into a hug. Backing up, she said, "Yes, but not as close as that. He really is too much of a gentleman."

Now I was laughing. "You don't know me well enough to say that. You might change your mind. Sit down. I can't believe Melanie is the friend you wanted to introduce me to. I mean, she's . . ."

Melanie's latest bout of laughter ended abruptly. I think she realized where my thought process was leading. She stood there, watching me in silence now while twisting those rings with the other hand. I looked away.

"Wine," said Val. "This calls for a celebration. I can't believe this. Yes, Melanie is the friend I wanted you to meet the night you saved me from Fred."

"How is Fred?" I said, grateful for the change of subject. "You had quite a story to overcome there."

"Tell you all about it later. He's become quite the gentleman," Val said. "How about that wine?"

"Sorry, I only have beer and coffee."

"I have some wine in the car," Melanie said. Val turned and gave her an odd look. Melanie continued, "How about something to eat, Michael? Have you had lunch?"

"No, but if you give me a few minutes to change, I'll take

you girls out. I don't have much here to eat."

"No, no," she said. "How about a picnic? Give me your umbrella. I have something in the car."

Val cocked her head with a questioning glance. Something was up, but Melanie chose to ignore it.

"Give me the keys and I'll get it," I said.

She held up a key fob. "There's a basket in the trunk. I'll open it for you when you get to the car."

I stepped close to Melanie on my way to the door. As I did, I whispered, "Did you see me at Orlando's last week?"

"No, I had no idea Val was talking about you."

As I stepped outside, Val moved closer to Melanie. "Wine? Food?" The look on her face told me to take my time.

No way. It was pouring. I hurried to the car, wondering what I was missing.

Once Melanie had unpacked the picnic, we gathered around and chatted amiably while devouring delectable munchies along with the wine. Melanie had included weird stuff I'd never eaten before: hummus, tabbouleh, and more. *Soy cheese?* Surprisingly, I enjoyed it all though I was really a meat-and-potatoes man.

Val sat across from me at the small dinette table while Melanie sat at the end of the table, close to me. One of her knees touched my thigh, but she didn't pull away. A rush of her energy ran through me with the touch. I glanced at her as we came in contact but held my position. What the hell was she doing?

I was terribly aware of her. Her overall presence was enough, but the knee touching me was driving me crazy. It was all I could do to keep from grabbing her, taking her in my arms regardless of Val's presence, and devouring her.

The ladies probed gently to find out more about me. Nosy women. I loved it, loved being here with the two of them.

"So, you're doing some remodeling on this place for someone?" Valerie asked.

"More like reconstruction, I'd say, but yes, getting it in shape to sell. It looks great today compared to the jungle it was back before Nathan and Nan became the caretakers. They've done a great job on the outside. The place should bring a pretty good price when the house is finished."

"I'll say," said Val. "I used to be in real estate before I married Henry. We're talking major dollars here, just for the land. So, who are Nathan and Nan?"

"They're a couple who live here in an apartment over the garage. They take care of the grounds and odd things that come up. A really great couple, friends actually. This place would be a mess without them."

"So, who owns it?" Val asked.

Melanie burst into laughter at the question. We had already been here.

Val looked at her oddly. "What is wrong with you, Melanie? You've been acting odd all day."

Melanie stood up at the question. "Yeah, Michael, tell us who owns it." *Oooo, wooo, hooo* sounds came from her lips as her hands rose, palms up. She started to shake them as she bent forward at the waist. Her hips and shoulders found a coordinated motion in some crazy pantomime of the mysterious. Laughter bubbled from her relentlessly as Val and I looked back and forth from Melanie to each other. Val shrugged her shoulders as if to say she'd never seen her like that. Finally, Melanie bent farther at the waist, trying to catch her breath, hands still up but fluttering now, as her head, still bent, shook from side to side.

What the fuck? I glanced at Val, scared to take my eyes off Melanie for long. Was she ever going to take another breath? Val shrugged her shoulders again as Melanie fought for breath.

"You need to get her out more," I told Val.

She nodded and kept her eyes on Melanie. It was clear Val had never seen her friend like this.

Melanie, with tears in her eyes, finally got control of her laughter and, with Val still looking on in awe, said, "Sorry. Tell Val who owns this place, Michael."

"I can't. It's a secret," I said.

"See," Melanie said, and once more tried the *oooo, wooo, hooo* sound, but she couldn't contain the laughter and lost her breath again.

I moved around her and motioned Val to follow me. We stepped outside under the awning.

Melanie tried to ask where we were going but couldn't in the midst of her uncontrollable giggles.

Finally, as Val and I reentered the trailer a few minutes later, Melanie looked up with tears in her eyes. From all that laughing, I guessed. Still trying to catch her breath, she said, "I'm sorry. Please don't go. Can we move on now?" Slowly she regained control as Val continued to stare at her.

Melanie wiped tears from her eyes as she looked from one of us to the other. "Where'd you guys go?" she managed to squeak out.

"Michael wanted to tell me who owned the place, but it was too noisy in here, so we stepped outside."

"Nooo," Melanie said. "Who?"

"I can't tell you, honey. Michael swore me to secrecy."

Melanie looked bewildered for a moment. "Not from me. Why would you keep it secret from me? Why wouldn't you tell me and Gail before, Michael?"

I remained silent, and Melanie turned back to Val. "You're my friend, Val. Please tell me since Michael is being so mean."

Val looked at me, and I nodded.

"It's owned by a very wealthy man," she said.

"Okay, but who?"

"I don't know. Michael wouldn't tell me."

"You rats! Why did you do that to me?" she said as we started laughing.

"Because you were having all the fun," Val said. "We wanted to have some, too."

"I was really getting disturbed to think you would tell her but not me, Michael," Melanie said. "I mean sure, you've danced with Val, but you and I have moaned and groaned and sweated together." She barely got the last out before the laughter took her again. This time we joined her.

Finally, Val said she had to leave. She wanted to see the house later though and let me know she was going to do some research into who owned it.

"As long as you don't find out through me," I said.

"It sounds like the rain is letting up," Melanie said. "Can you go with me to drop Val off? I'd love to stay and see the house if that's okay. Her car's just up the road near the bank."

"Sure. Sorry you can't stay, Val. We'll do it another time."

We drove Val to her car using Melanie's since mine was filled with work materials. Val positioned herself in the rear seat. Melanie kept looking in the rearview mirror and nodding as she drove. Once, she laughed and looked over at me with a little smile.

"I'm feeling left out. What's the secret joke here?" I asked.

Melanie looked at me. "No joke, she's just making faces at me." She gave Val a stern look in the mirror.

When we pulled up to Val's car, I got out of the passenger

side and opened her door for her. As I escorted her to her car, she stopped and turned to me.

"I am so happy you met Melanie," she said. "I'm sure my instincts are right about you, but . . . Well, I love her. She's an innocent."

"Hey, I'm not a bad guy," I said.

"No, but you're experienced, I'd say. She's separated, but she is married. She doesn't know what she's doing and neither do I. This is what I wanted for her, but I'm not sure now. Damn it, Michael, she's vulnerable."

"I kind of figured it was something like that. I like her, Val. I really do, and I'm not sure we need to be anything more than friends."

She laughed, surprising me.

"It's not you I'm worried about," she said.

Then she got into her car and waved as she pulled away.

"But I am," I said to her taillights.

***

Melanie and I drove back in silence until we parked in front of the trailer. It was still raining lightly but steadily, like it would last for a while. As Melanie shut off the engine, she turned to me. I reached over and pulled her close. Her eyes closed and she presented her mouth to me, but I didn't kiss her. My hand pressed against her back. I felt her heart beat furiously. She opened her eyes, her breathing rapid.

"Are you sure you know what you're doing?" I asked. My cheek moved, touching her, nuzzling her, absorbing the feel and smell of her, my arms around her. Her breath was shallow, hinting at desire. She didn't answer, but her tightened touch spoke to me, and I brought my lips to hers for the first time.

I was excited by her touch, barely controlling myself, gently kissing her lips, feeling her tongue caressing mine until I sucked it into my mouth.

Then I kissed her savagely. I couldn't hold back. I needed to devour her. Pulling apart, our eyes locked. Mine didn't waver as I reached for her, pulling up her short skirt.

"No, no, I can't," she said with tears in her voice. "Please, not yet."

Her eyes pleaded, wanting me, trusting me.

"I want you, Michael," she whispered. "But I can't right now."

I relaxed back in the seat, adjusting myself for the painful erection I had. I smiled at her and reached out with my left hand to caress her cheek. Her face pressed into it. Her eyes closed for a moment, and her breathing eased as her hand came up to play her fingers across mine.

"It's all right," I said.

I pulled her to me and kissed her forehead. It seemed a long time before I released her and opened my door.

"Now that I can stand again," I said, "we've got some exploring to do."

"Sorry," she said softly.

"Come on."

Then I was at her door, helping her out of the car. She smiled shyly at me as she took my hand. "I'm sorry. I'm just not ready for . . ."

"Shhh, not now." I held her hand and led her through the light drizzle.

Once inside, we explored the house together, spending a couple of hours walking around the porch, poking into every corner of the place, inside and out. I kept up a description of my plans, explaining things and listening to her, admiring her perspective on things. She was cautious with her comments, which were just short of suggestions. I marveled at her ability to succinctly appraise the place and find simple, appropriate solutions.

At the end of the tour, she turned to me.

"Thank you for sharing this with me, Michael. Whoever owns this place is very fortunate to have you. I can see how you love it."

I reached for her, pulling her close. "I do love it. I hadn't realized how much until we looked at it tonight, but I do." She released her head to my shoulder, resting it there.

We held each other. I closed my eyes and, for a moment, we were together in Italy, holding each other in Pisa. We strolled the plaza around the tower, one of many couples. I didn't feel alone anymore. I didn't want it to end; Venice waited.

"Come on, baby, it's getting late." My voice, which had turned husky, felt like it was coming from the bottom of a well. "Let's get you to your car."

As I started to move, she held onto me. "I didn't mean to be a tease. My life is mixed up right now, but I'd like to see you again." She didn't look at me. It was almost as if she expected rejection.

I pulled her closer and kissed her cheek. "I'd like that, but I want you to remember, my life is complicated, too."

"I know," she said. "'Complicated' means married, doesn't it?"

I guess it wasn't that big a mystery, but hearing her say it aloud startled me.

"We'll talk later, Melanie."

Chapter Eleven

I didn't like this. In just a few weeks, and especially in the past twenty-four hours, it seemed that Melanie had taken control of my life, my emotions. Everything had become a mess since I first saw her posing as a sumo to get into my head. I'd gone from resolute in avoiding her to some crazy exhilaration at seeing her again and, finally, to my present confusion and sense of loss.

She'd only driven away moments ago, and I just didn't know what to do about her. I was weak, rational realization tumbling away from me as emotional need of her took root. Just when I'd once more committed to staying away from her, some quirk or design of life had decided no. And I was weak.

I was shaken, too. I'm no angel, but I hadn't been with another woman since my relationship with Stephanie began, not even a kiss. Two years now I'd been with Steph, and today was more than a kiss, yet I hadn't felt any guilt. Shouldn't I feel bad? The kiss consumed me, stole my breath as my heart pounded, demanding more oxygen before leaving me weak but surging with adrenaline. I was still tingling with all that had just passed between us.

She had sought me out, brought an unwitting friend along to meet me. I laughed and leaned back into the cushions of the settee. It was all so crazy. *I'm too old for this!*

I laughed again, almost hysterical, remembering Melanie

being unable to control her own laughter. Poor baby must have been as nervous as me. Then there was the look on Val's face when Melanie said there was a picnic basket and wine in the car. Oh, yeah, that night at the club Val had wanted us to meet, but now she was apprehensive about her friend and me. Reality can be such a damn kick in the face.

I glanced at the clock over the stove. It was only six, and the storm was long over. I grabbed my truck keys and walked out. I was going nuts. I needed to move, talk to someone. Someone more screwed up than me, someone who could be objective about issues like problems and relationships that weren't his own. My problems he could understand though I hadn't been prone to taking his advice in the past. Not initially anyhow, but eventually I always did. I'd learned to trust his judgment.

I turned south on San Jose Boulevard and drove.
Married. She's married, damn it!

Maybe so, but she's separated. She never said she was separated though. Val told me that, said Melanie was separated and vulnerable. Val! Damn, what a surprise. And she hadn't a clue, surprised as I was at seeing one another. This definitely wasn't about casual sex. I didn't get that sense from either one of them. Whatever it was between Melanie and me was more. Today was just too intense, and she went out of her way to set it up: the picnic, Val, everything.

San Jose turned into Hwy 13 as I drove. Finally, I turned right onto a shady little entry road under a canopy of huge oaks and undergrowth. There was a sign with fading and missing letters. If you counted on it to find your way, you'd be lost. My mind automatically translated, just as it had years before: "Welcome to the Friendliest and Best Darn Do-It-Yourself Boatyard and Marina in the South." I pulled over into a little alcove under the trees for a moment. Get my head straight.

I turned off the engine and relaxed in the truck seat. So, was she truly separated, or was it living-together separated? I had read that this was becoming more common. Couples were finding the expense of divorce, even separation, too costly for many reasons. Health insurance alone forced many social and economic decisions. No, she appeared to have financial means; they weren't living together.

Damn it! I enjoyed being a single guy, going out and having a good time, listening to music, dancing even, but that was it. There'd been no other woman but Stephanie in a long time, and I still loved her. Why the hell did I need to be here looking for someone to tell me the obvious? I already had it made.

After a few minutes, I knew it was useless. I was just thinking in circles. I drove forward, and as the canopy of trees diminished, a new world opened up. Boats, all kinds of boats, appeared: sail and power, newer and older. All were blocked up, resting on their keels and jack stands, held upright on the hard as being out of the water is called. Through the somewhat haphazard assembly of boats, I caught sight of the porch and a glimmer of the river in the moonlight. A crowd had gathered. My timing was excellent. Too long away, it felt good to be back.

And then it welled up in me, the need to go to sea, the desire for the rise and fall of the ocean beneath me. I longed for the endless horizon, the smell of the ocean and the drift of life, too often now the rot of civilization, floating on the surface of the water.

I pulled into a parking space in front of the circular tables and chairs sprawled out in front of the porch. The veranda, as it was called, was merely an extension of the small porch. The rules that applied to the porch extended out another thirty feet or so incorporating the veranda and beyond. Odd to think about real rules here in this funky little place, but they existed. No cussing, damn it, was one.

I opened the truck door and stepped out into the crowd. Some I knew, others I didn't. It was always like this, new people coming in while others left for a time, cruising south to the islands in the winter before coming back. Everyone came back. Then there were the ones I knew well. Some of them were here, but I didn't see Nemo. I needed him today. That or I needed to run away, far away from Melanie, and Steph, too.

I grabbed the cooler out of the truck bed and headed for the porch under an assault of voices.

"Hey, Mick, where you been?" "What's happenin', dude?" "Sailor walking. It doesn't look good, folks." There was laughter all around and hands held out to shake or pound my back. It had been a while since I'd been back. I was always welcomed—most were, once accepted—but the place picked you. I hadn't heard "Mick" in a long time, but it was natural here.

Reaching the top step of the porch, I set the cooler down. A slim, almost emaciated man sat on a tall stool overlooking everything. "You're late," he said. "I take it that's Budweiser you have there?"

"Bud Light. I heard you were on a diet, Ben." The porch roared with laughter as the marina manager stepped down from his perch and gave me a hug. He popped the top on one of the Buds and raised it in a toast.

"To another lost sailor found his way home."

Ben and I caught up on things then. I let him know I was in Jacksonville working on the house. We had known each other for a few years now and shared much. I was living at the marina when I bought the river property. He'd called me

Mick—named me Mick is more like it—the first day we met, and that's who I am in the marina.

"Haven't seen Nemo this afternoon," Ben said in answer to my question.

I must have shown my disappointment.

"Got his rounds to make, you know. He'll be along, Mick," Ben assured me.

"Ah, I'm not surprised. He's always in demand. Seems to find the balance somehow."

Ben raised his beer. "Absolutely. A master he is."

I raised my beer, too, and looked around at people.

"Ready to put Cay Tam back in the water?" Ben asked. "Got a place for her right out there." He pointed to an empty slip in the marina. "Can do it in the morning."

"Not yet, Ben. Maybe in a couple of weeks if you still have room."

"Just call me. I'll have the below decks checked out, make sure she's watertight, and she'll be in the water when you get here."

"Thanks, Ben."

Then I was mingling with old friends, being introduced to new, and having a few drinks along the way. We had all been to, or were going to, many of the same places throughout the Bahamas and Caribbean.

About an hour after arriving, I felt a tug on my arm and turned to find a well-groomed, bearded, and mostly bald-headed man with a lopsided smile looking up at me. He wore a gold earring in his left ear, a simple hoop. The last of his hair was pulled back tightly along his skull and held there with some kind of leather device. He wore a long-sleeved blue cotton shirt.

"Where the hell you been?" he asked.

I hugged the older man to me. "Nemo."

He pulled himself away and straightened his shirt. He must have a half dozen of those faded blue shirts. "You don't call. You don't write. You just show up." As he spoke, he waved his hand in a backwards-circular motion that ended in a short dismissive flip of the fingers.

"Good to see you, Nemo. Miss me?"

"The hell with you, mate. I'm up to my ears in listening and advising the lost."

"Then I've come to the right place because I am totally fucked up and lost, buddy. Spitting into the wind as they say."

"Sounds like woman issues to me," he said, snickering. He bit on his pipe as he spoke, smiling up at me with one eye squeezed shut against the smoke.

"Boyce, I ah . . ."

A hand popped up in front of my face, silencing me.

"Let's take a little walk," he said.

We walked down the old pier a way before he turned to me again.

"Nemo, Michael." His jaw was set, his head cocked with determination. "Cap'n or Nemo, or Cap'n Nemo, damn it."

Nemo was the only one in the yard who occasionally called me by my given name. He definitely wasn't the follower type. Ben always scowled at him when he called me Michael, but Ben never said anything to Nemo. I hadn't called him by his given name in years. Where had that come from? I deserved the chewing out I was getting.

"Nobody remembers me as Boyce, Michael. Hell, Boyce was a boring old accountant. Took me a second to realize you were talking to me."

Then he laughed, stamping his foot along with the laughter as he held his pipe in his hand. "I love this life. You can be anything or whoever you want to be, Michael. And I'm Cap'n Nemo."

I nodded in agreement. "Sorry, Cap'n."

"Boyce was uninteresting. Cap'n Nemo is romantic." He exaggerated the last with another backward roll of his hand, fingers extended, bowed at the waist with his head slightly lowered. Always with the smile. I thought I saw a front tooth flash as if to emphasize the point. He was Cap'n Nemo, the part of him I needed to talk to. He was right about his former life as Boyce. Nemo could help me; Boyce couldn't.

"Now, what's going on, Michael?"

I shrugged my shoulders.

"You know, you don't come around enough. Every day somebody asks about you. And Cay Tam, Qui Tam—however you want to spell her, is wastin' away, sittin' over there on the hard, all proud and wanting like a good woman waitin' for her man."

I laughed at the analogy and looked across the yard to the storage area. I could just make out the bow as Cay Tam sat there blocked up. And in that moment, I decided.

"You're right. I'm going to put her in the water."

"Good. Now, what's up, brother?"

"I've met someone, Cap'n, maybe the one."

He didn't move, just stood there watching me as pipe smoke whisked around his head in thin tendrils. "And how is the lovely Stephanie?" he asked quietly.

My stomach flip-flopped. Damn him for making this difficult. I should have known he'd try to knock me off balance. "Steph's okay, but it's not her. Well, it is, but . . . well, I've met someone else, and it's all damned complicated."

"Stephanie is a lovely woman, Michael. I don't know how a man could do better."

I groaned and ran my hand through my hair. "You're hitting me hard. This isn't easy for me."

"You know life. It's not always about easy. And reality is best not faced alone sometimes, too hard to be objective about ourselves. But that's why you came to see me, isn't it?"

I nodded as he continued to smoke the pipe, watching me closely.

"I'm glad you came to me. How complicated is it? Is this woman single?"

"No, that's part of the complicated. She's separated but not discussing it, and she doesn't seem the type to have an affair. That big ring on her finger speaks to me, Nemo."

"Still wears the rings, does she," he murmured, more as a statement than a question. He cocked his head to the side, jaw reaching up again, his mind obviously racing. Connecting dots probably. "And you're not intimate, are you?"

"No, we haven't been intimate, and . . . and . . . Ah, hell, I don't know."

Nemo smiled and fired several conclusions at me at once. "Nice girl, struggling with herself. I can see it. You'd like that, respect that. Bring her by. I'd like to meet her."

"Yes, I like that about her. I know she's struggling, and maybe I should leave her alone, Cap'n. Let her find her way without confusing her life."

"Maybe," he said. "You lost harmony a long time ago, Michael. You know this goes way back, back to Millie. Eventually, you have to resolve what she did to you and your marriage."

I went stiff. "No, Cap'n. We're not going there. This might be right for me."

"It's not all about you though. As you said, it's complicated. Maybe you should let her go. Maybe Stephanie, too," he added softly.

I didn't want to hear that either.

"Don't look so surprised. Stephanie is a wonderful lady, but maybe you've had your time together. And why corrupt another wonderful woman when you know you're just repeating the same escape from your past? Your words, Michael. Not mine, yours. The past can't be denied. So, maybe you should go away somewhere and let life work on you."

His words triggered some invisible shield. I heard them and cast them out as my mind took me back to Italy, to the leaning Tower of Pisa. Not a very romantic moment in my life, but it was the keystone for my realization. I wanted someone to seriously share my life with. A partner. I'd shared much, but I'd never had a partner. I wanted Melanie to be the one, but I'd also wanted Stephanie to be the one. *Maybe* was the key now. *Maybe* meant that Melanie *could* be the one.

"I know, Cap'n. I do. Blessed, cursed, I don't know what I am. I hate to think about what I'm doing to both of them. Melanie is an innocent, and I've seduced her. I'm really torn, but I just can't bring myself to walk away. I need to talk to Steph, explain what's going on, that I've met someone."

He took a few moments, observing me through the smoke of his pipe, smiling at me with that one eye closed against the smoke milling around his face.

"I've been a little hard on you, Michael. As long as I've known you, you've been searching for something, maybe something you've lost or something you thought you had. I don't know except that it goes back to your marriage, to Millie. You have to work that out or it will forever haunt you."

We talked quietly on the dock, away from everyone except the occasional boater making his way home to his boat. Nemo drew it all out of me, or most of it. He knew enough about my past and my early marriage, but not all. Seemed he didn't need it all, that he had enough to push my buttons and make me go back and at least give what he called the beginning a look. Beginning of what, the end regarding relationships? What? He planted the seed, probed around but wouldn't come right out and shove my face in it. He probably figured I'd do that later, but I wouldn't. Not for a while.

"I just know you're searching, Michael. You've planted good seeds in life. Perhaps you're being rewarded. In spite of yourself, you are a good person. Harmony will find its way back to you when you work at it a little. The lovely Stephanie will be all right. You've brought each other much, I suspect, but perhaps she's not the one and she knows it. Start there. Talk to Stephanie. You need to do that."

I nodded, my head in a daze, and turned away without even thinking to say goodbye. When I got back to the porch, Ben was still there, sitting on his stool as always.

"Time for bed," he said and stood. "You're staying, I'd say." He held out a key. "Little Bob's trawler. You know where it is."

"Thanks, Ben." I took the key. "I'll see you in the morning."

I joined a group of liveaboards I'd known for years and quickly put Melanie and everything else away, at least for a while before heading down the pier to Little Bob's boat.

I woke before daybreak. Waves gently lapped the hull as I bolted up on one elbow. *Water music.* Why was I on a boat? It all came back in a moment, a few too many drinks for sure. At least I'd still had sense enough to take the key from Ben, recognizing the subtle advice to stay. Now the night was just giving way to the gray tint of morning. It couldn't be six o'clock yet.

I'd slept on one of the settee berths, lying back onto it with a cushion for a pillow, and had a few kinks in my shoulders this morning. After stretching, I straightened up Bob's boat and went to the porch. Only Ben was there at this hour, having a cup of coffee with the TV on for company as he played a hand-held computer game. He kept his head down, concentrating on the game.

"Everything okay, Mick?"

"Just fine," I answered, setting the key down beside him. "Thanks, Ben."

He merely nodded as I poured a cup of coffee.

I sat down, looking over to Dwight's monster of a barge. No one home now that Dwight and family were at their home in the Virgin Islands. I reminisced about old times there in the quiet of the morning as Ben continued to play his game. We'd done this a lot in the past. I'd lived here for over a year on Cay Tam. Lots of great friends and stories. What was today going to bring?

"Ben, go ahead and put Cay Tam in the water."

"She'll be there tomorrow," he said, never looking up from the game.

Chapter Twelve

I drove in the gates around seven thirty, plenty of time for my meeting with Joe the carpenter at eight that morning. Nathan would be wondering if I was all right. He was already gone when I pulled in. He wasn't used to my being gone overnight unless I let him and Nan know, and most often then it was because I was going out of town. An image of them peeking out their window yesterday popped into my head. Lots going on with the storm, cars coming and going then coming back again before leaving one last time. Now I'd been out all night. That had to have them wondering.

Joe and I spent the greater part of the morning finalizing the work plan after he had time to determine the involvement and practicality of what I had laid out. After we agreed on the changes, he set to work and I hit the shower. I'd thought off and on during the day about Melanie, and under the cleansing spray of hot water, I finally made up my mind once more to put some time and space between us. Nemo was right.

Changing after the shower, I decided to go out for a late lunch and pick up some groceries. I snagged the running list I tried to keep adding to and put it in my pocket with a triumphant, "Gotcha!"

My cell phone rang as I reached the door. It was Melanie, and everything else around me evaporated. Damn it, my heart jumped like crazy and my mind went blank. I was powerless to ignore it, even as some part of me chided my weakness.

"Hello?"

"Michael, this is Melanie." Her voice sent little pangs through me. Some kind of stupid happy shit. Meanwhile, my more mature side thought she sounded nervous. Alarm bells went off. *Here it comes, dumping me before we're even seeing each other. Good!*

"Hi, how are you?"

"I'm fine. I was wondering if you were free later. Could you join me for a late lunch?"

"Sure, I'd love to."

Oh, yeah, I was strong and resolute, damn it. And I didn't even have a hard-on. I was going downhill fast. So much for time and space,

***

We met at the parking lot where Val had previously parked her car. Melanie brought the picnic basket to my truck as I pulled up. I couldn't even get out before she was there. Darn it, girl. Momma wouldn't stand for me just pushing the door open. I got out and walked around to let her in. As I opened the door, she kissed me on the cheek.

"Friends," I said.

"Yes."

I reached across and buckled her seat belt. Her eyes commanded my attention.

"What?"

"Nothing, just no one's ever buckled my seat belt before." The lush green of those eyes pulled me in. I couldn't resist. As I backed out, I brushed my lips against hers and continued to pull out of the truck even as her arms were coming up to me. I was getting stronger, but now my dick kicked in, trying to rise for some attention.

As I got in the driver's side, she said, "Okay, I've made the lunch. You get to pick the location."

"Too much responsibility. We'll find a place together."

"Okay."

There it was again, that word and the way she used it. Just a quick, snappy *okay*. I would come to love that response. It had meaning somehow, agreement but more. It was her "we" as in *we'll work it out*, not simply *whatever you say*. I liked it immediately the first time I heard it. Something else to like about her, damn it. *Okay*.

As we drove, I said, "That's always my first move."

She looked confused. "What do you mean?"

"Lock 'em in with the seat belt, then off to the woods to have my way with them."

"Okay."

I laughed. My little secret. *Okay*.

She smiled.

"Yeah. Get me worked up, and then you want me to forget lunch. No way. I want my free meal," I said.

Melanie became silent, and when I looked over at her, her eyes were a little teary.

"I'm sorry, Michael. I'm not like that. I didn't mean to tease last night. I don't even know what I'm doing here now."

"I know you don't. I'm sorry for saying anything. Let's just enjoy ourselves."

She leaned into me as I wrapped my right arm around her shoulder.

We ended up in a little park near the river. She had brought a blanket, a radio, and the basket of food. She proceeded to spread everything out on a picnic table positioned at the V of two narrow, one-way roads and concealed by trees. The roads were more like paths, really, with just enough room for one vehicle at a time. She surprised me again, bringing a bottle of Merlot and a few bottled waters. The real surprise was make-your-own peanut butter-and-jelly sandwiches plus pretzels and a couple of watermelon slices.

"Do you like peanut butter and jelly?" she asked.

I spread peanut butter on two slices of whole wheat bread. My favorite.

"Love 'em, almost as much as pizza."

"Really?"

"Absolutely."

As I finished cutting one of the sandwiches diagonally, I raised my right hand and shook my knife at the sky. "Take that, Mom."

I smiled and raised an eyebrow as I looked over at Melanie. "Would you like yours cut?"

"I don't know. What was that all about?"

"An old ritual, something to do with me and my mother." I cut her sandwich and passed it to her. "One of those little mysterious things you hate."

"Oh, no, you don't. Not again. Tell me."

Taking a bite of the sandwich, I savored it for a moment before telling her my childhood sandwich story.

"One morning, I was having my oatmeal when I looked over at Mom making my school lunch. I told her all the other kids had their sandwiches cut diagonally and asked if she could cut mine that way. Well, she looked at me and then put down the knife. 'No,' she said, 'but you can cut it that way from now on when you make your lunch. You're a big boy now.' She always found opportunities to give us more responsibility."

Melanie nodded. "Smart woman."

We enjoyed the afternoon together, talking easily, exploring each other with little questions, sitting close, touching, kissing passionately, and then taking a walk through the park holding hands.

The afternoon was great. She had to work the next day, but we left the parking lot with the understanding I would call her after she got off work to see if she could spend the day after with me. When I called, I told her to dress for canoeing or kayaking and to bring a bathing suit.

"Really? I haven't been canoeing since I was a Girl Scout," she said.

I could hear the excitement in her voice.

"Once a Girl Scout, always a Girl Scout," I said. "I'd like to go early if you can make it."

"Okay, I'll pack a lunch."

"No need. We can go to a little place I know."

"Okay."

Chapter Thirteen

*T*he parking lot at the supermarket again. Was I really just here a couple of days ago? I got out of the truck to meet her as she pulled up beside me.

"Nice legs," I said. She was wearing khaki shorts and a green pullover top. I couldn't help noticing those pretty red toes in lime-green flip-flops.

"Well, thank you," she said.

She proceeded to exaggerate her movements as she settled in, wiggling her butt into the seat as I leaned over to connect her seat belt. As I snapped it in place, I looked up, intending to admonish her for being provocative. Seeing those playful green eyes and those smiling lips, I kissed her instead, snaking my tongue into her mouth. I kept kissing her, and she pulled me to her, wrapping her tongue around mine.

She said she'd been to St. Augustine many times in the past, having brought her children to the beaches there for years. She talked about how she still enjoyed the little town though it was becoming more and more touristy and artificial.

Unless you knew where to go and what to stay away from, I told her.

I drove through town and across the Bridge of Lions, which spanned the Intracoastal Waterway where boats of all kinds were at anchor on both sides of the bridge. The city marina, its docks extending out into the waterway, lay on the southwest side.

"I love the freedom those sailboaters have. Can you imagine what it's like to slide through the water with no engine running, the quiet and peace of just the wind pushing you?"

My interest perked. "Have you ever sailed?"

"No, it's one of the things I plan to get to," she said.

She couldn't have known how that pleased me. I glanced at her, watching as her eyes soaked up the tranquility of the scene.

Going past the lighthouse, I turned into the state park. She was aware of the park but generally preferred to go farther down to the beach where she could drive on it and park if she was going to have to pay a fee anyhow, she said.

I pulled over to a covered pavilion area with grills and, beyond it, a small hut with kayaks, canoes, and other watercraft.

"Let's take that table in the shade," I said.

I helped her out of the truck and retrieved most of our stuff. Melanie followed with a small bag and a radio. She set things out as I walked over and greeted the attendant at the boat rental. After a few moments, I walked back.

"Ready to go?"

"Sure," she said. Raising her arms over her head, she slipped out of her t-shirt and shorts to reveal a blue bikini. I watched in awe, my heart beating madly as she jogged to the water's edge.

Pulling on a baseball cap, she looked back. "Which one, Captain?"

She wore a Florida Gators hat. I smiled and pointed to one of the canoes.

"That one. Did I tell you I'm a Gator? Class of . . . Well, I got a late start."

"My son would like that. He's the Gator."

As we moved through the water, I sat in the back of the canoe, admiring her slim form and graceful movements. She was definitely in good shape. The little she wore now amplified the womanly hardness of her body. Her femininity was overwhelming, even in this setting. With difficulty, I adjusted myself as I came alive again.

She eased her paddling and watched a couple of windsurfers skim past on their boards.

"That looks like fun." She looked back at me. "Thank you for bringing me."

"Next time, we'll try it."

"No way," she squealed, suddenly turning completely around. "Whoops," she squealed again as she held onto the rocking canoe. "Okay, but you first, then maybe I'll try."

"Okay," I said.

I was busy keeping the canoe upright during her sudden movements. As soon as I started paddling again, the boat steadied. The view of her from the front was even better.

She gently paddled backwards. Then she stopped and looked at me strangely. "You already know how to windsurf, don't you?"

I laughed. "A deal's a deal. One lesson with Richard and you'll be off with the wind as they say."

She looked skeptical. "Next time, right?"

"Right. You're going to love it. You're a natural athlete."

She shrugged and took a long look at the windsurfers in the distance. "I can try."

After putting the canoe away, I introduced her to Richard. He explained a little more about windsurfing, and she seemed more comfortable with it. Afterwards, we ate and lay in the sun until it clouded up. We had just finished packing the car when it started to rain. I backed out and headed for the gate just as it really let loose, a typical Florida thunderstorm.

I couldn't see more than a few feet in front of us, so I pulled off the road again and switched the key off.

"We may as well—" with a whoop she climbed over everything in the cab of the truck until her slender body was in my lap, her arms hugging me.

"What are you doing, trying to kill us?" Little kisses peppered my face as I tried to unwrap myself. "This seat doesn't go back any farther, silly." My hand found what I hoped was the hazard light switch, and I pushed it.

"I had such a great time today. I loved it. Thank you, thank you, thank you," she said as she continued to kiss me.

I gave up trying to untangle myself and just laughed as I held onto her. "I loved it, too, baby. We'll do it again soon."

We held each other as the storm raged. Holding, laughing, and kissing, wrapped up in each other. Finally, it stopped, and I drove the short run to Beachcombers, a small out-of-the-way bar and restaurant. It was right next to one of the beach access tollbooths for those driving on the beach.

We reached across the table, holding hands as we waited for our meal. Her toes gently massaged me as her bare feet rested on top of mine. We talked quietly, barely conscious of others. The waitress startled us when she came with our food, laughing at us, then with us, as she set our plates down.

Later, arriving at her car, Melanie raised her head off my shoulder. It was almost dark, and I was reluctant for her to leave. She reached up, pulling me to her, and kissed me hard, her little tongue igniting me. "I've had a wonderful day. I promise to try windsurfing if we can go again."

"Okay." I pulled her to me again, holding her, kissing her strongly.

As we finished packing her car, a woman came by walking

a small dog. I said hello.

"Hi," replied the woman.

I knelt down, holding out my hand, and the dog immediately came to me, sniffing cautiously.

"This dog is so ugly it's cute. Where did you get this thing?"

The woman laughed, and I joined her. I looked over at Melanie to find her face relaxing from what appeared to be a look of horror.

"I don't mean to offend," I said. "He is cute."

"No, you're right, and you're the first person ever to tell the truth about him," the woman responded.

I stroked and baby-talked the dog.

"He is ugly," she added, "but I love him."

"That's the way love is," I said.

The woman was still laughing as she continued on her way.

Standing outside her car, Melanie turned and snuggled into me.

"I just love it, Michael. I love the ease you have with people and how they take to you." She lifted her head and kissed me again, passionately.

"I love your passion for life," she said. "I just love that."

Chapter Fourteen

*T*he next day was a blur. I went to the gym, had a good workout, and started on some of the jobs I could do by myself. More and more, I found myself eyeing the dock. Finally, I walked down and started to inspect it. There wasn't much of a tidal change here, but it was low anyhow, so I took a good look at the pilings, the ones I could see, and knew immediately they would all have to be replaced. I jotted down figures as I made estimates in a small notebook I carried. Probably ninety feet of dock, I figured. Major expense if I replaced it all, but it didn't need to be that long unless I wanted to bring Cay Tam to it. I hadn't decided yet, but that was the driving force now, fueling my focus on the dock. I liked the marina and trusted the people there to look out for me, but it would be nice to have Cay Tam here, at least some of the time. Or I could shorten the new dock and put a mooring ball down in deeper water. Keep it out of the navigable channel and it would be okay. That would be good for short periods of bringing her here.

I pulled out one of the lawn chairs that Nan and Nathan kept against a tree near the water and sat down. I closed my eyes, intending to think about the cost and whether I should just let the new owners, whoever they might be, decide, but it was wasted effort. I knew I would never sell the place. I needed to accept that, stop fighting it.

I relaxed. It was nice there under the tree, looking out across the water. Soon, as I had so often lately, I was thinking about Melanie, smiling again as I remembered how she'd scrambled into my lap during the thunderstorm. I flashed momentarily on her being so happy at such simple things.

Then, it was back to work.

***

Later, the phone rang as I was finishing my shower.
"Hello."
"Hi, Michael, is this a good time to talk?"
"Who is this?" I asked.
"Why . . . why this is . . . is this Michael?"
"Well, yes, it is, ah, Melanie, right?"
I laughed at her pause. "Sorry, Melanie, I couldn't resist a little fun. I knew it was you, baby."
"Now it's 'baby,' huh? I am really going to get you one of these days. How are you? Up to anything special?"
"I'm all done for the day. I'm just drying off from my shower. How about you?"
"There's a visual," she said.
I loved the laughing that went with our banter. "Don't just stand there looking. Hold on, let me turn around so you can do my back."
"Oh, no, stay where you are. I can dry your back from here," she said.
"Okay, sexy one, that's enough. I can't take anymore of where this is going, but I'd like a rain check."
"I'd like it, too. Real possibilities there," she said.
"Are you working tomorrow?"
"No, do you need some help? I'd be glad to help with 'hey,

girl' kind of stuff, or I could dry your back or something," she said and giggled.

"I'm going to ignore that for now—but not forever. How much time do you have tomorrow? I've got something in mind for a few hours."

"Well, I need to go to the gym in the morning, but then I'm good all afternoon."

"See you at the gym. Bring something comfortable to wear," I told her, then paused to grin. "And a bathing suit."

***

The kickboxing class that morning was especially good for me. I was gaining endurance with the regularity of my workouts. Melanie looked wonderful, full of fun and life. Once more, I was aroused, so I ignored her. I concentrated on the movements, thinking about today, wondering how she'd respond to the place, to the people.

Afterwards, I pulled off my sweat-stained Mickey shirt and jumped in the shower. After changing, I left the gym and drove the truck to a Walmart where I was to meet Melanie.

As I waited, I thought about things. I had to stop fooling myself. We were on a path to jumping into bed together, and I didn't want to stop it. Yesterday had been a real exclamation point for me. I really wanted to be with this woman, and if today was another indication of that, then I needed to make some decisions.

But there was only one decision to make, and I made it. I owed it to Stephanie to tell her the truth of the situation. I would drive to Orlando tomorrow no matter what. I'd call her tonight, I decided. If she wasn't available, I'd stay over until she was.

And what is going on with Melanie's marriage? Is it important? Of course, it is. If she can work it out with her husband, then that's what she should do. But no, why is she seeing me like this if she's trying to do that?

Too much thinking. I shook my head to escape from it all. I was left realizing once more how much I wanted a partner, someone to share my life with, and it couldn't be Stephanie. I'd always known she wouldn't leave John, and I wouldn't want her to. I had to talk with her.

Melanie was like a wraith, suddenly there and in the truck before I could get around to her and open the door.

"You're too quick. I was raised to help a woman in and out of the car. You've gotta stop doing that," I chided as I climbed back into the driver's seat.

"Okay, I'll try to do better. I'm just excited," she said so fast it took the argument out of me. "Hey, got a new adventure ahead. Let's do it!"

I noticed she hadn't buckled up. I shook my head. "Spoiled already." I leaned over to pull her belt across her and buckle it.

"Oh, I didn't think about that," she said.

I gave her a look that told her the mock innocence wasn't working.

"Actually," she said, "I guess I am spoiled, and I like it."

I had to chuckle as I drove out of the parking lot and headed south.

"Going back to St. Augustine?" she asked.

"Nope."

"Another park? I don't see a picnic packed."

"No again, but lunch is in the cooler," I said, motioning with a thumb over my shoulder. "Be patient. It won't be long now."

"Guess you need to know I'm not patient, either," she said.

She raised her eyebrows, and her lips seemed a little tight, pushing out her cheeks so that her dimples showed more.

I laughed. She folded her arms across her chest, a picture of impatience. I looked down to see if her foot was tapping. It wasn't.

"Too bad." I continued to drive, eyes on the road, ignoring her. A few minutes later, I pulled onto the marina entry road. Melanie immediately sat up straight, looking around, eyeing everything, absorbing. Such little things excited her. I began to wonder what she and her husband shared together beyond a home and children.

As the canopy of trees opened to reveal the boats on the hard, her natural excitement exploded. "Wow, I never knew this was here. And I've driven by it hundreds of times. This doesn't look like a windsurfing day to me."

It was a full-up workday in the yard, owners mostly, working on their boats, some that would never see the water again. I pulled up to the porch as I thought about how many boats just sit at the dock or in a boatyard or even on trailers at homes, seldom used. I didn't understand it. Like the body, boats needed to be exercised regularly, or they would go bad just sitting there. I was guilty of it, too. I hadn't taken Cay Tam out in a while, either.

I got out of the truck and brought Melanie to the porch where Ben came out of the office to greet us.

"Welcome back, Mick," he said, shaking my hand. "And you, too, lovely lady. Welcome to the porch."

"Melanie, this is Ben. Ben runs the place. Ben, this is Melanie."

"I am pleased to meet you, ma'am, no matter how it is that you have come to know this rogue and lost son." He bowed at the waist to kiss her hand. Some of Nemo had definitely rubbed off on him.

I laughed and quickly pulled Melanie back to me as Ben had tucked her arm in his and was making for a chair. Definitely a Nemo move.

"Oh, no, you don't, you old hound dog. Get your own woman."

Ben gave a good-natured shrug and released her to my pull.

"He knoweth me too well, lovely lady. Perhaps in another lifetime then," he said with a bow. "Till it be morrow, sweet princess."

Melanie looked from one of us to the other as Ben and I laughed, then she joined in.

"She's in the water, Mick, and Phillip has checked her out," Ben said as he headed towards the porch steps that led to the active part of the yard. On the second step, he paused and turned towards Melanie. "I'll see you again, young lady." And he was off.

"*Mick?*"

"Next time we have a workout together, remind me and I'll explain." I took her hand and started for the dock.

She stopped. "Too many mysteries, Mick, I'll have it now, please. I'm beginning to wonder how many lives you're living. I need to know your real name, at least." She arched her eyebrows, questioning me.

I shook my head at her insistence for an explanation. "Okay, I'll come clean. Mick is short for Mickey. Now, let's go."

"So, is your name Mickey or Michael," she asked, clearly puzzled, "because I know Mike is short for Michael, but Mick? Do they call you that as a nickname for Michael?"

"No, they call me that because I used to run a lot here and I sweat funny." Her face still showed her confusion. "Next time we work out together, check out my shirt. Mickey Mouse appears as I sweat."

"You're kidding! That's why they call you Mick?" She laughed and bent at the waist, slapping her hands together, her mouth open and her eyes shining. "I can't wait. I never noticed that."

"Of course not, you're too busy looking at my butt," I said. Laughing with her, I pulled her along to the dock that extended out for some distance. "Actually, the Mickey Mouse sweat thing came out after Ben named me. He does that," I told her. "Names people."

This time she just nodded.

We admired the boats, both sail and motor vessels, as we strolled along the pier. Some of them were being worked on as we went by. Finally, I stopped alongside Cay Tam. I climbed down the ladder attached to the dock and reached a hand up for her.

She didn't move, just stood looking at the boat.

"Did you rent this for the afternoon?" she asked. "That is a big boat. Do you know how to operate it?"

"Come on down, and then we'll talk," I said.

Slowly, she climbed down the ladder with my hands on her all the way.

"Welcome to Cay Tam," I said as she stepped onto the deck. I turned her towards me and wrapped my arms around her, pulling her tightly to me. "This is where I like to be, sailing her, living aboard, going to places I've never been. Want to go for a sail?"

"Can we really?" She looked around, slowly turning before hugging me. "It's beautiful, Michael. Whose boat is it?"

"She's mine."

"Yours! This is your boat?" She looked up at me.

"Yes, she's mine. Has been for several years."

"Can we take her out and sail her? Really?"

I was pleased with her excitement. I was wondering how she would react. I'd wanted to bring her here ever since seeing her reaction to the boats in St. Augustine.

"Come on, we need to get the lunch cooler out of the truck, and then we're off."

After stowing our lunch and taking a tour below, we prepared to depart, disconnecting the electrical cords, then all the lines but two. After checking everything below, I showed her how to start the engine and what to check for. Then I briefed her on what I needed her to do and what I would be doing, making sure she understood.

After the engine had warmed up and I had Melanie stationed forward with a boat hook to push off from the dock, I released the last lines and returned to the cockpit. The light wind was ideal as it continued to push the bow gently away from the dock with Melanie's push. I motioned her back to the center cockpit and gently throttled forward to move around the boat forward of us.

"Here," I said, "take the helm while I check on a few things."

"What? No, I've never driven a boat before!"

"You can do it," I told her. "Here, just take the wheel and aim us towards the center of the river."

She gripped the wheel so tightly her knuckles turned white.

"Easy there," I said, "Just relax. I'll stay right here until you're comfortable."

"You better," she said. She glanced at me with those big eyes, but only for a moment as she shifted back into responsible mode. I watched her take in everything around her again, getting her bearings.

I explained the simple controls to her, talked about the wind and its effects on the boat and, finally, as I was going below, said, "Look out for crab traps and avoid them."

"Hold on. I don't know what a crab trap looks like!"

I looked back as I started down the cockpit stairs again, laughing this time. "Okay, so don't hit anything. I'll point one out when I see one." Then I went below to check out the boat.

I examined the bilges for water leaks, then the engine room, looking and listening throughout the boat for anything that wasn't right. Going back topside, I found her relaxed.

"I like this." Her face was lit up with the joy of it. "I like the name, too, I think," she said. "Well, maybe I would if I knew what it meant. Cay Tam, what does it mean? And how do you pronounce it?"

"It's a restaurant in southern France. I liked the name, so I just eliminated the Le. And it's pronounced, K Tam." A little white lie, pronunciation and all, for now. Melanie didn't need to know the underlying history, that Cay Tam was really Qui Tam, a bit of misdirection needed after my friend, Dwight, called my attention to the provocativeness of it to some in the world. He'd insisted that I was arrogant to name my boat after a type of lawsuit that had brought me a fortune due to the corruption and greed of others.

He was right. The pronunciation was the same, Qui Tam or Cay Tam. It just wasn't so much in your face if you were to know about things like that. And I could always say it was actually pronounced "Key Tom," instead of Tam, after a small island in the Caribbean that's not on any charts in case someone who knew how to pronounce the name of such islets should ask. Of course, I was careful to just pronounce it K Tam for now. Because of nosy women.

"Well, I like it, too, then," she said.

She reached over and kissed me quickly before turning her eyes forward again, looking for crab pots or whatever else might be floating in the way.

"Cay Tam. That's the name on the card you gave me, isn't it?"

"Yes, SV Cay Tam. SV is for sailing vessel."

"Okay, got it. What's next, Captain? I'm ready," she said.

"All right, let's do a few things. Bring the throttle back and put the boat in neutral."

She did and then went to reverse as directed.

"Checking her out, are we? How long's it been since you had her out?"

"Yes, checking her out. It's been way too long," I said. "Feels good to be on her again."

I pointed out the gauges and explained them, ending with the depth gauge. I wanted her to understand that it was set to show the depth of water under the keel, the lowest part of the boat, not the actual water depth.

Her finger tapped the top of a joystick-like control on the pedestal. "What's this?" she asked.

"That's a bow thruster. Move it left or right . . . whoops, I mean port or starboard . . . and the bow of the boat moves in that direction."

Her forehead wrinkled. "Guess we'll get to that 'port' and other thing later. Why didn't you use this thruster thing to get off the dock?"

"Because you have to learn it the hard way first. In case the darn thing doesn't work when we want it to." I liked that she caught that detail.

"Slow down all the way, and we'll check it out," I said.

We continued like that, putting the boat through a

checkout, with Melanie learning as we went along. I took it slow, allowing her to absorb the boat, the water, and the wind, feeling it, growing with it as she learned new skills. Finally, I pointed to a spot ahead but off the channel. I told her to slow down and make for it but to watch the depth gauge carefully as the water would quickly become shallower.

We put out the anchor, another learning experience for her. I had her man the helm while I did everything manually to drop the anchor instead of using the remote control from the cockpit. For some reason, I wanted her to know how to do things the hard way, the way we'd have to do it if things went wrong, like if the windlass should fail. Experience had taught me that life was most often Plan B. It was best to be prepared.

We had lunch in the cockpit on a table that she hadn't realized was there until I unfolded it from the steering pedestal. "So much to learn," she said.

After lunch, we enjoyed a glass of wine. She leaned back in my arms, and I felt a pulse of intense pleasure course through me. I was rising, getting hard as she asked if we could put the sails up.

I laughed. "There's enough up right now."

She turned in my arms with a questioning look. "There's no sail up."

"I didn't say sail. I said there's enough up."

Slowly, a smile appeared, and she brushed the back of her hand against the bulge in my pants. Then she pulled her hand away, and glistening moisture showed in her eyes. "I'm sorry, Michael, I didn't . . ."

I smiled and pulled her to me in a hug. "It's all right. Now, about the sails, we need to keep to the basics this trip. But next time, I promise, we'll put up the sails."

"All right, and then we can go out into the ocean and really sail her. Right?"

Her enthusiasm was stimulating. "No, baby, that'll be another trip."

"Oh, come on, honey, please." She used her eyes to sway me.

"Do you know how long it takes to get to the ocean from here on a sailboat?"

"No, but it can't be that long. It's not that far."

"How about thirty-five miles. And we'll be doing five or six knots."

"What's a knot?" she asked.

I explained a knot as a measure of speed in nautical terms, then the realities of current, tides, and boat speed as well as bridge openings and distance until she stopped me. Her shoulders slumped under the weight of the knowledge I'd placed on her.

"Okay, you've beaten me down. How long will it take?"

"Seven hours on a good day."

"Great." She came back strong, energized as a new thought took her. "Okay, how about we take one day out, one day on the ocean, and one day back? Let's see, that's two nights, so we'll pick a long weekend. We make a list. I'll go shopping, and we just do it."

Her enthusiasm and excitement drew me in. I laughed, then laughed harder when I looked up to see the serious look on her face as if she couldn't understand what was so funny.

"I love the way you have it all worked out," I said. "Just do it, right?"

"Right, we'll just do it." She hopped into my lap, hugging and kissing me so spontaneously that I think she even surprised herself.

"You're beautiful, my lovely one, and I love having you

with me on Cay Tam."

Her face was so alive. I could feel the depth of her pleasure in being here. It scared me for a moment, then I was lost in her. Until she went limp.

"Are you all right?" I asked at the sudden release of her arms.

"Yes, I guess I just feel a little guilty enjoying this and you so much." I saw her vulnerability then, and my heart jumped.

I pulled her back to me. "Are you ready to talk about it, about us and where this is going, maybe about your marriage?"

"No. No, I'm not ready," she said. She looked at me then, exploring my face, silent. I wondered what was going through her mind.

"You know what, baby? I want you, and both our lives are complicated." I added a smile as if things were humorous though she must know I didn't feel that way. "I can be a much better friend than lover, and we're moving towards lovers."

Her words were muffled as she snuggled into my shoulder. "I know. I want you as both," she said.

"Don't forget I tried."

***

Late in the afternoon, I maneuvered Cay Tam to the dock. Melanie was positioned on the bow where she threw the spring line to Ben on the dock, then turned, picked up the bow line, and threw it to someone else. Turning, she came aft to handle the stern line. I was already throwing it as she hurried back. Her hands went to her hips. "My job!"

"I had a little extra time back here since you did so well," I said. I reached for her hand as she moved aft. We were secured to the dock, and I would adjust the lines before we left.

"Thanks, guys!" I shouted. Ben gave a wave and moved

back down the dock in his golf cart.

I took Melanie by the hand. "Greg, I want you to meet Melanie."

Melanie smiled. Her smile assured me I wanted her to be a part of my life. "Greg lives on the trawler forward of us," I said.

"Good to meet you, Melanie. Look out for Mick," he said, grinning as he moved towards his boat.

"Good to meet you, too, Greg," she said.

Melanie hugged herself to me as if she enjoyed being a part of my world, a world that was getting bigger very quickly. "This was all a major surprise today. I really don't know you, do I, Michael?"

"Of course, you know me. You just don't know all of me, like I don't know all of you."

As I drove back to Melanie's car, she shifted her head off my shoulder and turned as best she could to face me in the seat.

"Michael, I'm going to Daytona weekend after next with Val for a dance thing. You could get a room at our hotel and we could see each other if you'd like."

I looked at her for a moment, then pulled her close, keeping an eye on the road.

"You think about it first. If you still want me to come, let me know Monday and I will, but only if you're sure. You have a husband," I reminded her.

"And your relationship is complicated."

"Do you want to talk about it?"

"No, so you be sure about this, too, because I'm sure now. Just come to me if you're ready."

It was Thursday. We parted with her knowing I would be out of town a few days. The concern at that was plain on her face, but I didn't explain.

Chapter Fifteen

I left early the next morning though I knew I wouldn't be able to see Stephanie before five that afternoon. I'd called her the night before, explaining I needed to do some business there today and would like to see her if she had time. She called me back, said she could see me but couldn't spend the night.

I called Curt, my friend and accountant. He could work me in at one o'clock, and we agreed to meet and go over a few things, including a review of projected costs I had compiled for my Jacksonville property. I wanted Curt to be current on a few things, especially the house. I was less inclined to sell it now as Nathan and Nan had apparently known all along. I needed to talk to someone objective about that aspect, and I'd always found Curt's financial advice just that, sound and objective.

By four, I had seen Curt, completed all my errands, settled into the condo, and taken a shower. I was nervous. I wandered the rooms, looking out over downtown Orlando. *Why did I build this place?* But I knew why. I loved it. Loved how the city was being cleaned up and how it was attracting more residents to the revitalized downtown area. Orlando was one of the success stories of downtown restorations.

What to say to Stephanie—that was the thing. I knew it would come when needed. What did I expect to come out of this? I'm seeing two married women. Why do they need to know anything, really? For a moment, I rationalized that I should just see them both. What did I really owe either of them? I immediately regretted the thought. I respected both women, regarded them highly, and knew neither of them had become involved with me casually. They weren't that way, and I loved them both. Being with me was a significant twist to their married lives, a twist brought on by extraordinary circumstances in each case. Otherwise, an affair, or any relationship with another man outside their marriage, would be out of the question for them. I knew I was in their lives intimately only by some breach in their marriages. I understood Stephanie's, but what about Melanie? What was really going on in her marriage?

I didn't know enough. Maybe it was simply part of life's ongoing struggle, sorting out everything, continually seeking harmony. That's what Nemo would say. I smiled at the thought of him. Even he would say I couldn't have them both. He would call it selfish fantasy, hormonal rationalization, not harmony.

Finally, Stephanie arrived, and we held each other. I poured us some wine.

"Well, this was a nice surprise," she said. "I just wish I could stay tonight, but I can't."

Smiling sensuously, she moved into my arms and kissed me deeply.

"I do have a couple of hours," she added with a purr in her voice.

"Whoa," I said, easing away. "Let's have a glass of wine."

"Okay." She looked at me oddly, probably sensing my nervousness.

She was concerned for me immediately. I could hear it in her voice.

"What's wrong, Michael, are you all right? Has something

happened?"

"No, no. I'm just a bit off balance right now."

After a moment of silence, I turned to her. "Honey, I've met someone."

As we sat looking at each other, she took a drink. Realization had not sunk in.

"Okay, so is everything all right?" Then her eyes got wide as I remained silent. "Oh, my God, you mean another woman."

I could see the pain stirring in her eyes, the realization taking hold. Veins in her neck stood out, and her face flushed red, completely enveloping her creamy skin. "I . . . I guess I knew it would happen one day. I haven't been there for you enough. I always knew you needed more, but I couldn't. I just couldn't." She fumbled with the words as her breathing quickened and her eyes welled with tears.

I pulled her to me, holding her close, talking softly to her, trying to sooth and ease the pain I'd caused.

Awkwardly, hesitantly, I spoke.

"It just happened, Steph. I mean, I . . . I don't know what I mean, but I had to talk to you about it. I couldn't *not* tell you. I had to talk to you. I'm sorry, honey."

"Oh, my God, Michael, I'm not prepared for this. I need a minute." She eased herself from my arms and walked towards the bathroom.

I couldn't help but admire her, still graceful and dignified despite the soft crying as she left the room. I loved this woman. What was I doing?

Minutes later she returned, her eyes damp but under control. She sat with me and took my hands, our knees touching.

"How far along is it?" she asked. "How close have you become?"

I stammered and looked away. "I can't talk to you about that, Steph. I don't know where I am with it. With her."

She was patient. "Michael, it's important for me to know how close you two are."

"We're intimate," I said. I looked into her eyes, and I felt my own start to tear. The full realization of it hit me then. "Intimate but not sexually involved."

She let out a deep breath she must have been holding. "Thank you," she said simply. "Thank you for respecting us. I want to be happy for you, I really do, but I am so sad about us."

My God, her grace and poise was like a hot poker through me. How could I be so stupid as to give up this wonderful woman?

She squeezed my hands in hers. "You know I love you, baby. I really thought we'd be together. That one day, John would pass naturally and we'd be together. In the back of my mind, I guess, I always realized this could happen. But it wasn't real. It was never real, Michael."

Then she let loose, and the tears flowed. She tried to choke them back, but the dam had broken. I could only hold her and fight my own tears, but I, too, lost the battle.

"I know," I said as a choking pain grabbed my throat.

Minutes passed, then she stood abruptly and returned to the bathroom again.

A couple of minutes later, she was back and composed. Only a trace of redness was apparent in her eyes.

"Are you staying or going back?" she asked.

"I'm staying, probably for the weekend. I need to do some things here."

"Yes, you do. You need to think and so do I, baby." She leaned into me so our heads were touching, resting against each other, and reached out to caress my jaw with her hand.

"You probably need to take Cay Tam and go away for a while," she said.

I smiled at her observation. This woman knew me so well. She was right, and so was Nemo. I really did need to get away.

"I don't know what to say. I need to think, Michael, but I don't want to leave it, leave us, the way it is now. John and I have plans this evening. I really must go, but I'd like to come back in the morning."

"I need to see you, too." I took her into my arms again, holding her, afraid to let her go.

***

My cell went off after she left. Damn, it was Nan. I hadn't said anything to her or Nathan, and I'd driven the Porsche. "Hey, Nan, what's going on?"

"You, Michael. You're going on, worrying Nathan like this when he doesn't know where you are."

"I'm sorry, Nan. Really, I just got busy and didn't think."

"I know," she said and laughed. "Just wanted to make sure you're all right."

"I am, and thanks for keeping me straight. I'll be here all weekend, I think."

"Okay, just one more thing. What's going on with this man Joe? He says he's working for you."

"He is. Sorry about that, too. I should have introduced all of you."

"Are you all right, Michael? This isn't like you, and we haven't seen much of you lately."

"I'm all right, Nan. I'll explain when I get home next week. But all is okay. How about you guys?" She knew I meant Hannah, too.

"We're all well, no problems. I knew you were in Orlando,

but Nathan was a little worried. Hannah called and told me she talked to Curt, and he said you were seeing him there today."

I felt bad. I never treated them this way. "Yeah, I've got to get my head out of the clouds. Tell Nathan I'm good. I'll talk to you all next week."

Later, I called Melanie. She picked up on the first ring. I could hear music in the background. "Hello, Michael? Can you hear me?"

"Yes, I can hear you." I tried to sound casual, forcing it a bit, trying to keep things light though I felt miserable. "Soon as I'm out of town, you're off dancing with other guys."

"Hold on a sec," she said. A moment later, she was back and there was less noise. "Well, I haven't been dancing, but I can now that you've called. I didn't want to be away from the phone in case you did. No more excuses for Fred now though. He saw me take the call, darn it."

I laughed at the mention of Fred, and she joined me. I could visualize him waiting, lurking in the background, tall and lanky with that shock of dirty blonde hair overlapping his left eye. "I'll bet he's a good dancer, isn't he?"

"Yes, he is, just annoying in other ways. I wish he'd get a regular girlfriend. He's really locked onto me and Val lately."

"Who can blame him? Two beautiful women, both with great legs. Yeah, I can understand it."

"Well, thank you. I guess that's a compliment. I'll tell Val. She'll love it. You know she's still checking out the house thing, right?"

"I'm afraid she's going to be very disappointed, baby."

"She's having fun. I hope it's not annoying you."

"Not at all. Let her have her fun." I didn't care that Val might discover certain information about me, but it did annoy me to have someone digging into my private life. It was more than a game to her, I realized. She was protecting her friend.

"Are you coming home tomorrow?"

Home? Where was home? "No, probably not for a couple of days, but I'd like to see you next week if you're free."

"You know my schedule. If you're flexible, we'll find time."

"All right, go give Fred his dance and say hello to Val for me."

Hanging up, I took my drink onto the balcony, looking out over the "city beautiful" as it was advertised. I hadn't wanted to talk to her, but I needed to hear her voice. I guess I needed reassurance, a validation that I was on the right path. I still had serious doubts but felt better somehow. Regardless of Melanie, my time with Steph was ending.

My heart clenched at the thought.

Chapter Sixteen

*S*tephanie came back the next day, but she didn't want to talk about it. We lazed around, chatting about things going on in our lives. Then we made love, savoring it, letting the pleasure build and spread over us, taking in the smells and feels of one another as if we could store the other within. Later, we grilled out on the balcony, and she said she wanted to stay the night. We made love again and slept holding each other.

The next morning, she wanted to talk.

"What are we going to do, baby? What are *you* going to do?" she asked.

"I don't know. I only know I had to come to you, to tell you."

"You should go away, Michael. Get away, away from both of us, and stay away for a while. Go to Europe, that place you love in Italy. God, I wish I'd been able to go there with you. Or go to the islands. Just get away."

"Or I could just be with you both." I couldn't help it. It had been there on the periphery of my mind all along. Not seriously though, and I felt a big smile spreading across my face.

She laughed, hard, a belly laugh, releasing all the tension, all the misery.

"Only you could come up with that solution." She continued to laugh, turning herself out of my arms to face me. "What was her reply to that?"

"I haven't asked. We're not that far along."

"What do you expect it to be?"

"The same as yours. *No way.*"

"You are so right, but I wavered for a moment," she said, allowing me to pull her back to me. "So, what are you going to do, Michael?"

"I don't know. If I can't have both of you, I'm going to stay away from both of you, I guess. Sure you won't reconsider?" I asked again, pushing my luck but feeling oddly mischievous in the midst of this miserable time.

Her look was one of amusement. "I'm beginning to think you're serious. No," she said again, "I'm hurt and I don't want to lose you, but no, that's not going to happen." She hugged me to her tightly. "Oh, Michael, I love you so and we are so good together."

Then she pushed back from me, still holding my shoulders, and looked at me hard, her eyes penetrating me, going deep into places only she knew but had treaded lightly until now. "I thought about things a lot last night, this morning, too. I know you, Michael. There's something you're not telling me. I couldn't figure out what it was till now, but I..." Her voice had begun to tremble and rise as she spoke. She held my gaze with haunted eyes. "Damn you, she's married! She's married, isn't she, Michael?"

I remained silent, still looking at her.

"My God, Michael! What are you doing? What are you doing to us? What are you doing to her?" she asked.

Her words, her look of pain burned through me. Still, I said nothing. I was powerless to give her an answer.

"Damn you. I could give you up for the right woman, a single woman. But this? This is not right, Michael. Don't you see how you're punishing us? Punishing every woman you've been with for what Millie did to you, punishing us for loving you?"

I stood there, mute, absorbing the battering I deserved. I hadn't even thought about there being a difference whether Melanie was married or not. Now I saw it through Stephanie's eyes, through her pain.

"Oh, Michael, think about what you're doing. Think about her. Look at me, Michael," she demanded, pulling me back as I turned away.

Her voice became very low, just above a whisper. "You've seduced her, Michael. You know you have. Let her go, Michael. Let *me* go. Let life come to you, and the right woman will come into your life. Stop punishing us, Michael."

I remained silent, and Stephanie finally turned and went outside to the balcony.

Coming back in a few minutes later, she was composed. She led me to the couch and sat with me, taking my hands as if I were the one needing comfort.

"Look at me, Michael, please," she said softly. "You're important to me no matter what happens, but I have to talk to you."

"I know, baby, I just don't know what to say. As much as I see this is hurting you, I just don't know what to say."

"Just talk to me," she said. "She is married, isn't she?"

"Yes, she's married, but separated, Steph. That's all I know."

"It doesn't make any difference, baby. Don't you see what's happening? She's vulnerable right now. Surely you can see that. She's probably in her forties, right?"

"Well, yes, I'd say late forties."

"Think about it, Michael, just please think about it. She's at a difficult time in life. Kids grown and the husband's probably not around much. They've drifted apart. She has too much time on her hands and is feeling her way through life right now. She's adjusting, and you're interesting. You've seduced her, even if you won't admit it, even if you don't realize it. Her marriage may still be salvageable. Are you ready to destroy that possibility?" She squeezed my hand, hard. "Talk to me, Michael. Talk to me, damn it!"

I remained silent, in turmoil over all she had said, letting it sink in painfully as I absorbed it all.

"You need to think about this, honey. Are you ready to be responsible for her and all that that means? Are you ready to marry her?"

Then she was silent, still gripping my hands while I sat there stunned, unable to speak.

She got up, and I still sat there, listening to the door open.

"I love you, Michael. I want to be happy for you. I really do. You need to leave us both, my love. Leave us both and open yourself to life, allow a single woman into your life. Let Millie go."

And then the door closed.

Chapter Seventeen

*T*he rest of Sunday passed somehow. I must have been in a zombie state, like driving to North Carolina or some other place and wondering how I got there on arrival, all points in between lost.

As the sun began to set, I started to come out of it. I sat out on the balcony as the traffic below invaded me, the faint noise of it suddenly there, penetrating where nothing else had. Where had the day gone?

I tried to call Stephanie on her cell. It went to voicemail. I thought about calling her house. Instead, I relived all that she had said. She was right, unselfish even, and I thought of the hurt she was going through.

But I had to see Melanie again.

The evening was miserable, and I wallowed in it.

I called Melanie as I drove home Monday morning and told her I'd like to see her.

"Yes, I want to see you, too," she said.

"Are you free tomorrow? I'd like to spend some quiet time together."

"Yes, I'd like that. Just tell me what you want to do so I know how to dress. I never know how to dress with you." She sounded upbeat but maybe a little reserved, probably curious about how I spent the weekend.

"Hey, life is Plan B, love. Get a little bag and be prepared.

But for tomorrow, how about we just walk around downtown Jax for a while, see how the place is developing? You know, explore a bit. Have some coffee and lunch later."

She hesitated. "Michael, I can't. I know people there."

"Oh, I guess I never thought of that." My voice must have sounded hollow. Her words had taken my renewing spirit with them. There it was, the first time for us to come face-to-face with the inherent obstacles of the relationship we were entering. *You need to leave us both and open yourself to life more, to single women.*

"Michael? Are you there?"

"Ah . . . yes, just thinking," I said. I shook Stephanie's words out of my head.

"How about Jacksonville Beach then?"

Again, she hesitated. "Same thing, honey. I'm sorry." Her voice told me things. She had to know what these limitations, this need to protect herself with secrecy, was doing to me. "Would St. Augustine be okay?" she asked.

"Sure. I'll pick you up, same place about ten in the morning. How's that?"

"Good. See you then."

I drove and thought about the conversation, how life has a way of putting a bump in your path when everything appears wonderful. This was a big bump. We were seriously involved, our relationship developing quickly, going much deeper than a little flirtation or the simplicity of sex. Love is hard, damn it. Sex is easy.

I'd had casual sex before, just a sharing of pleasures for a short time with other women, inconsequential to us both in the end. This was major. I knew Melanie didn't take it lightly. I realized the enormity of what was developing. We were both approaching this as a courtship as though she weren't even married. Nothing else was important. Everything was us, our developing feelings and the overwhelming need for one another.

Then life intruded. She may as well have said, *Michael, I can't. I'm sorry, but we might run into my husband there.*

Reality, with consequence. Stephanie's words speeding across the distance between us as though she were there with me. *Her marriage may still be salvageable, Michael.* More followed, the realities, all of it cascading down on me. *Let what Millie did to you go.*

I pulled into the next rest area along Interstate 95. I walked around, thinking, pushing fragmented pieces of Stephanie's words away, but they kept coming back . . . *what Millie did to you.* Looking up, I discovered I'd walked quite a distance from the car, away from people and distractions, too. I sat at a picnic table and tried to think of something else, but there are times when old memories won't be denied, especially when they relate to war and love and loss.

I'd been excited to be going home. I hitched a chopper ride to the nearest USO to make a call back to the States. Calls had to go through a radio operator to another radio in the States and then a long-distance phone-call hookup, depending on which radio operator was raised. There was no privacy, and like with any radio, it was transmit, listen, transmit, saying "over" each time.

"Sorry, that number has been disconnected. Would you like to try another? Over," the radio operator said.

I remember my knees buckling as flashes of painful anxiety bolted through my body, feeling my free hand go to that space between my eyes, trying to numb the pain suddenly pulsing there.

"No thanks," I said, moving away from the field phone,

distancing myself from others waiting to call loved ones while a terrible fear became shocking reality. Silently, I moved on, cursing God. Who better to blame? Not her, something terrible had happened to her. Where was the fucking Red Cross? Why hadn't they contacted me?

But I knew. I'd seen it with other guys. Just like this, when they were close to ending their tour in Vietnam and going home.

I lived that phone call, those horrible moments, over and over. Two days later the letter came. It was from Mom. I was nervous; the last two days had been hell. I thought I had mastered the pain, the ache of abandonment, but was nervous to the point of nausea holding that letter. Creeping in were thoughts that everything was okay, but I knew better. The last two days had fortified me with a resolve and coldness normally foreign to my nature, and the pain eased.

Mom's letter told me to come home, that she loved me and all would be well. Then she went on, saying Millie and Robbie, our son, wouldn't be there when I returned. Mom hated to tell me in this manner but couldn't see any other way.

Millie really was a bitch. She'd even had her sister call my mom and take the letter for me to her. Mom wrote that the poor sister was embarrassed, even apologized for Millie. Christ! I wanted to rip that letter into little pieces and cry.

Instead, I opened it.

Millie had met someone, and things just happened. They were in love and leaving to start a new life together. Please don't try to find her. She would be in touch. She wished me well and asked that I please understand that some time needed to pass before I saw Robbie. He didn't really know me and was very comfortable with Tim.

For a moment her voice was yelling at me. *I've met*

someone! Tim. Over and over again it came.

Damn it! *Tim who?*

I remembered the shame of failure and loss. Even worse was the humiliation of my mother having to be the one to tell me. And I lived it again in that moment. Robbie, my son, was comfortable with . . . *Tim!*

I had sent a card home to my family but didn't go back for two years, and only then because Mom was ill.

I'd never respected guys in affairs with married women. So why had I become one? Adultery is just another form of corruption. I blanked it all out, denying the psychology I had later studied so intensely for a few semesters at the University of Florida. Even the married psychology professor I eventually slept with couldn't provide the answer.

As I pulled back on the highway, I didn't know what I was going to do beyond a determination to talk to Melanie about her marriage.

Then I thought again about Stephanie. I thought of her pain—and mine in telling her about Melanie. Steph and I had been so close, still were, holding each other, kissing, making love even while knowing we might never see each other again. She would never let on to John, but he would know soon enough. The pain was there to see. She told me he had queried her that Friday I talked to her. She was dismissive, saying it had been a bad day. He would ask again because she was such a part of him. He would know soon, but not now.

Already the cost of my involvement was too high. I thought about it all, reflected on it over and over. I'd hurt someone I loved, and I was heading down the same path with Melanie. Only more pain could come from our involvement in the end.

But Stephanie was wrong about me. I was not

punishing women for what Millie did to me. Still, I might be compensating for it. I wouldn't allow myself to be in that position again, but I was not punishing them. That was the one thing I had resented Steph's saying to me. But none of that mattered if Melanie was the one.

Was she?

***

She wore a simple sundress of bright colors, orange and yellow in some complicated pattern with just enough lime green to mollify it a little. Then there were the flip-flops, a different pair today, orange to match the dress. Where did she get them? The straw hat was perfect, subduing the otherwise colorful outfit just enough to complement her natural state of simple elegance. She was beautiful. I brightened to her smile. I could see the pleasure of my appreciation coming to her eyes. She blossomed in it. I felt myself rise with the vision of her. I wanted her.

We spent the day in St. Augustine, this time exploring the little shops and cafes on St. George Street. The street was a joy to wander along and people-watch. This was a walking street with cars interrupting the throngs of people only at a couple of small intersections that crossed it.

Later, we stood on the small sidewalk that bordered the bay just south of the old Spanish fort. I pointed out and explained the red and green markers that marked the Intracoastal Waterway and the inlet from the ocean.

We walked on, going through the narrow streets in an old residential neighborhood, finally finding a small, shaded park with benches. We sat there and talked, sharing a bottle of spring water, enjoying the day.

"Melanie, yesterday when I wanted to spend the day—"

She was there before I could finish. "No, shhh," she said, gently putting her finger to my lips. "I know, Michael, and I hated it when it came out. That we might run into someone I know. I hated it when I said it. I hated the reality of it."

She was frantic, her eyes pleading with me, desperate. "Please, I can't talk about it now. I promise I will, but please, not now," she whispered. "I want to be with you. The only thing I need to know right now is do you want to be with me?"

I felt sorry for us in that moment, just another tragic love story developing.

"Yes, you know I do." I breathed into her ear with the words. "But there's more than us involved here, there's—" and again she interrupted.

"Not now, please. After this weekend, I promise we'll talk. Please, let's just forget about my marriage and your complicated relationship for a little while longer."

"Are you sure you want me to come with you to Daytona?"

"Yes." She grasped the hand I had around her and smiled. "I thought about it a lot this weekend. I want us to be together in Daytona. It feels right, you know. We're right."

"Yes, I know." I pulled her to me, holding her, letting my head rest on her shoulder for a moment.

I had decided. I was emotionally drained, but for once, I wasn't burdened.

Chapter Eighteen

I drove down in the truck, laughing to myself as I pulled into valet parking at the Marriott on Daytona Beach. The valet wasn't going to take any joy in driving my old truck. Melanie and Val had come earlier in Melanie's car. I had a reservation for a room on the same floor as them but far enough away to allow more thinking. I planned to talk to Val as soon as possible. The guilt I felt, and I did feel it this morning, was about how I'd hurt Stephanie, not about this. This was different, this was no longer about Stephanie, but the guilt was there, and her words still haunted me.

We had dinner together, the three of us, at a little Japanese place down the street from the hotel. Both women looked lovely. Dressed simply, they were nonetheless alluring, Val in a tan dress with matching short jacket and Melanie in a simple navy-blue A-line dress trimmed in white. The swell of her small breasts barely showed. It was enough. There was a glow about her, a radiance that emanated from her smile and drew me in. Perfect except for the damn wedding ring. If she were so sure of us, why was she wearing the damned thing?

They carried themselves as the dancers they were, backs straight, shoulders back with heads held high, graceful posture. Any man would feel proud seated next to them. The exotic meal featuring seafood and nori was accompanied by light conversation centering on the next day's competitions that Val had entered with her dance partner. Her husband had opted for a fishing weekend on the west coast of Florida with his buddies. He was supportive but had been to these events with her before, Val said, and would really rather be relaxing on the water with a fishing pole in his hand. Her partner, Danny, was due in the next morning, but she had a small get-together to go to in another hour. An earnest discussion of my guilt would have to wait.

Finally, Melanie excused herself to go to the restroom. She paused as she stood and looked expectantly at Val. Val declined going, either because I bumped her foot with mine or because she was waiting for the opportunity to speak to me, too. Melanie looked back at us as she rounded a corner. Immediately, Val turned to me and we started in.

I jumped in first. "Val, I tried to back out. She's so innocent. What's with her and her husband? I'm not sure I . . ."

"Whoa, slow down," she said. "She's having second thoughts, too, worried that she's caused a problem for you and your girlfriend. And she is an innocent, but she wants to be with you. So, the question is, why are you here? I can see you care about her, but how much?"

"Too much for a man who's been single most of his life. Too much to be involved with an innocent, especially a married one. I don't want the responsibility of what happens between her and her husband."

"She loves you. Do you know that? She wouldn't describe it like that, but she does, and I think you love her, too."

"Okay, but where is it going? I don't want her hurt, or her husband. I've already hurt one person this week. And then there's me."

Val kept her eyes on mine and slowly nodded. "Yes, there's you, Michael, and I'm afraid you could get hurt. She's very traditional and loyal. Very loyal."

We were quiet for a moment, lost in thought. Then she smiled.

"I agree you both could get hurt," she said, "but think of all the fun you could have in the meantime."

I shook my head at her. "This is serious, Val. We're not just meeting for drinks and dinner here."

"God, I hope not!" Suddenly, she laughed. "I was hoping you'd get a connecting room so I could listen." She kept laughing but contained herself as she became aware of those around us.

I wasn't buying into the humor, and she knew it. So, finally, she said, "I can't talk about her husband. That's up to her. I can say that he doesn't see her. But it's more than that. As a couple, there is no oneness about them, not in the most important places—the heart, soul, and being—where a loving couple should reside together. If it ever existed, it's lost between them now. I think she realizes that. I wouldn't have thought she could handle an affair though. I've kidded her about having one forever, but now that it's real, I'm shocked. But I'm happy, too, really happy for her because you're the right one. You must be, otherwise it wouldn't be happening."

I sat back in my seat, suddenly tired again, overwhelmed with what was going on. I was used to having control, and I'd lost it. I was along for the ride now with Melanie dictating the terms, in charge of the outcome.

She approached the table with a big smile.

"And what are my two best friends up to?" she asked, looking expectantly from one of us to the other.

I stood and helped her into her seat as Val spoke.

"Just small talk, honey. I was questioning Michael about the house again. I did some checking. Some corporation owns it. There has to be some dirt here. I want there to be, but I can't dig anything up, darn it."

I was surprised at the response but didn't indicate so. She had checked things out, all right, and I appreciated her segue from the obvious nature of Melanie's question. Then I realized just how devious Val's response had been. She had tried to catch me off guard.

She gave me a little smile, and the tip of her tongue appeared for a second. *Take that!* zipped through my head. I laughed, but they ignored me.

"I'll have a friend do some more research, then we'll know Michael's secret," she added.

"Great, call me as soon as you know," Melanie said.

Both of them looked at me as if I were cornered. I merely smiled.

"It's no big deal, ladies, just someone wanting his privacy," I said, adding a pointed, "Privacy should be respected more."

"You made it a big deal when you said it was secret," Val said. "We hate secrets."

She stood.

"I guess Cay Tam is no big deal, either," she added. "Seems the same corporation owns the boat. Makes a girl wonder . . . Oh, and the name Cay Tam. Boy, did that prompt some hits on the internet. Maybe you should come clean, Michael. You may not want me going deeper." With a smile and wink over her shoulder as she turned, she said. "Gotta go to the girls' room, then I'm off to my ice breaker. See you two later." She bent to give Melanie a hug before leaving.

I laughed as she walked away, annoying her even more. I wanted to shake her a little, but I was concerned. I didn't want Melanie knowing I was rich yet.

Moments later, Melanie and I walked out also and turned

towards the boardwalk, drawn to the sound of the ocean.

"So, what were you two talking about?" Melanie asked.

I smiled at the question, feeling her arm link with mine. "You, of course. You and life and how complicated it can be."

"Did you talk about how right it can be, too? It can be, you know, like right now." She stopped and turned into my arms.

"Yes, it can be, and we did talk about that." I held her close, kissing her cheeks and her ears softly.

"It is right, honey. We're right," she whispered.

I led her down a couple of streets, turning into a small club off the boardwalk. Soft music drifted from it, enticing me. Inside we found a table and ordered drinks, sitting close together, our thighs touching. I ached. We danced to a slow song, and she found my neck, then my ear, with her lips.

"I love being here with you," she said. "Thank you for coming. I know it hasn't been easy for you these last few weeks."

"Shhh." I backed away and put my finger gently against her lips. "Shhh."

Then we just danced.

***

Later we went back to the hotel and her room where Val was waiting. I didn't know what to expect from this point, but the girls quickly made me comfortable. We talked for a while and had another glass of wine. Val told us stories of her dance world experiences. Some of the characters who found their way into it were quite colorful.

It was a little before ten when Melanie excused herself to go to the bathroom. Val and I were able to talk.

"How was your evening, Michael?" she asked.

"Great, just like you knew it would be."

She laughed and reached out to hug me. "God, I wish I could help you both with this, but I can't. I'm just glad you're in her life." We talked softly for a few minutes, then Melanie opened the bathroom door and called for Val. When Val came out a few minutes later, she looked concerned.

"Is everything all right, Val? What's the matter?"

"It's Melanie. She's in a delicate place right now, a little fragile, I expect. She'll be all right."

I was dumbfounded. What could have happened?

"I . . . I don't understand," I said.

I looked to Val for help, but she wasn't giving me any.

"This is too much for her," I said after a moment. "Look, I'm going to pack up and check out. Tell her I'll talk to her tomorrow."

"No, please don't do that." Val put out a hand as though to restrain me. "She's just finding and accepting reality. Don't do this to her. She needs you even if you don't sleep together."

I stood and headed for the door.

Val grabbed my shoulder, holding me back. "Michael, she called her husband. Don't ask," she added, holding up a hand. "I can only guess it was a last attempt thing, looking for a sign that would cause her to change her mind maybe. I don't know."

Val paused. She looked defeated in that moment, embarrassed even.

"I'm not sure," she said, "but it's got to be something like that."

"It's okay," I told her. "What matters is she has doubt, and that's enough."

"Michael, we both know she's not experienced at this. Please, don't leave. Just go back to your room for now. Let her compose herself, and she'll call in a little while."

"I really think I should leave. I'm confusing things for her."

"No, no. She loves you, and you're good for her. This is right, but I told you before, she's an innocent. This is just part of it, part of her makeup as a person and part of her journey back into life. Please, stay the night. Just go to your room for now, and don't worry about her. I'll take care of her, and we'll see you in the morning, or at least I will. I promise. "

I lay awake long after returning to my room, concerned for Melanie, my feelings for her building. More than ever, I was determined to end it now, for her. I would just tell her I couldn't see her anymore. I'd leave in the morning.

There was a knock on the door. *Val?*

I slowly drug myself out of bed and cracked the door open. "Melanie!"

"I'm sorry, Michael. Can I come in?"

"Of course," I said. I stepped aside as she looked down the hall, nodding her head before stepping in. When I looked out, Val waved at me.

"I am so embarrassed," Melanie began. "I don't know what to say."

"It's all right." I pulled her to me, holding her, and felt something hard and cold in her hands. A bottle of champagne.

Her eyes lifted, searching my face. "I want to be with you. I've brought a peace offering."

She held out the champagne.

I nodded and kissed the hair against my lips as I held her. She smelled of roses and spice.

"Yes."

The room smelled of her, her scent, and now I noticed she was wearing a silk robe over a matching nightgown. She was stunning, wearing only a faint trace of red lipstick for makeup.

I took the bottle from her and let the cork out gently, allowing the champagne to open with a joyous pop. Her eyes never left my face as I poured the sparkling wine into glasses she held for me. I could feel her tension.

Setting the bottle down, I took a glass from her and started to raise it in a toast.

"Please, let me," she said, and raised her glass to mine. "To your patience and understanding, and to us, for what is so right between us."

We drank and were in each other's arms immediately, her sobbing and me holding and kissing her while realizing what I had almost forsaken.

We were emotionally drained, but the need was great as we slowly moved to the bed, exploring each other. Her breasts came alive as I pushed her nightgown aside. No panties.

I rose up on one elbow, looking down at her. She turned to me, her eyes trusting, her body wanting. I rolled one of her swollen nipples, holding her eyes with mine. It hardened even more. I took it between my lips and moved a hand to her thighs. She moaned as her eyes drifted closed. I eased her legs open. Her breath came short and fast. It was too much. I groaned as she opened for me. I pulled her to my lips and felt her back arch against my hands as I held her tightly to me.

"Yes, *yes*," she moaned as she pulled me into her.

***

Slowly, I became aware. Melanie was holding me, still a part of her though softening. She stroked my back and neck with her fingers. Small sounds from her lips washed over me. I moved slowly to separate from her, but her leg hooked around my butt held me.

"Oh, no, you don't," she said. "Stay. I want it again."

I didn't have the strength to resist. "You what?" I said, collapsing into her.

"You heard me. I want to do it again," she said and laughed.

I mumbled something she couldn't hear.

"*What?* I can't hear you."

"Samson and Delilah, I said."

"What? A new version?" She laughed again.

Rising slightly, I said, "It wasn't a hair thing at all. Delilah took Samson to bed, had sex with him all night, and took his strength into her as she turned him into an empty husk." I collapsed into her again after the effort. I wasn't kidding. I was worn out.

She laughed as I lay there, trying to gather strength. I felt like a feather as she easily rolled me over and sat on top of me. "Damn, woman, it's cold out here."

For a moment, she looked confused. Then she smiled. She raised her hips slightly and tucked me between the warmth of her thighs. "Oops! Sorry about that." She leaned forward, holding my shoulders down as her hair spilled to my face. "That Samson story may be true, but you did say they did it all night. So, come on."

I groaned into a pillow as she laughed and rocked on top of me. Finally, I had enough strength to pull her down to me. We held each other for a little before she hopped out of bed and poured the last of the champagne. As we sipped, she caressed my chest. Slowly, I felt the tingles of arousal coming back. I took her hand and placed it on me. When she just held me, I looked into her eyes.

"Stroke me. Squeeze and stroke me." She did, but timidly, as I continued to hold her eyes with mine. I saw her excitement build as I came alive in her hand. Her nipples swelled.

"Wrap your hand around me here." I showed her, and she stroked as I continued to grow. I marveled at her inexperience, even as the eroticism of her hand aroused me. She explored me as she sat Indian style with her legs crossed, her upper body bent forward over me. She reached out her other hand to my hip for support and seemed in awe, watching me grow as she slowly pumped and squeezed. I put one hand on her shoulder and gently pulled her forward. Her head bent with my tug.

She pulled back slightly but continued to hold me. In a very quiet voice, she said, "I don't do that, Michael. I'm sorry, but I've never done that." She looked down at me, her eyes wide, fearful actually, and looked into mine.

I reached between us. Slowly, I slid a finger along the outside of her lips before pushing her backwards and entering her quickly.

"You will," I said as her legs wrapped tightly around me.

Her hands grasped my butt, helping me pump. She whispered in my ear as we moved. I don't know what she said. Her energy drove my passion. My need for her blinded me to everything but my pleasure. She rode me, holding on with her arms and legs locked around me, stimulating the sudden powerful needles of pleasure flowing through me.

I awoke snuggled into her breasts. I had one arm around her and a leg over hers. Her arms were around mine, and she was kissing the top of my head. "Good morning, baby," she said.

I rose up on one forearm, my eyes still so full of sleep and a wonderful weariness that I collapsed back to her.

"I have to go to Val, my wonderful Samson," she said.

I continued to lie there. "I'm coming," I said, yawning.

"Well, how about a little enthusiasm then!" The whole

bed shook and seemed to turn upside down. When I got my bearings again, she'd rolled me over and was climbing on top of me again. "You can do better than that."

She started bouncing her bottom up and down. "Last night it was 'I'm cumming. Oh, baby, baby, I'm cuumiiing!'" She threw back her head, and her nails gently scraped my chest as she cried out passionately.

I could only lie there and watch her in awe. "What the hell?"

Suddenly, she collapsed on top of me. She was laughing so hard I finally joined in.

"I have to go, baby," she said. "I promised Val I'd meet her for breakfast and help her for a couple of hours."

She kissed my cheek and slipped away from me. I watched her pull her nightgown over her head and slip into the robe. I didn't move.

She looked at me. "Can you stay tonight?"

I pulled myself up in the bed. "Darn right. Meet me by the pool or on the beach later?"

"Okay, I'd like that," she said.

She gave me another kiss on the cheek and approached the door before turning. "I really loved last night." After a pause, she added, "and this morning." Then she squealed and ran back to my arms.

I laughed as her arms hugged me. "I did, too."

I got to my feet, fumbling with the covers before I kicked them away and, still nude, walked her to the door.

She turned and looked down at my nakedness, then back up at my face as she held the door to leave. Reaching out to stroke me for a moment, she said, "Don't get caught in the door," and giggled. I watched her hurry down the empty hall to Val's room.

I crawled back into bed but couldn't sleep, only dozed with memories of Melanie jolting me awake every few minutes. I had been surprised at how naive she was about sex. She responded enthusiastically but was so tentative about touching my cock.

Then it came to me. *Responded*, that's what she'd done. She only responded last night, yet this morning, she was so playful and provocative while simulating sex with me.

I hadn't pursued her giving me oral sex after the earlier try. I knew it would come at some point, but it bewildered me that a woman who'd been married as long as she had been didn't perform oral sex on her husband.

I thought of the stories I'd heard of married men going to prostitutes for oral sex. Some because their wives refused to do it and others because they thought it was too dirty an act for their wives to perform. Hell, it was probably still illegal in some states.

I shook my head as the thought went further. As far as we've come with civilization, there are still those who would burn others at the stake for suspected witchcraft or oral sex. People are so fucked up.

I wondered about him, her husband, what he was like. What was it they'd had together in the beginning that they lost? Why did they lose it? Was it him? Was it her? Was it both of them or just the realities of life? If it was just life, it reinforced my long-held fear. Would it just degrade for us over time, too? Then why the bond of marriage?

Yes, I wondered about him and whether marriage overall was archaic and doomed. I always wanted to feel that excitement upon seeing my partner, even if it had just been a few hours, a week, or a month.

Did he give her the gift of intimacy, the tenderness of love beyond sex that was natural between her and me?

***

I was lying on a lounge chair by the pool, absorbed in the sun, running from my inner turmoil when she found me. We had talked on our cell phones earlier and arranged to meet there for some sun and then have lunch. I sensed a presence and looked up. She was silhouetted against the sun, so I couldn't see her face, but the lovely shape and appearance of a large hat satisfied me it was Melanie.

"Is that you, Delilah? Is that you come to give me back my strength?" I stammered in a frail voice.

"Tis I, yes," she said in a superior tone, "come to take what pittance of you is left."

She sat on a lounger next to me and raised a foot to my chest in a gesture of dominance. I took the foot with my hands and kissed a pretty, red-painted toe. "Yes, strong, beautiful one, take what you will."

"Stop it," she cried out softly. Then she was laughing hard, trying to pull her foot back as her eyes searched the area around us.

I released her, rising to stand over her, and whispered in a strong voice, "You didn't stay for the rest of the story, wench. I have sucked my strength back from your toe. For it is written, I have prevailed, and you will be my slave wench and do my bidding this night as I may desire."

"Please," she whispered. "Take me to your chambers now, master. I submit. Take me."

"Later maybe," I said, plopping back down in my lounger. I closed my eyes and relaxed again. A toe pushed against my lips. Was she trying to give me more strength?

"You rat," she said. "I was just getting into it."

I smiled but didn't say anything.

"We need to meet Val in a little while before she has to go to the banquet."

"Come with me," I said, taking her hand as I stood. I had ordered lunch to be served in my room, and it was almost time.

Back in the room, we shared a plate of raw vegetables, pita bread, and hummus. I fed her a piece of wheat pita with hummus as I asked, "Am I the first since you were married?"

Melanie looked at me oddly as she chewed. "Yes, I've only been with my husband." She gave me a bite of the pita.

"I thought so. I'm flattered, but I'm sad, too. I didn't want to open Pandora's Box. I don't want to be the cause of your making a mistake. I mean, I don't think we are a mistake, but the time may not have been right."

"Michael, this is right. We're right, or we wouldn't be here together because of those values. This did not come easy for me, but then it did, because it's right," she said with a nod of her head.

I pulled her to me, suddenly uncomfortable with the conversation. This woman, this wonderfully sweet, innocent woman, deserved better. There was a knock on the door, and she got up from the table to answer it.

Val came in and started picking at the remains of our late lunch. She had a little time before her next competition and then had to get ready for the banquet and award ceremony that followed.

"I heard you slept in this morning while we had breakfast," she prodded and laughed at my awkward shyness.

"I was bitten by a little bug, I think."

"Yeah, a love bug, you rascal. I couldn't believe the energy in Melanie this morning."

Casually, she looked over at Melanie, who said, "It's a new Delilah thing Michael taught me last night."

I turned away, trying to keep from laughing. I knew she was quick, but she'd surprised me again.

"You want to expand on that?" Val asked.

"No." Melanie winked at me with a straight face, her eyes filled with mischief.

"Delilah thing, huh? I'll have to get it out of you later," Val said. "Have to go now, but we're not done, honey. Not done at all."

She stood to leave, gave us both hugs, and said she'd see us in the morning. Danny, her dance partner and instructor, would escort her to the room later.

Chapter Nineteen

I drove back the next day after spending all the remainder of my time in Daytona with Melanie except for the brief periods she attended the competitions to be with Val. I did little that afternoon except reorganize my plans for the week, committing myself to get down to work again.

I thought about Nathan and Nan, and Hannah, too. None of them knew Stephanie well, but she had made an impression the few times they had met her. They would be shocked to know I wasn't seeing her anymore, and, worse, Nan would be concerned because I had confided a little in her. They were probably confused already, having seen Melanie and Val over at my place the one night. It wasn't something that I did, bringing women over.

Yes, I needed to talk to them soon, but not now.

I had been invited to dinner with Nan and Nathan when I arrived home. I told them I couldn't, that I wasn't feeling well. Of course, Nan jumped in, telling me I couldn't play all the time and not expect to get weak and ill eating the fast food I loved, and . . .

I wasn't ill but didn't want to hurt their feelings. I needed time to absorb what had happened between Melanie and me in the last few days. I'd gone from not being able to do without her to letting her go for her marriage's sake to sleeping with her for two days. I didn't know where things were going, but I knew I needed time apart from everyone so that I could think and understand if possible.

Later that evening, she called.

"Hey, baby, I miss you," I said. And I did. I really did. Our time together had been too brief in the end.

"I miss you, too. I loved our time together."

"How's Val? Is she all right with everything, with us?"

"Yes, she is, and not just because she's my friend. She really likes you."

"I like her, too, even though she's way too nosy. I hope she knows that."

"What?" Melanie asked. "That you like her or that she's nosy?"

"Both," I said with a laugh.

"She does know you like her, and now she's becoming a real pain about that Delilah thing."

"Didn't you tell her?"

"No, and it's killing her." I could hear the mischief in her voice and pictured a big smile. "So, I'm not going to for another day or two even though I'm as nosy as she is."

"Yes, you are, but she is really aggressive. She surprised me with the Cay Tam thing. She needs to get a job or something to keep her busy."

"She's just having fun, honey. Is it really bothering you?"

"Not really. It's kind of fun watching her mind work."

"Good, I'm glad we're not upsetting you. Really, it's just in fun and curiosity."

"I know."

"Michael, I need to talk to you about something."

"Okay, let's talk."

"It's awkward for me. I, ah . . . I think I may have given you the wrong impression."

"About what, baby?"

"Well, about my experience with men."

Oh, I thought. Here it comes. I should have known the world isn't that simple. No one could be that naive. She'd been with someone else during the marriage. I should be ashamed, but the relief was immediate. Why was I happy about that? I should be saddened at this change in my picture of her. My wonderful woman was not so innocent after all. Even as I knew I loved her, I was running, running from responsibility once more.

Split seconds of thought pulsed through me and told me I was off the hook. I was privileged to have been with her, but so had others. No responsibility here.

In the space of a few milliseconds, I was saddened as these realities sank in and my heart sank with the validation that we were only having an affair.

"I've only been with Jamie," Melanie said.

I couldn't absorb the meaning. I was confused as she dropped the bomb, and it was a big one.

"I've never been with anyone but my husband, and now you."

Oh, my God! Shame enveloped me. Shame at my thoughts, at my cowardly relief from responsibility, my regret that I'd been with her, and now I was overwhelmed with the feeling of responsibility I'd sought to avoid. I was the first for her since she got married, but she'd never been with another before her husband—and now me.

And then I understood the nightgown, the shyness. She was creating a marriage night for us, the first time she was to give herself to her husband, me. Me, if only symbolically. That's what she'd done! My head was spinning. Thoughts and realizations pummeled me.

She held to the importance of her beliefs and values. She was creating another life, a parallel life with me. She wasn't giving me sex. She was giving me her essence, her soul, a special gift that only one other had known in her life. It all made sense now, her naïveté, her innocence, her inexperience but willingness to explore and enjoy and, especially, to give to me.

Responsibility weighed in on me heavily, and my thoughts tormented me. My God! What had I done by taking her innocence, by the selfishness of my seduction of her? Stephanie's words battered me over and over. *She's confused, and she's vulnerable now. You've seduced her, Michael. Have the moral courage to let her go.* But I hadn't, and now it was too late.

"Michael? Michael, are you there?"

"Yes. Yes, I'm here, baby. Must be a black hole in the trailer. I lost you for a moment." I didn't know how long I'd been silent. "I have you now."

"Did you hear what I was telling you?"

"Yes. Yes, I did."

"Michael, you did misunderstand me, didn't you?"

"Yes, Melanie, I did. I don't know what to say."

"Don't say anything. I just wanted to make sure you know me, to know how important you are to me. See me on Tuesday?"

"Yes, baby, I'll see you then. Good night, love."

"Good night, Samson."

I hung up, lost in the new reality of the relationship, falling deep into a place I'd never been. She held herself special, I knew, but on such a simple, unassuming level, and she especially wanted to be special to me. There was no need to tell me what she had tonight except that she held me special, too. It was important to her for me to know what she'd brought to our relationship.

How did I feel about this woman? How had I felt about her before I knew this? The same. I simply loved her. Anything I knew before this, I'd twisted and used to shield myself, to arm against the vulnerabilities she presented, the potential pain she offered. She had taken away all rights to my selfishness. She had presented herself to me in the rawest, most vulnerable form: a virgin.

This is what she had given me. Not in the traditional or the medical sense perhaps, but in the romantic sense. None had passed where I had now. Unknowingly, she had saved that essence of herself for me.

Chapter Twenty

*T*he next morning, I was sluggish. Probably because I hadn't slept long enough, or maybe there's something to that Samson and Delilah thing. Still, I was determined to get in a workout. It had been several days. Okay, it had been a week, probably. I couldn't think about it long enough to figure it out.

I ate a light breakfast, a handful of fresh blueberries and a banana, spooning peanut butter on the banana as I ate. I needed some protein.

There were plenty of spots open as I walked into the workout room. I was bent over, head down, stretching with my legs spread wide when she entered the room upside down. That was a rush. I'd never seen her from that viewpoint. I stood up, stretching other areas that needed it, and watched her continue into the room. She greeted people as she moved, full of energy, Samson energy. She looked strong, rested.

I gave her a neutral nod of greeting. She continued over my way, taking up a place alongside but a little in front of me.

"Good morning," she said. Her voice was loud enough to gain the attention of those around her.

"Morning, Melanie."

"You look a little tired, Michael. Tough weekend?"

Well shit, that's provocative. "Not really. I had a great weekend."

"Interesting. What did you do?" she teased.

"Yeah, tell us about it, Michael," said Annie, one of the soccer moms.

"No, really, it's nothing you old married folks would understand."

A collective groan came from the gaggle of healthy, fit women ready to kickbox me around the room.

"Whoops, just kidding." Damn, that was a mistake. A major one with this crowd.

"Too late for that," said Judy. She was one of those kick-ass older women who could probably whip my butt. "You're in trouble."

"Sorry, I promise I'll do penance later. I was just being discreet."

It wasn't working. They stood around me, shaking their heads. They might have lynched me if Gail, the instructor, hadn't popped in.

"Penance is here," Melanie said.

I hung my head in resignation. I got through the class, feeling much better after the exercise, and tried to sneak out the door when Melanie called out.

"Hold on, Michael." I turned towards her, and she moved a couple of steps closer.

"I thought that's what I saw. Look at this, girls."

"What? What's going on?" someone asked.

The other women gathered around Melanie, looking at me. This was not comfortable.

"Do you see it?" she asked the others.

"My God, it's Mickey Mouse on his shirt," Annie said.

"Yes, I see it," others chimed in.

I looked down at my shirt, then at Melanie giggling off to the side. "Where? Are you sure?" I asked.

"Put your shoulders back and raise your arms a little," one of them said.

I did what she said and turned slowly in the middle of the crowd of mostly women.

"Yes, yes, it's Mickey all right," they said.

I brought my arms down and faced them. "I guess a guy who sweats Mickey Mouse on his shirt can't be all bad."

As they laughed and shook their heads, I moved in. "Come on, am I forgiven?" I brought my arms back up and took another small turn around for them.

"Huh. Maybe if Mickey comes back twice. See you, Michael," one of them said.

She started an exodus. Guess my little pirouette for Mickey wasn't working. That left only Melanie and Gail with me.

"Coffee, or are you two abandoning me, too?"

"Not today. Got to work," Melanie said.

"Me, too," Gail said. "Maybe next time." They both turned to the door, leaving me alone. I was a little dejected after that.

Minutes later, as I was leaving the parking lot, Melanie called, laughing again as she went back over the Mickey Mouse episode. "You really do sweat Mickey on your T-shirt."

"Yes, but you didn't have to tell everyone."

"Sure, I did. That is just too special not to share. You handled it well, by the way. You should thank me for getting you out of trouble after that 'old married folk' comment."

I laughed then. "You're right, except that you prompted it. I'll watch my mouth in the future. When can I see you?"

"How about tonight? Can I make you dinner at your place and maybe stay the night? I can get away."

"I'd love it, but should you really stay the night?"

"Are you worried about your friends?"

"Some, but I'll talk to them. I'm more concerned from your side of things. Are you sure this is wise?"

"It's all right. No one will even know I'm gone. How about six thirty? Oh, do you have a grill?"

"Six thirty is good, and yes, I have a grill." I shifted to a more serious tone. "We need to talk, Melanie."

"Michael, please, let's not have the talk right now. Can we just have a little more time together? Give me that, and I promise we'll talk soon."

"Sure," I said.

Why bring on pain today that can be put off till tomorrow?

***

We grilled the salmon she had marinated earlier in olive oil, pepper, garlic, and some secret ingredient she said she might share with me someday—*if* I behaved. We grilled outside at the picnic table. The weather was good, so we ate there, too.

Melanie had put a romaine salad together before she came over. We relaxed and enjoyed ourselves afterwards, talking about many things but not "the talk" as she'd put it after our workout class. We didn't always agree on the issues we discussed. That's the yin and yang in life, but our intimacy allowed us a willingness to listen that opposing politicians could never achieve. We each took the view of the other and absorbed new aspects into our individual foundations of belief. Being stubborn and opinionated, I was surprised at myself.

Later, as we were cuddling on the settee, Melanie excused herself to use the bathroom. When she came out, she was wearing a T-shirt that I'd left hanging on the door. Peeking out just below it was a pair of thong panties. Her hair was down, and she stood shyly in the doorway, her eyes on me. I took her in, all of her, before looking into her eyes.

She liked my eyes on her. I could feel it.

"Turn around," I said. "Now, lift the shirt and face me." I felt the rise of desire for her. "Again, slower," I said. My voice took on a firm tone, gentle but dominant as I guided her with a circling finger.

She turned slowly, keeping her eyes on mine as long as she could. Then she brought her head smoothly around to me again through the turn. A dancer's turn.

And we were dancing in a way, very sensuously. I could feel her excitement growing, matching my need.

She stepped towards me. I reached for her, caressing her through the thong before I pulled it aside. Her breathing spiked, and her hands reached out to circle my head. I leaned back, locking my gaze on her eyes. "I need you."

"Yes," she said. Her head fell back, and her eyes closed. Mine roamed over her.

The thin cloth of my shirt outlined her nipples. She had risen slightly on her toes, giving me more access, and reached out for my other hand as I pulled her onto my lap. Her lips found mine as my hardness throbbed against my stomach.

***

I awoke to her caressing my chest and continued to lie there, absorbing her touch, feeling her shyness give way to her need to know me. It was early morning; a faint graying of the darkness was visible through the roof hatch of the trailer.

Slowly, her hand moved lower, finding me, and I grew with the touch. Though timid, she was comfortable. She knew I was awake, that I welcomed her exploration. My body's response was for her. She held me gently, slowly stroking me, bending to look. I knew she wanted to please me, and she did, taking me into her mouth, into the intimacy and innocence that was Melanie. She gave to me as she desired, exploring in the process and seeming pleased with my response. She became more adventuresome, teasing, probing, and heightening my need for her until she must have sensed that I could no longer hold back. She mounted me quickly and rode me to an exquisite level of pleasure that was familiar but so new and rewarding with her.

I slowly woke the second time to the sound of the shower running. She had become important to me, special in my life. Almost thirty years single, and now, I was smitten. I smiled at the word. *Smitten.* Maybe not the language of today, but it suited me. I lay there thinking, taking inventory of myself. *Us!* I saw that her sexuality was developing through her relationship with me. She'd opened up through me, enjoying her womanhood. A new sensuality grew about her, and her growing confidence was frightening.

I wanted her for myself. Had I opened Pandora's box? The fear that had originated long ago in my life, the fear of infidelity, came back to me now. Fear rooted in my early and ill-fated marriage. Fighting those bonds and finding a release from them was critical. This woman had become my life. It scared me.

I struggled up, pulled a towel around my naked hips, and turned on the coffeepot. Everything went dark. No power.

I groaned. "No, no, no. Not before coffee."

"Hey, where's the light?" Melanie called from the shower.

"Hold on. Blew the breaker, I think."

I checked the circuit breaker. Everything looked good, but I reset it anyhow. Still no power. My head flopped to my chest. I wasn't good at dealing with things before coffee.

"It must be off at the pole, baby," I called out. "Can you see well enough to finish?"

"No problem. It must be late. There's plenty of light coming through this ceiling thingamajig."

I laughed. Plan B again, real life, but I accepted it grudgingly this morning. I pulled out the old stovetop percolator, filled it with water, and added coffee. That's enough thinking without coffee. I lit the propane stove, turned it to low, and crawled back into bed.

She came out of the bathroom. "Hey, day's a-wastin'. Can a girl get a cup of coffee around here?"

She was always up, positive and energetic about life, one of the many things I loved about her. Even so, I hadn't had my coffee. I rolled over on one elbow and looked at her through eyes that didn't want to be open.

Damn, she was lovely. She had her hair wrapped in one towel and another circled her hips, just below her waist. Her hands rested on those hips, fingers tapping as if demanding an answer. Her small breasts held my attention; they stood proudly, bare and lovely in the morning light. Her breathing increased as I looked, and her breasts rose and fell gently. She smiled. Such a cruel woman. I groaned as I felt another pang of need. A man needs to respect his limitations. Wisely, I collapsed back into the pillows.

I closed my eyes. "On the stove."

She laughed and crawled back into bed. Her long legs straddled my butt. She moved her hips around before leaning forward, lying down on my back. Damn it, I needed coffee.

Her breasts pressed into me as she whispered promises in my ear. No, I was too weak to endure all this. This was a mean, mean woman. Her wet tongue caressed my ear, and gentle slurping noises radiated through me with the erotic touch, stirring me more.

Then she was up. "Okay, love, rest. I may have need of you later." I lay there and groaned, trying to hide from her as she laughed.

"Yum, smells good. I've never made coffee in one of those," she said.

I managed to open one eye and found her examining the percolator atop the burner. I snuggled back into my pillow. This was too good. Maybe she would go away.

"I like this. You just get your strength back, and I'll take care of it," was the last I heard.

I must have dozed because I woke with a start. She was talking to me. I rolled over, barely awake but aware. I started the journey back when I caught a whiff of coffee. "Is it done?"

"No, still perking. This thing is slow."

"How long was I out?" I yawned in the middle of a good stretch. The smell of coffee lifted me. I could take her now. I was stronger, I told myself. *Coffee.*

"Oh, about ten minutes, I guess."

"And the coffee's not done?"

I sat up, shaking off the sleep that held me. I had been floating with dragonflies, in awe of being able to fly upside down. God, I needed some rest. She was killing me. I smiled at my good fortune even as I silently complained to myself.

"No, it's still perking. Shouldn't be long now," she said.

I risked a peek. She wore a lovely smile along with the towel. Beautiful. I noticed she had two cups and all the makings laid out. I rubbed my eyes to clear the sleep and looked over at the pot. "What do you mean, it's still perking? Is it done?"

"Can't be. It's still perking."

It hit me a moment later as I felt growing panic. "Baby, it will perk until we turn it off. It's done. Turn the burner off. It's done, probably been done."

She jumped up and shut the burner off. She turned back to me, her eyes wide with hands up, palms facing me. "I've never used one of these. Doesn't it just stop perking when it's done?"

I fell back into the pillows and rolled in them with laughter. I couldn't believe my ears. She squealed, and the bed sagged as she jumped into it.

Then I felt her sit on my butt again. "What's so funny? I never had a coffeepot like this before. I thought it would stop perking when it was done."

I couldn't stop laughing. She gently beat on my back. "What's so funny?"

"Ow, that hurt!"

"You're not laughing now," she said and gently kissed the ear she'd just bitten.

She raised her hips as I rolled over. "I'm sorry, baby. I don't mean to laugh at you," I lied.

She smiled. "Okay."

"Think I can have a cup of that coffee, black?" I asked.

Her face glowed as she smiled down at me, taking her time getting up. Her hips moved, gently gyrating against my groin. It was painfully delicious, but I was strong. I ignored this cruel woman until she finally got up. "Like I don't know how you take your coffee."

She brought me a cup and I took a sip. "Ah, I needed that," I said and took another sip.

I set the mug aside on the ledge by the bed and pulled her to me. "Careful there, girl . . . I'm getting stronger."

Her face lit up. "Good, I'll make another pot then."

I scrambled out of bed, pushing her back into it with a laugh. "No, you've done all the work so far. How about I make you a cup and tell you how this gas percolator thing works?"

"Deal," she said. She was smiling, but I could see she was still embarrassed.

I made her a cup, stirring in cream and sugar the way she liked it. Handing her the cup, I reached back for the percolator and sat down with her.

She sipped, and her face grimaced. "Strong," she said.

"Yeah, we'll make another pot in a minute."

She bent to take another sip. Her eyes gazed at me over the lip of the cup. "Guess I better pay attention."

"Yes. Now, when the coffee water starts boiling, the heated water rises up into this glass bulb and spreads over the coffee grounds. It gets darker and darker until . . ."

"It's done!" she yelled, finishing for me. She threw her arms over her head in victory and burst into laughter.

I loved it. She only had the towel on her hips, and I was almost finished with my coffee, stronger with each sip.

***

We went to the marina and talked briefly with Ben before driving down the pier to Cay Tam. As we got out of the truck, a beat-up blue car puttered towards us and stopped. The driver got out and gave us a squinty-eyed once-over.

"So, you didn't wait for me last time. Just brought a beautiful woman here and avoided me," he growled as he walked past me to Melanie. I grinned, watching as he bowed and she naturally curtsied. With a slight turn and nod of his head, he took her hand and kissed it.

"Hello, my lovely, I'm Captain Nemo. I'm pleased to make your acquaintance," he said, smooth as always.

"Melanie, kind sir," she responded, performing an elaborate curtsy.

They both laughed, and he released her hand as she came back to me.

"You've done well, Michael. She's a fine woman, I can tell. You're excused now, lad. I'll call if I need you." Turning back to Melanie, he moved to her side and grasped her hand again.

I laughed as Melanie's eyes went wide. Then she joined in as the captain laughed also. We talked for a while, Nemo declining the invitation to go sailing with us though he did stay and help us disconnect the power cables and all the lines but one. Then he was off with a flamboyant flurry of hand movements and a bow for Melanie.

"I like him," she said as Nemo drove away.

"I think he likes you, too, baby. Now, let's get going," I said.

She moved forward to take up position on the bow, boat hook in hand.

I called her back. "Let's do it the other way."

"Bow thruster?" she asked excitedly.

"You take the helm and leave it in neutral until I tell you to go forward. Okay?"

"Okay, Captain."

She came to the cockpit and started the engine as I watched. I went below and checked things out. Going topside, we talked as I checked the gauges periodically. Everything looked good, so I took a position on the port side of the cockpit and removed the aft spring line from a cleat. I pulled on the line, easing the boat backwards a few feet. "Okay, baby, take the bow out a little at a time, but look behind you to make sure the stern doesn't hit the dock."

She gave the control a short push as I'd taught her, and the bow started slowly out. Looking aft to check the angle of the stern and closeness to the dock, she gave the joystick another short push and checked position again.

I was watching, too, and threw the spring line on the dock as she maneuvered the boat farther away. "Go forward and throttle up slowly."

She moved through the motions, looking fore and aft to check her alignment. Turning the wheel slightly to starboard, she cleared the boat forward of us easily and took us out into the river.

I eased into one of the cushions and relaxed as she looked for crab traps, reinforcing everything she'd learned. This was the conservative, friendly woman I'd come to know. I wondered at it all, how we'd come to be together and the change that had come over her. There was a new confidence, an enjoyment, a playfulness that had been building during our time together.

She surprised me again. She looked back at me and suddenly pulled her shirt off and threw it, and then her bra, at me. I was stunned but made a big show of folding them neatly and not commenting.

Her eyes were full of mischief as she looked back at me playfully once more. "Well?" she said.

"Keep your eyes on the water ahead." She looked disappointed but turned forward.

"Nice tits."

"Thanks," she said, keeping her eyes on the water as a smile grew on her face. She quickly glanced back at me. "Do you like them?" she asked.

"Love 'em."

"They love you, too," she said.

There was no wind for the sails, so I had her motor to a good anchorage in a large bowl of the river near Julington Creek. She was going through the shutdown procedure when

I dove into the river. "Come on in," I called as I floated on my back.

"Aren't there alligators in the river?"

"Yes, but not this far out. Come on in, but first untie that line on the aft ladder and let it down." She did and prepared to come down the ladder with her shorts on.

"Hey, no fair. Take those shorts off."

"I don't have a swimsuit," she called back.

"Me either." I turned my body into a shallow dive, bringing my bare butt out of the water as I did.

She whistled. "Wow, nice butt."

Moments later she was beside me, her body curling with mine as her arms came around my shoulders.

"I've never been skinny dipping before," she said and glanced about as though looking for voyeurs. "I can't believe I'm naked!"

I laughed at her seriousness and swam away. I loved the way she had blossomed, the way she had opened up to life, embracing it. She chased me until I floated on my back, then she turned onto hers beside me and we just floated there. "We need to get some of those floaty things. I don't remember what they're called," I said.

"Floaties," she said.

I cocked my head and gave her the *Huh?*

"Okay, spoilsport, they're called noodles. They're great for kids in the pool," she said. "I'll pick up a couple."

"I don't know," I said. "How much are they?"

"Forget it, cheapo. I'll buy them." She splashed me and sprinted for the ladder.

We made a light lunch of the meager groceries I'd brought from the trailer and ate as we sat in the cockpit, drying in the sun with towels around our waists.

"Michael, can I ask you a private question?" Her voice was shy and low.

I shifted, turning to face her directly. "Sure, but then I get to ask you one. Are you comfortable with that?" We both knew we needed to get to this point, but now it was from a real need to know more about each other rather than just curiosity mixed with motives of self-preservation.

"Your complicated relationship," she said tentatively. She avoided looking at me directly until she finally came out with it. "Is it complicated because she's married?" She looked into my eyes then, probably feeling my discomfort. "We don't have to talk about it if you don't want to." Her eyes never wavered from mine now that it was out.

"No, we need to talk about it." I scooted over and drew her to me. "Yes, she's married, but it isn't that simple." Why did I have to say the last? Was I defending myself?

"I thought so. How close are you? Does she know about me?"

"She does now. I talked to her about you last week. That's why I went to Orlando. We were close, very close."

She moved into my arms. "What are we going to do, Michael? Are you going to keep seeing her?"

My jaw rested lightly on her hair as I held her back against my chest. I couldn't live in this heavy emotion. I'd been here too long. I had to break out. "I guess I'll see you both."

"What!" she exclaimed and eased from my grasp to look back at me.

"Well, you're both married, so I'll just see you both."

"No way! That's not going to work."

"Hold on," I said, laughing. I pulled her back to me. "I don't mean together. Well, not unless you two agree. Wow, I like the visual. It could be fun."

She wasn't laughing. "Michael, that's not going to happen, no way."

"That's what she said."

"Really, she said that?"

"Yep."

"Well, I think I like her."

"Great, so we can do it, the three of us?"

"No! But I like what I'm learning about her so far. Is she beautiful?"

"Of course, she is, silly. She's the most beautiful girl in the world besides you."

"Okay, I shouldn't have asked that," she admitted. "But she is, isn't she?"

"Yes, love, she's beautiful inside and out, just as I'm finding you are. There are other things, but for now, you should know that her husband knew of us."

I felt her sharp intake of breath at that and held her tightly as she wriggled, trying to turn. "It's complicated, Melanie, not kinky. I'll explain another time, but it was never just about sex. It's more . . . like us in a way."

"Thank you," she said. This time I let her turn. She hugged me, turning her face up to me. Her eyes were tearing. "Thank you for being truthful with me. I'm so sorry I've made it more complicated. I want to know more. I want to know it all."

"I hate that I hurt her, but she had to know before Daytona. If you weren't married, she would be happy for me, that I found someone. That you were married disturbed her greatly. It disturbs me, too, Melanie, but it hasn't stopped me."

I was back where I didn't want to be. Once again, guilt washed over me. I'd wanted to keep it lighthearted. Stupid. So much at stake here, so many lives involved, and I was weak.

Melanie was sobbing now. I watched her struggle,

trying for control. I knew she was lost in the emotion of my experience, my complicated relationship, and our own. We sat quietly for a time, holding one another.

Her cell rang. "Whoops, forgot to turn it on vibe." She didn't move to answer it.

"Perhaps you should answer that. It might be important. You can take it below for privacy."

She looked at me, and the phone stopped ringing.

"We've had enough drama for one day. If it goes to message, I'll check it," she said. She scooted back into me, hugging against me as if she needed the security of my presence at that moment.

I wrapped an arm around her. "This might be a good time for me to ask about some things."

The damn phone went off again, a different ring, probably a voice message. She got up to check it and started below, looking back at me.

"Saved by the bell," I said.

"Could be," she said, laughing over her shoulder.

A few minutes later, she returned and snuggled back into me again. "I'm sorry, Michael. I can't see you tonight."

"All right. Is everything okay?"

"Yes," she said, turning slightly to look back at me. "That was my husband. He wants to see me for dinner tonight. I have to see him, Michael."

I sat up at that, still holding her. "Well, of course, you do, but I don't understand."

I was determined to get some things out in the open. "Don't you see each other every night? I mean, you've only come to me once overnight except for the Daytona trip. I thought he was out of town then or something."

She had never mentioned her separation though I knew of

it through Valerie. I wanted it to come from Melanie, for her to tell me, to talk to me and make it all right for the first time. It was already too real, and it all came rushing at me though I didn't let her see my anguish. *Damn it, you knew she was married, you idiot. You've been playing 'let's pretend.'*

On the surface, I had been asking to have the talk, but I hadn't really wanted to, I realized. No, I didn't. I didn't want to face this. I just wanted her, and my attempts to talk to her had all been superficial.

I remembered that whenever I would bring him up, *us* up, she would press a finger to my lips, shushing me, telling me it was our time and no one else's. Her way of avoiding the talk, and I buried my head every time.

"We're separated, Michael, and have been for a while. He asked for it; I didn't. I was kinda shocked . . . thought we should talk. You know, go to counseling, but he said we'd do that later. He said we needed some time apart first, that we'd see each other on dates, start anew, and work things out."

She paused for a moment, then took my hands and looked into my eyes. Searching my face for understanding, I guess, maybe worried about what I must think of her.

"I didn't even know there was a problem. Later, I looked back on everything, our lives together, and I could see that we needed to work on our marriage. I mean . . . well, something was obviously missing." She looked off to nothing in the distance and grew quiet.

I let her go, let her sink into herself and reflect, do whatever she needed to reconcile this time in her life. I remained silent.

"We were really more like two roommates than anything else, I guess. I just thought it was normal. We had warmth but no passion, partners in everything material, but that's all. Sex was . . . was . . . well, I don't want to go there," she said.

She quickly looked away, then back to me. "There is no way I'd let myself become involved with you, no matter how attracted I was, if my husband and I were together."

"I know," I said and felt terribly sad. Stephanie's words again haunted me. *She's at a difficult time in life with the kids grown, the husband not around much, probably drifted apart, and too much time on her hands. You've seduced her!*

I thought of my role in this, in allowing and fueling our relationship to develop. "She was right."

"What, honey? Who was right?"

"Nobody, Melanie. It's just a thought." I pulled her close. "Have you tried to work it out with him?" *Him?* I knew his name, but using it would have made him become more real to me than he was now. I didn't want him to be real. I wanted him to go away, to have never existed. "I mean really tried. Have you told him you're lonely, that you need to do things together, asked him what he thought?"

Blindly, I was trying to help now as guilt overcame me. Even though I had known she was separated, I wasn't ready for the reality of it, the reality of her being married at all, and I still didn't know what "separated" meant. I was confused and shielded myself from any responsibility. I tried to push Stephanie's insightful assessment of Melanie's situation away, but it wouldn't go. I had only complicated life for her, added to her torment, and now I was helpless to do anything but try to do right.

"Sorry. I don't mean to put the whole burden on you. Marriage is a two-way street, a partnership. Knowing you, I know you've tried."

She smiled, but it was troubled, weak. "Michael, don't take this in too much. This has nothing to do with you or with us now. Yes, I tried, and I asked for us to spend more time together. Last weekend, I called him from the room and asked if he would come down the next day." Her eyes were pleading with me now. "I'm sorry, honey. I don't mean to hurt you now, and I didn't mean to play games with your feelings then. I wanted to be with you. I wanted to make love to you, but I had to give my marriage one more chance. I am so sorry that I used you that way."

"It's all right. I guess I understand. Val told me that you had called him. I suspected something like that. I was surprised when you came to me."

"Yes, I came to you, and I will always be happy that I did."

I stayed silent, patient for once, as I could see she was soul searching.

"Michael," she said as she looked into my eyes, "I have come to enjoy and feel life so much more since you've come into it. He was too busy to come down, told me we'd get together soon. He said he was just so wrapped up in an important project that he hadn't had time to see me as he'd planned. 'It'll get better,' he said, but it never does."

"I'm sorry, Melanie. I don't mean to pry. I have no rights here. I know I'm just the outside man and . . ." *Oh, my God, the outside man! That's what I've been, what I've become.*

"Michael! Michael, are you all right?"

I blinked to find her holding my face, concern showing in hers. I'd gone away again. "I'm all right, but I'm realizing how much at fault I've been. I've complicated your life and confused things even more."

"I knew you were going to take things badly, honey, but really, in my mind and in my heart and soul, these matters are separate. I have to deal with my situation, my husband, yes. But in my heart, we were already apart, divorced in all but the legal sense. I just didn't see a need to take it further," she said. "And then you came into my life, and I found I needed you, Michael. Somehow life brought you to me when I needed you, and I need you still."

I know I was making a leap, reading between the lines, but the need thing bothered me. She needed me, but for how long? Forever? Until her husband wanted her back? Until she found the church, or her family wouldn't like it? It had to be more than need. I pushed it down.

We were quiet and just held each other for a while. The talk had taken a toll.

* * *

We never got to sail that day and eventually motored back to the dock. Melanie was reluctant to go as we put her things in her car. She knew I was trying to sort things out, just as she was. We agreed to get together later in the week.

She called me late in the evening. "I had to call, honey. I know you're still concerned with our talk earlier today. He was here today and . . ."

"No, baby, that's entirely your business," I said, cutting her off. "I mean, of course, I'm concerned, but . . . well, it's your business, honey." Damn, she was still screwing the son of a bitch.

"He's my husband, Michael."

There it was. There was the reality in so many words. She was still sleeping with him, had to be. How could she while she was sleeping with me?

"I don't know where I'm going right now and . . . I want to keep seeing you, but I have to see him, too, and . . . he's having lunch with me and our daughter after church this Sunday. He's never done that."

"What are you going to do, honey?" Immediately, I regretted the question.

"I don't know what you mean. There's nothing I can do right now. I just don't know. This is all so new to me. Can you understand that?"

"Of course, I can. I'm sorry I asked. I know you're going through a lot right now. I'm just kind of struggling with my own thoughts."

"I know you are. That's why I knew I had to call. Can we just go slowly with everything?"

"I'm not going anywhere. All of this needs to go slowly."

But I was concerned and lay awake thinking about it.

Stephanie shouldn't have to wait. She deserved to know as early as possible about my feelings. My growing attraction for Melanie was a breach in my relationship with Steph, one that I hadn't expected. For a long time, I had believed Steph and I would be together one day as husband and wife. I never communicated the thought, but I felt the expectation was there for both of us.

I wondered again how she was doing.

Chapter Twenty-One

I actually got some work done the next few days. I arranged schedules and a work plan with an electrician and plumber, making sure there was no conflict. They were good, responsible workers. I was appreciative of their skills and reliability. Too often, the past few years, I'd discovered pride and ability lacking in the building trades.

Melanie called Wednesday during a break from her work. "Hey, what are you up to today?"

"Just getting some things done around the house." I chuckled as a vision came to me.

"What's so funny?"

"I sounded like a housewife just now. You know, just getting things done around the house."

"Yes, you do." She laughed. "I just have a few minutes," she said, "but I wanted to talk to you."

"Okay, what's on your mind? Hold on, we have to open the garage door."

"What?" she asked, laughing again. "What are you up to?"

"There, got it," I said, raising the door. "Hey, we gotta keep working here, so I'm taking you with me. Don't you love these cell phones?"

"Yes," she said, "I do. I'm with you . . . got my eyes closed. Where are we going now?"

"We're off to the master bedroom."

"I like that. Can we get a bed soon, a big one, and open up those French doors to the veranda?"

"You devil, you're excited again, aren't you?"

"Yes, I am now, and I have to get back, darn it. Molly just signaled me a patient is waiting. Can we pick up here tomorrow? I want to see you."

"Sure. Whoops, almost dropped you, honey. You all right?" Her laughter as she hung up lit up the phone and my day. She always made my day. Then I stopped and sat down. What was I doing? I'd made the right decision, the responsible one, and I needed to tell her. I continued to sit there, miserable now.

Nathan came looking for me that evening. He found me in the torn-up kitchen. I was measuring an area that looked like it might get some cabinetry one day soon.

"Where have you been? We haven't seen you, except driving in and out, for days."

"Hi, Nathan. Sorry about that, just been involved in things."

"Nan sent me to bring you to dinner. I think she's curious, figures you're seeing that pretty lady we noticed you with. All night," he added, coughing a little as though embarrassed to bring it up.

I smiled at Nathan's discomfort but didn't let him off the hook. "I'd love to have some of Nan's cooking . . . and your company. I guess I'd better bring you both up to date before the rumors start throughout the community. So, what time is dinner? I need to clean up."

"You got an hour."

"In that case, look at this and tell me what you think."

He followed me across the room. "I said *you* got an hour. I only have five minutes. We married guys have other responsibilities if we want to stay happy, you know."

"I've heard." I bent over the worktable and went over part of the plan and a rough sketch, showing him what was bothering me. Nathan looked for a minute and quickly pointed out the solution. "Thanks, Nathan. I guess I was just too close to it."

"The place is looking good. Darn shame you're going to sell it."

I was still bent over the drawings. "You're right. I love this place. Maybe I should just keep it and move in."

"You will," Nathan said as he walked away.

I stood, watching Nathan leave.

He looked back with a big smile. "Less than an hour now, Michael."

I was sure he was rushing back to tell Nan what I'd said about keeping the place. They both kept telling me that one day I'd change my mind and stay.

I took a shower, dressed in a pair of shorts and pullover, and was out the trailer door. I slipped into a pair of old boat shoes that lay just outside on a piece of green indoor/outdoor carpeting, then turned back and went inside for a notepad in the pocket of my work shirt.

Hannah answered the door, surprising me. I didn't know she was there though I should have. She didn't climb stairs here too often. I was glad to see her. I had neglected them all too long.

"Hello, Michael. Good to see you."

I hugged her and got a kiss on the cheek. "You, too, Hannah. How is everything?"

"Very good," she said. I led her by the hand into the small living room where Nathan sat watching a game show. We exchanged waves as I helped Hannah get seated. Then I went into the kitchen to see Nan.

I took in the kitchen aromas. "Smells good, like pot roast and potatoes or something."

"You have a good nose, Michael." The pressure cooker whistled, and Nan turned the stove off, then gave me a hug.

She held me by my shoulders, examining my face. "What have you been up to? Is everything all right?"

I had to laugh at her intensity. They had all been determined to see me tonight.

"Yes, life just gets a bit complicated at times, but all is fine."

"Tell me about it when you're ready." She turned back to the pressure cooker, taking it to the sink to cool it with fresh water.

"Can't fool you, can I?"

"Just want to make sure my landlord is all right. I hear you might be staying." She turned and smiled over her shoulder as I headed for the living room.

Later, after clearing the table, Nathan and I did the dishes and talked about what we had going on while the ladies sat working on some kind of new crochet stitch. "Michael, I've got a young guy working for me that I think will be a good investment," he said, referring to the Foundation. Nathan was on the advisory board and took it seriously. He knew how a little bump of encouragement and enablement could make a big difference in a person's life.

"Yeah? Tell me about him." We talked quietly. Nathan's judgment was always good, but I wanted to hear about the young man. Nathan didn't mess around with the undeserving, and I wanted to know what prompted him to act on the youth's behalf.

As Nathan and I came back into the living room, Nan and

Hannah put their crochet stuff away. "Sure was nice of you gentlemen to do the dishes," Nan said.

"Anything for my lovely lady," Nathan replied.

Nan beamed as Hannah just shook her head.

The evening was not going to end without my talking about Melanie, so the ladies brought out wine to loosen my tongue. Sometimes you just have to go with it. Is that part of the harmony Nemo talks about? I don't know, but this was my family. I shared a little with them. I kept waiting for a question as I brought them up to date on what was going on, but they didn't interrupt.

It was awkward for me as I stumbled through. My mind reached out in many tangents as I tried to stay focused. It was nerve-wracking, but finally, I finished.

"Is Stephanie all right?" Nathan asked.

I noticed Nan and Hannah give approving nods, like a couple of bookends. I laughed and shared my thought with them.

"Bookends?" Hannah said, moving to a chair across from Nan.

"Sorry, it was a momentary vision. You two sitting on either side of Nathan and . . ." It was just too funny, and laughter overtook me. I hadn't let go like this since I was in Vietnam when I smoked my first cigarette and unknowingly ate my first special brownie on the same night. I gave up the cigarettes, but there are times I long for those brownies. They made the world right for a while. "And you were both"—I gasped for breath— "nodding at the same time." I paused once more to inhale. "Bookends," I finally got out.

They weren't laughing. *So much for levity.*

I cleared my throat and sobered my facial expression. "Stephanie is good," I lied.

They wanted to know when they could meet Melanie. I told them soon but that things were a little complicated.

As if on cue, my wonderful bookends looked at each other and, at the same time, said, "Complicated?"

Nathan laughed. Pillows pummeled him from two sides as he moved to sit with me.

"Dang, Michael, you always get me in trouble."

"We're both in trouble, buddy. It was funny," I said. More pillows were thrown, and Nathan moved back to his seat.

"Yes, my lovelies, 'complicated' as in 'married'—married but separated. Separated and not living together. I've discovered there's a difference," I continued. "I want you to meet her."

We left it at that for the night.

***

As I walked the short distance to the trailer, I thought about it all. I pulled one of the plastic chairs from under the awning and positioned it so I could see the river. It was very dark, but I could make out the movement of water by tufts of white foam kicked up by the breeze.

I was glad that I'd talked to them. They were family. Maybe not together all the time, but close. Only these three and a few others were able to contact me at any time.

I've had a hell of a life. Many acquaintances, but few friends, and even fewer close friends. I counted many at the marina as friends but not close ones. Ben was, and Dwight, but we didn't talk on a regular basis. Nemo was close, but still, it was different. He was a trusted confidant, wanting nothing from me but the mutual respect we enjoyed even if we didn't see each other for months at a time.

I was social, loved people, and was very open, but being kind of a loner, I'd never been one to surround myself with superficial friends. Tonight, I'd been with close friends, family.

The past won't be denied, somehow insinuating its way into things at the darnedest times. Like harmony, I suppose, it has its course and schedule, finding its way to us for a reason.

My life started with good family, yet I'd abandoned them for a while.

After graduating aircraft mechanic school in Ft. Eustis, Plan C changed to Plan D. I moved to Georgia and took a job with one of the major defense contractors around Atlanta. But I did start night classes under the GI Bill. Two classes a semester was going to make for a long time getting an engineering degree. I just wasn't comfortable yet with thinking I could live solely on the GI Bill while attending school full time.

That changed sooner than I'd planned, and I was back to Plan C again.

After working as a mechanical technician for almost a year, I became aware of an anomaly in some hardware test data. Initially, I reasoned it was probably an error in the associated criteria. Surely, the hardware was all right. Things like this happened, but it required investigation. I brought it up for resolution through my supervisory chain. I was surprised when I was suddenly moved to another project after being told it had been resolved months earlier. Occasionally, I queried one of the supervisors about the issue, only to be met with a cursory brush off. "Don't worry about it, Michael, it's taken care of."

Having a security clearance had helped me to gain employment and now provided after-hours access to documentation I wanted to see. I conducted my own investigation and discovered bogus mandatory inspection validations. Critical heat treatments hadn't been applied on some high-grade bolts. The bolts were used on military aircraft that required very high fabrication criteria along with stringent test and inspection requirements.

Two of the tests had not been performed but were technician-stamped and signed off as having been done. The tests involved tens of thousands of very expensive bolts used in a variety of military aircraft. I had discovered that the ability to perform the critical tests did not exist within the plant, and I could find no evidence that the material had been sent out for the testing at any certified facility. I understood the significance of what I had found, knew the possibilities of failure in flight of this hardware.

Wary now, I approached supervision again with a bolt and the test data. The next thing I knew, senior management had me on the carpet. They told me the company was well aware of what I had brought forward and had resolved it as a nonproblem.

They confiscated my evidence, threatened legal action if I brought the issue up publicly, and escorted me out of the plant, fired for wasting company time or something. Later, I found out they took additional actions to discredit me and have my security clearance quietly suspended within the company.

No, I wasn't a stranger to greed and corruption. I was then, but that was the beginning. Being wary early on, I had carefully collected data and made copies of everything, including a couple of the bolts. Then I sought to collaborate with a machinist who was close to the issue. That bit of innocence of the world was really the end for me in the company. The machinist cooperated, confirming my suspicions, even acknowledging that he had questioned the issue, too, but had shut up and moved on when politely told the problem had been resolved. After thinking about it and becoming concerned about what I might do, the machinist must have decided he had better tell supervision. Better to save his job than worry about my wild goose chase, I guessed. Hard lesson, but it served me well in the future.

I did more research and discovered the original supplier had gone out of business after it was discovered they had never done any of the required testing.

The company where I'd been employed would have suffered minor embarrassment and significant cost associated with recalling and correcting or validating the hardware, but it would have recovered. Instead, they chose to manage the problem away. Unfortunately, there were lives lost that I believed were related to the questionable bolts.

A friend taking law courses advised me to approach the local US Attorney's Office. After a few phone calls, they stonewalled me, promising to look into it further.

Yes, they were determined to make me rich. I laughed there in the night as I watched the river, but I didn't feel a lot of humor.

The law friend introduced me to qui tam, or whistleblower, lawsuits after my discouraging meeting with the US attorney, and I filed suit against the company and its subcontractor. I was angry and frustrated with the government and blamed them as much as the contractor. I had money saved up and most of the GI Bill, so I finished my classes, packed up, and moved to Florida.

The US Justice Department later got involved in the case and took it to conclusion with me. As I became more informed and experienced in qui tam lawsuits, I learned that was a normal part of the system when they determined a valid case existed. It took almost four years for the case to be resolved, and by that time, I'd earned a civil engineering degree from the University of Florida and was well on the way to another in accounting.

As in most cases, there was a negotiated settlement, but this one was for tens of millions of dollars. I found myself a very wealthy man with the percentage I earned as the relator, the legal term for my role in surfacing and filing the suit. I stayed on at Florida and finished the degree in accounting. Then I worked for a few years, still learning and applying what I'd learned in college. During that time, I learned enough to start a small construction company with my brother.

Robert, the Justice Department attorney who took over and finalized my qui tam suit, and his bosses didn't leave me alone, however, and I'd worked for them indirectly over the years as they gained information that needed developing. Hey, the government can be sneaky, too. In most cases, I took on an active advisory and investigative role for a number of whistleblowers going through their own horror experiences in industry. Some needed counsel, guidance to develop a claim when the government didn't feel there was enough for them to step in. I had firsthand experience and cost less than an attorney. So, I worked with the whistleblowers, often undercover, for a percentage of their relator's fee.

Many years later, I bought a boat and ended up sailing the Caribbean for a few years before Robert popped up and recommended Fools Cove Marina to me. We were old friends by then. I'd also worked directly for the Justice Department a few times since that original case, always driving hard bargains. Hard money bargains though I didn't need the money.

Another time and I'd have done it for wages, just put

me on the payroll. But not later, not after seeing how the corruption may have even extended to the US Attorney's Office when I'd gone to them for help years before. I'd learned from that lesson. No, when they came to me for help after that, I accepted lead-in information, mostly unfounded suspicions of fraud, but I was on my own. The deal was they would cover me with credible manipulations of my own identity, and I'd hire on with the company and investigate from within. Then I would file under the provisions of qui tam, and they could take over the case and pay me the relator portion when the case was resolved. I earned a lot of money that way across several agencies.

Corruption is relentless. People just need to read their local paper to find out how normal a part of life it is. It may not be in terms of millions of dollars all the time, but it's significant, constant, and sometimes deadly at every level of business and government. Churches seem to have their own unique problems, but even there it comes out regularly.

I yawned as I stood and stretched. Everything was dark at Nathan and Nan's place. Tomorrow was a workday. I went to bed at peace with myself for once.

It lasted for three hours before I woke to the guilt of my own corruption: wrong relationships.

Chapter Twenty-Two

*T*hursday, I met Melanie at a shopping mall parking lot. She'd called me earlier. "How about a late picnic?"

"Sure, I love your picnics. Can I bring anything?"

"No, I have it all. Wine good for you?'

"Great."

I pulled in beside her and went to open her door, but she stopped me, calling out through the passenger side window of her car. "Hop in, honey. I'll drive today."

Sliding into the passenger seat, I automatically reached for her.

"Did you have a good day, baby?" she asked.

"Now it is." I nuzzled her cheeks and kissed her lips.

"For me, too." Then she reached over and fumbled the seat belt around me. "Hey, I'm the car commander now. It's my responsibility to take care of you."

She smiled at me as she buckled my belt. I laughed, but she remained serious and didn't join in. I laughed harder, and she ignored me.

"All right, we're ready now." Putting the car in gear, she backed out of the parking space. She was wearing another simple sundress, not as bright as the last one but still colorful and pretty. It gathered just below her breasts, and she wore no bra, I noticed. Looking down, I found the flip-flops, of course.

"Lovely." I closed my eyes and sat back in the seat.

"What? What did you say?" She looked over at me quickly, then back to the road, with those big eyes.

"Lovely, I said . . . you're lovely." I brought the hand she had placed on my wrist to my lips and kissed it. Her cheeks turned red as she glanced at me.

She pulled my hand to her cheek and rubbed it as she drove. "Thank you," she said.

We went to the park we'd discovered together and sat at the same table as before.

She had picked up sushi-to-go from Publix. "You do the wine, and I'll have this ready in a minute." She handed me a bottle of cabernet and a corkscrew.

Melanie opened small packets of soy sauce, poured it into a plastic bowl, and mixed a small mound of wasabi paste into it, stirring until it was almost liquid again.

"Wow, quite a production," I said.

"Never had this before?"

"Only at a sushi bar. This is great."

After lunch, we took a walk down to the water, watching boats on the river. I held her, enjoying the view, the simple things.

"Are we ever going to sail?" she asked.

"Maybe when you stop running around naked."

"Hey, you're always trying to get me naked, skinny dipping and not allowing me to wear a bra on board," she said. She leaned into my arms, her fists balled against my chest as I held her.

"Me? Who took her top off, baring her boobs for everyone to see? We were barely away from the dock, you exhibitionist."

"What?" she squealed. "I am not an exhibitionist." She looked at me defiantly before her face crumpled. "I am, aren't

I? I do like getting my top off." She gave it more thought. "Okay, I am an exhibitionist, but only with you. You bring it out in me," she said, laughing. Then she got serious. "God, I love the freedom I feel with you, Michael." She put her arms around me and hugged me closer.

Finally, we cleaned up the area and packed up the car to leave. It was early, a few minutes after seven, as we drove away. I leaned back in the seat, enjoying not driving for once. I closed my eyes, comfortable in our time together, loving that she was so near to me. I wanted to ask her questions, but it wasn't a good time. We needed this, this simple being together right now.

Moments later, I opened my eyes and sat up, turning to her. "I got pretty relaxed there. You can drive all the time if you like."

"No way," she said. "I like the old truck. My seat is getting worn out though. When are you going to get something else?"

"Never. I love that old truck. You're embarrassed to be in it, aren't you? That's why you're always scrunched down in the seat. You're hiding, aren't you?"

"No, I love it, too, for work things, and it's good for picnics," she said. "And I am not hiding all scrunched down in the seat. I sit low because it's worn out, you rat. Next time, I'll drive it and you sit on the springs. How's that?" she said, glancing over at me.

"I'll get you a cushion to sit on."

No reaction. I was disappointed, but all I got was a quick side-glance.

"Okay, I'll go out and buy a car."

"No, no," she said. "Don't do that. I just thought you might have something else in Orlando."

"Actually, I do have another car. It's in the garage at the

house. We'll take it next time we go out. How's that?"

"Okay," she said. I loved that easy, up-for-anything response.

As we drove, we became dangerous. The roles were reversed. I normally did the driving. My seat belt stretched as I moved to be close to her. She drove with one hand while the other continued to touch me, pulling me to her while I nibbled her ear, kissed her cheek, and then massaged her breast. She looked over at me then, her eyebrows arching as if she were questioning the wisdom of what I was doing. Gently, I released one of her breasts—small, beautiful, and delighted at my touch and kiss. Her nipple responded, desiring more.

"Hey," she said, "trying to drive here, getting a little distracted." I looked up at her smiling face, still squeezing the nipple gently, and she was responding. We were in traffic, and I reluctantly sat back. I still held her breast, breathing hard. We continually glanced at traffic and each other as she drove.

"Oh, God, what you do to me," she said once again, and I knew, for it was the same with me. We both loved this, but she was right, and I placed the lovely breast back in the folds of the dress top.

"Bear with me, honey," she said, glancing at me. "I want to show you something. Sit back and relax a minute."

"Sure." I leaned back but couldn't take my eyes off her. I was lost, my focus tuned to her alone and the feelings that were especially overwhelming on that night. The next time I glanced out, I noticed we were in a residential neighborhood. "Hey, where are we going, honey?"

She didn't answer.

I had a bad feeling, and it suddenly came to me where she was taking me. "Baby, this isn't a good idea."

She looked at me with those big, beautiful eyes. "Please,"

she pleaded. "I need to do this."

She pushed a button and pulled into a driveway, easing into a large garage as it opened. When the garage door closed, she switched off the ignition and reached for me, pulling me close. She teased me with a delicious kiss, which somehow only fueled my anxiety, and then she was bouncing out of the car.

"Come with me." She was passionately joyful, so happy to be sharing her home with me.

I was miserable.

She led me into the house, turning on lights and giving me a tour, starting with her kitchen. She was proud of it for sure, and so happy to be sharing it with me that I didn't want to spoil it.

"I wanted you to see this. It's a part of me, and I want to share everything with you. I want you to know where I'm sitting when I send you an email. Where I'm listening to our music and thinking of you. Where I'm sleeping curled up, imagining your arms and legs around me." She wound her long body about me and pulled me close, searching my face.

I don't know what she saw there, but it didn't dissuade her.

"Come on," she said.

She was full of energy as she pulled me through the house. Room by room, I invaded her husband's home, *their* home. I could see how important this was to her and tried to allay the awkwardness. As much as I didn't want to be there, I didn't want to spoil it for her, either, and I liked the thought of knowing her surroundings. It's just that . . . I closed my eyes and pushed it away for a moment. I could see her sitting at the kitchen counter, bent over the computer that sat there, burning a CD with music. I remembered her jumping in the truck and twisting around to give me a kiss while her free hand

was searching to put a new CD in the player. She fumbled
with it, releasing me only for a moment to turn her head and
find the insert slot. Then she was back on my lips as the music
began to flow.

I liked that visual, all of it, and now I could relate fully.
Still, I was extremely uncomfortable.

Then we were in their bedroom and into her closet. She
was excited, loving this sharing as much as I was hating it.

"These are my kids, and those are my parents, married
fifty years last June," she said. She proudly showed me picture
after picture throughout the house, and my heart grew heavy.
The guilt began to overtake me again. *She's vulnerable,
Michael. Let her go.*

Finally, it was over, and we were in the car, not quite as
close as before, lost in thought. Pulling up to my truck in the
mall parking lot, she switched off the ignition and turned,
pulling me close.

"I'm sorry it bothered you so much. I was just so excited to
share with you. It was important to me for you to be there, to
be a part of me, to have your presence there for me now when
I'm alone."

She was crying softly as I held her close. Tears came to my
eyes, too, and my voice choked as I spoke. "It's all right. I know
how you meant it and how important it was to you. It's just . .
. it's . . ." I was unable to talk for a moment. My throat ached
from holding back the sob trying to burst from my chest. "It's
just so much more real now. I can't help it, Melanie. I guess
I've been playing 'let's pretend,' and now I've gotten a very
harsh dose of reality. I'm sorry I spoiled it for you."

"Oh, my God, Michael, I am so selfish! But I'm not sorry. I
want you to know me, need you to know me."

There was too much between us now for our parting to

be anything other than tender, but still we were strained. I drove away in a daze. I'd been in denial, selfishly locked onto the good aspects of relationships. Ever since Millie, I'd lived a life carefully shielded from pain and responsibility. I'd never truly shared the ups and downs life presented real partners. I was never really a partner. I only enjoyed the good times in my relationships, never the bad, and sharing both is what it means to be a true partner. That's the essence of what I faced going to her house. *Their* house. The photographs served only to drive reality through me like a stake through a vampire's heart.

Turning a corner, I found myself at Harvey's. It was time for a drink and a quiet place to think. No, I didn't want to think; I wanted to drink and not think. I wasn't ready to go back to the trailer. I didn't want to be alone, but I didn't want to be with people, either. At Harvey's, I could not be alone without having to deal with people.

There were quite a few customers, but I found a high table in the shadows outside the dance floor. Moments later, Jigger placed a glass in front of me. "I hope I wasn't presumptuous, Michael. You still drink Dewar's and water, don't you?"

"Hey, Jigger. Yes, thank you. Can I buy you a drink for once? Please, join me for one drink." I knew she wouldn't without a push and maybe not even then. She looked over her shoulder, then slid onto the stool with my help.

"Let's see, you're going to have a . . ." I leaned over and glanced to find that she was wearing heels again tonight.

"Okay, then, a martini it is," I said to her laughter.

She was such a lovely woman. Her eyes sparkled. I was troubled and thankful for the distraction she offered. I really didn't want to think about things just now.

"So, you're still on the heels and martini thing even though Hannah says bunny slippers," I commented.

"Absolutely, you've made me a believer," she said.

I liked that she seemed comfortable with both the conversation and me. In the back of my mind was that day at the gym when she'd seemed to get oddly sad.

"I can't help it," I told her. "When I think of martinis, I see you in heels." She laughed as I stood to order her drink. "I'll be right back."

Becky, one of the bartenders, was waitressing tonight and took my order. She looked over my shoulder and, after a moment, nodded. "One special martini coming up."

I noticed Jigger's timid smile when I got back to the table.

"That should start them talking," she said.

"Why?"

"Because I never sit with a single guy and have a drink here." She looked at me with that shy smile again. "They'll be all over me later."

"Uh oh, am I causing a problem? Is your husband going to be upset?" Becky was at my shoulder as I spoke.

"No, Michael, everything will be fine." A look passed between her and Becky as Becky set the martini down and left.

"To martinis and good advice," Jigger toasted.

I bowed slightly and enjoyed the smile I felt on my lips. "Thank you, madam. And to a lovely, elegant woman in heels who appreciates them," I added.

We sipped.

"Thank you," she said. "What brings you out tonight? I haven't seen you since you were here with the rest of the gang and introduced me to Robert. And thank you for inviting me into your group that night. I enjoyed it."

"Any time, Jigger. We enjoyed you, too."

My eyes went to my glass then. The pleasant moment was over, and reality came intruding.

"So, what's been going on since then?" she asked.

"Well, I've been busy working on the house—and a complicated relationship."

"Oh," she said, so quietly that I looked up at her.

"Sorry. I don't mean to cry on your shoulder, lovely as it is." Quickly, I added, "I'm not coming on to you, Jigger. I didn't mean to get personal."

Her laugh was full of energy before she got serious. "It's all right, Michael. Thanks for the compliment."

It became quiet for a moment. "Everyone goes through bad times," she said and raised her glass again. "Here's to the good times, may they always outweigh the bad."

"Here, here," I said. I drained my glass and looked over to Becky for another. Becky brought another scotch, and I sipped in silence. I felt Jigger's eyes on me. I never should have whined in front of her.

"I always wear heels now when I drink martinis," she said. "You were right. Our talk that day helped me more than you know. So, now I'll tell you something." She paused as though to be sure she had my attention. "Don't drink when you have emotional baggage to deal with."

Downing the rest of my scotch, I nodded towards Becky before turning back to Jigger. "The next drink will be my last. And I apologize. I didn't mean to burden you with my personal issues."

"No problem, Michael, but that one"—she nodded towards my empty glass on the table—"should be your last tonight."

"One more, really. Then I'm out of here." I looked over at her. "Hey, you've barely touched that martini."

"I don't normally drink here, remember?"

"I remember. And thanks for tonight."

She was charming. Her husband was a lucky man,

probably a true soul mate.

She nodded and took a small sip of her drink. "This is good, and so are you. Don't let whatever is bothering you eat you up," she said.

My turn to nod. "Jigger, do you think you can find your soul mate and not be able to share a life together? Or if you can't share a life together, can you really be soul mates? You see, I don't know. I thought I did, but now I don't know."

Suddenly, I was embarrassed and rose to leave. "Sorry about that, Jigger. Didn't mean to throw my problems at you. You're just too easy to talk to, I guess."

"Just sit for a few minutes, please." She looked over her shoulder and shook her head as Becky approached. Becky pulled up as if someone had grabbed her shoulder and did an about-face with my drink, returning to the bar.

"Hey!" I laughed. "You're cutting me off."

Jigger placed a hand on my arm. "Only for tonight. This isn't the right night to drink. You have something to work out. Be patient. Don't push it is my advice. Let life come to you, and it will."

I thought about what she said for a moment, this lovely woman sharing the wisdom of Cap'n Nemo with me. "Thanks, Jigger. I've enjoyed this." I reached for my wallet.

"Please, my treat. But you owe me another martini."

She had a way of bringing a smile to me. "I'd like that."

I stood to leave. "Thanks again, Jigger."

She raised a hand in goodbye.

Lovely woman, I thought as I drove away. Her husband was a lucky man to have her. Why did she always have that tinge of sadness about her though? Poor woman had to cut me off the scotch to get me out of there. I knew better. She cared about people. But why so sad? I wondered again as I turned into the driveway.

I beat it around late into the night, the morning actually, sober and rational, though emotions still prevailed. How many times had I been in a situation like this? Too many, but this was different. I'd been breaking up with this woman, for all the right reasons, since before we were lovers. I'd known what I should do all along, even before Stephanie told me.

I knew better than to become involved with hurt women. They had too many things to work out first. Unfortunately, they didn't always realize that, often seeking an immediate new relationship. Love was tough, and I could understand their requiring some validation that they were not the cause of the breakup, divorce, whatever. I had seen that they often resented the men who came to them as if the women themselves were not done with their own self-loathing and assumed these men were even more unworthy than they. Were they punishing us for getting involved with them?

Whoa, was I punishing women because of Millie? Was Stephanie right? That drew me up short. It seemed a terrible endless cycle for some, and that could include me.

The door I'd kept securely locked now splintered with these thoughts. I tried to push them deeper, away from me, but it was too late. Everything spilled before me, and thoughts unleased regarding hurt women became personal. I could no longer dismiss the realities that everyone but me could see so easily. The association was so clear and undeniable that the impact finally hit me on a conscious level. I was just like these hurt women. And hurt women hurt men, of course. Why couldn't I see and accept this before? Now, it wouldn't let me go. I was suddenly exhausted.

Yes, it was the same for me and, I'm sure, for other men who had been jilted in the same way. Somewhere in all of this,

I had forgotten myself except in the "poor me" sense. I needed to take care of me: to live, breathe, and absorb life. Just for me. I needed to open myself to life as Jigger—and Stephanie and Nemo before her—had said. *Don't push it. Let it come to me.*

Something else kept coming at me, something intangible but familiar, way out there on the periphery. It escaped me. Something to do with Jigger and her sadness. It wouldn't come, a dot without a connection.

And then I lost it.

Chapter Twenty-Three

*A*t some point, I must have slept, waking with the dawn and too little sleep. Sluggishly, I got out of bed long enough to start the coffeepot before crawling back in. It came to me floating on the energy of coffee perking, a simple word. *Harmony.* And with it was a vision of Nemo. He was winking at me. I needed the harmony.

I got to work and completed a number of small projects. Then I went over the work planned for the real professionals the next day. An air conditioning guy was scheduled for tomorrow, plus the electrician. I looked over the work the electrician was doing. If the AC guy turned out to be half as good as him, I'd be happy.

I was satisfied, especially since I'd been neglecting things a lot since Melanie. That was crap, so why was I blaming her? Hell, I'd been totally enriched by her, and she was willing to come here and just do some work so that we could be together.

I called her late in the morning and left a message on her cell. I told her I'd be with my brother the rest of the day but would like to see her in the morning if she could make it. It was a lie. I needed time, time to rest and to absorb and accept my intentions before I saw her.

She called back later. "Hey, got your message. I didn't know you had a brother."

"See how little we know about each other? Yes, I have a brother."

"I have both a brother and two sisters. Now we know all about each other," she said, laughing.

"Catholics, taking over the world, one child at a time." I couldn't help kidding around with her even now that I knew we couldn't go on together. I was too comfortable with her.

So right, damn it. Why does it have to end?

It just does!

We agreed to meet at the park at nine the next morning.

I was sitting on the picnic table when she pulled up behind the truck. She rushed to me as soon as she was out of the car. I wrapped around her, kissing her as I led her to the table.

We sat on the tabletop, knees touching, holding hands with our feet on the seat. "So, how was your day yesterday?" she asked.

"Good, got a lot done and the guys are working now. It was a good workday. How about you, how was yours?"

"Well, I went to dance last night, or practice, I should say. Val picked me up, and we went to Orlando's. We stayed for the practice session and left right afterwards and had dinner."

"Good. Did you have a good time?"

"Yes, except you weren't there." She squeezed my hand then and turned to kiss me on the neck.

"Val says hello and sends her love," she added. "She says something is fishy with the house you're working on. Says you better make sure it's a good friend because she can't find out anything beyond it belongs to some corporation."

I had to laugh at that. "She's really obsessed with it, isn't she? It's really no big deal."

"Then tell us who you're working for. Who owns the house?"

"I can't. The owner insists on privacy," I said truthfully.

"All right, but Val will find out one of these days.

"Oh," she added, "I can't see you tomorrow." She had turned her head at an angle and shrugged her shoulders with her mouth tightened and her eyes opened wider as if to say she didn't understand it herself. "My husband wants to go to church with me for some reason, and then we're having lunch with our daughter. I'm free tomorrow night though. How about you? How did dinner go with your brother? Am I going to get to meet him?"

She was so bubbly about everything that I almost decided not to tell her that day. It could wait till Monday. I struggled.

No, Michael. You need to do it now.

"Baby, my brother wasn't here yesterday."

"What do you mean? Is everything all right?"

"I lied about him coming, Melanie. I . . ."

"Why? Why would you lie to me?"

Obviously stunned, she stood and faced me. It was slow motion as I watched her look away from me and tug the bottom of her blouse down around her hips.

"Because I needed some time," I said gently.

"Oh, no, Michael." I could see the realization reflected in her eyes as it hit her. "It's the house! Oh, my God. I never should have taken you to the house. I told Val last night and she was angry with me, told me it was stupid. I am so sorry." She was looking at me wildly with those big green eyes.

I reached out and pulled her to me. "Honey, your house is beautiful, just like you. I know it meant a lot for you to take me there. I'm sorry I lied to you, but I needed time to think."

She tried to pull back from me, but I held her.

"Listen to me, Michael . . ."

"No, baby, shhh. Please. You need to listen. I have to say some things, and it's not easy. Please." I could feel her heart pounding against mine, or maybe it was mine as I held her.

"Baby, I can't see you anymore."

I felt that she heard the words before I said them as if she knew. "I can't do this. Stephanie was right. I seduced you. You need time to work things out with your husband."

She tried to pull away, and I held her tighter. I was afraid to look at her. I didn't want her to see the tears in my eyes.

"No," she said, "no, it doesn't have to be like this."

"Yes, it does." She became stronger and pulled away to look at me. Oddly, she seemed under control though she had been crying all along. Now she stopped.

"Let's talk about this, Michael. You didn't seduce me any more than I seduced you. It was meant to be, you and me. It's right between us, and you know it."

Finally, I grasped her shoulders and gently shook her. "No! Listen to me, Melanie. I know you now. I know the core of you and what you're about, how embedded some things are in you. You need to work on your marriage, finalize it somehow without me as an influence."

"No, we can work things out. We just need some time, Michael. I know you feel about me the same way I do about you."

"No, you're wrong. I don't!" My voice was stronger. I knew that if I didn't do it now, I never would.

"Go home to your husband, Mrs. Langstrom. You're fucking him. That's where you belong! I am sick of married women."

I turned her and guided her towards her car. Her feet carried her as though she were unaware she was walking. I could feel the madness of it all, so wrong and overwhelming to her.

She was crying softly, and I fought to hold back the sobs building deep within me. I hated this. Hated my life, the pain I was bringing her. Hated my loss, hated me!

I put her in the driver's seat, but as I tried to back out of the car, she grabbed my forearm. Holding it tightly, she wiped her eyes with the back of her other hand. "Please, just talk to me about this. Please." I buckled her seat belt and backed out of the car as she sat there immobile.

I got in the truck and drove away, keeping a constant check on the rearview mirror, but I never saw her car. Concerned now, worried about her and terribly tormented, I pulled into a parking lot and parked out of view of the street. I'd done the right thing, finally, but was she going to be all right? I knew she would recover, but I was worried for the short term. I started to back out of the lot and go back when I saw her driving slowly by.

The rest of the day without her was miserable with guilt over seducing her and feeling horrible at the pain I'd caused once again by breaking up with her now. Emotionally, I was a wreck. My thoughts jumped wildly, desperately seeking a solution that wasn't there, aching for her, yet wanting to purge the image of her, the essence of her, from my soul. What a horrible path to harmony.

Only time and distance could heal me, and I couldn't leave now, not with the house this way, but I could disappear. Change everything: gym, store, phone, everything. It wouldn't be fair to either of us to be around each other.

She called later. I let the phone ring. She didn't leave a message. I was afraid there would be one, and then I was miserable when there wasn't.

How much has one person, one woman, affected my life? Is she the reason I'm the way I am?

I had poured a scotch and water and was walking down towards the dock, but the evening breeze stirred the bamboo, drawing me to it. The soft whisper of its sway in the wind was seductive and inviting. I sat in the swing that Nathan had strung from the thick overhead branch of an old oak, seeking the harmony. For a while, I was lost in the music of the breeze and the bamboo. The sounds were mesmerizing, like the flickering flame of a fire though its breath was cool on the night.

My ex-wife, Millie, still had too much power over my life. Stephanie was right about that. And then there was the kid. That was the real issue. I should have been stronger there, should have developed a relationship, damn it. I'm his father. But I never knew the child, a man now, poisoned against me from the beginning.

Why? Why turn the kid away from me? Still the equation came out the same, the ultimate sum of my marriage: a child I never knew and failure to commit with women.

I was afraid of that commitment, and though I'd seen my son several times over the years, we were not close. I hadn't tried hard enough to bring us closer together. It was all too much after being denied visitation rights for such a long period of time, denied because I had not known how to get in touch with them after coming back from Vietnam.

Early on, after a few attempts to see my son, I gave up. I had contacted an attorney only to find out the fruitlessness of my efforts given the laws of the state Millie was in. So, I signed the divorce papers when they finally came and sank deep into depression and drink for a time.

Now I realized that while I resented her, hated her, actually, I ended up resenting the boy as well for being a part of the betrayal. Ridiculous. He was an innocent child, but I was unable to overcome the poison of his mother in later years.

Somehow, I had pulled something together back then. By

the time I left Vietnam and landed in California, I had a basic plan. I called Millie's sister to get Millie's address or phone number. The sister hung up on me after saying she was sorry but couldn't get involved. So much for Plan A. I moved on. I could go home, and do what? I discarded Plan B and took on C, thinking it all through.

As other Vietnam returnees stood around calling me "lifer," "loser," and worse, I reenlisted—or enlisted, I guess. I joined the Army Reserve, pushing for training as an aircraft mechanic. It didn't take long for approval to come through after I completed tons of paperwork. Then I joined another group and processed through the lines for a new Class A uniform, ID, and military orders. The orders required me to report to Fort Eustis, Virginia, in thirty days, plus a couple of days' travel time.

Then I was off to Las Vegas where I got wasted on drink, weed, and gambling. Fortunately, I had been smart enough to purchase a plane ticket to my next duty station when I got the ticket to Vegas. I had also opened a bank account and put a thousand dollars away. I reported to my training station early, after only eight days. I was nearly broke except for the nest egg in the bank. I recovered, determined to move forward in life. Many weeks later, I graduated and traveled to report to my future unit for one weekend a month plus two weeks a year.

I needed to stabilize. I'd realized that while pondering Plan C there in the Vietnam returnee out-processing facility. Plan C included school. The savings I'd made during more than four months of aircraft maintenance school, along with the GI Bill, should enable me to get there.

The sea breeze was lying down when I'd had enough of the past. I made my way to the trailer and crashed.

***

It was Sunday. Melanie would be in church, the church I passed on the way to the gym. I had to go; he was going to be there. Maybe it was to see him, see them together, and reinforce my actions. Maybe to see her again, to know she was all right. I don't know.

For many years, church was a familiar place to me. Different churches, actually. I'd never found God in any of them. I had felt the presence in my life in many other places while exhausting the answers of organized religion. I believe, and I needed God in my life.

I arrived as late as possible and slipped quietly into one of the last rows, just inside the pew. I looked for her, of course, as unobtrusively as possible, scanning the large room until I saw her. Yes, she was sitting with a man. I supposed it was Jamie. He appeared tall, taller than me, with dark hair, almost black except for a tinge of gray, neatly trimmed.

My pounding heart sent fresh blood straight to my cheeks, and I felt like a lighthouse in that moment. My soul pulled at me, demanding that I race forward and claim my woman. But she wasn't my woman. She was his. His wife.

I ached for her and barely contained my emotion. How had this woman become so much, so important to me and so quickly? Why was I here now, on the brink of emotional disaster, afraid she would see me yet wanting her to in a way I didn't understand? I was afraid she didn't really know how much I cared, how much I wanted to be with her. I was a mess.

I tried to lose myself in the church and the ceremony. I missed much of it, lost in my self-pity, but caught enough to realize again the importance of it to our lives. This was a fundamental need and represented only a moment in our lives to attend and become involved. A regular cleansing act that could allow us a new beginning at any time we chose. Such a natural thing, really, once you came, but it hadn't worked for me.

The sermon wasn't important, at least not to one such as I, lost in my own misery. I blamed God for my misery, of course, like we all do. Then I prayed for forgiveness and for peace, for her, and down deep that we could get back together. Pitiful, I thought later, but so human.

The shuffling of those around me brought me back from my reverie. The priest asked all to stand and greet those around us. I panicked that she might turn and see me. The gentleman on my left turned to me with his hand outstretched. His face seemed startled as he looked at me. I knew my eyes were red and puffy with grief. The rest of me, who knows? He seemed to sense my burden.

"Are you all right, sir? Can I help you?"

"No, but thank you. I'm Michael," I said, reaching for his hand. "I've recently lost someone."

"It's all right, Michael. I'm Don. I'm sorry for your loss."

"Thank you, Don." I turned away and slipped quietly out of the pew, making my way to the door under the scrutiny of more fortunate souls.

My God, what was I thinking coming here?

Chapter Twenty-Four

*T*he phone rang later that afternoon. Melanie! I couldn't answer. It was too soon. The call went to voicemail, and I had to listen.

"I have to see you. I can't let you go like this. Please see me, Michael. I have felt you with me all day. I need to see you." Her voice was calm, and I felt relief at that. *She's all right.*

"Michael, please talk to me. See me, just for a while."

I did see you, I thought, at church, and I wanted to come to you. Then I turned off the phone.

Later that afternoon, I drove to the park and wandered aimlessly. I took a seat under a shelter built over the water and found a sense of peace. Birds drifted on air, going nowhere in particular, like me. A turtle poked his head up for a moment, and the water gently cascaded away in ripples, the only evidence of his ever having been there.

I sat for a long time, going over it all again, knowing I was right in my decision. But I also realized it was because of the visit to her home. That was the catalyst. Too much reality to ignore.

The phone rang, startling me. I had forgotten that I'd left it on after listening to her message a second time. I answered.

"Michael, I want to see you. We have to talk."

"I did see you," I managed to get out. "You were with your family."

"Oh, my God, I knew it. I thought I saw you. I felt you.

I looked for you when the service was over. We need to be together, Michael. We need to talk. There are things you don't understand."

I was miserable, but more than that, I was weak. I listened and shouldn't have.

"Michael, are you there? Talk to me, damn it!"

I smiled. She never used bad language. "Stop cussing. I'm here."

"You knew I was married before we got together, honey. Separated, but you knew I was married. And yes, vulnerable. Don't you think you agonized enough before we became intimate? Don't you know that you had already come to terms with things? Don't you know that I was going through the same thing?"

She paused, but still I kept silent. Gently, she started again.

"Michael, you are not the cause of where my marriage is, and I think you know me well enough now to know you would not be the cause of a divorce. I think you're protecting yourself, baby. I think you love me and you're afraid of getting hurt, and I can't promise you won't. We both could." She spoke haltingly as though feeling her way. "We are meant to be together somehow, honey. See me."

"No," I said with as much resolve as I could muster. "That's not what we should do. I'm hanging up now, Melanie. Don't call again."

I continued to sit there on the bench feeling terrible for treating her that way. I closed my eyes. *I gotta talk to Nemo about this harmony shit.*

"I can't believe you hung up on me. Made me drive all the way . . ."

I didn't hear anymore. I looked up, and she was rushing at

me. Then she was in my arms, and I held her tight.

"Melanie! How . . . what are you doing here?"

She continued to hold me. "I came down here with a bottle of Merlot to whine. And here you were. You didn't see me drive past you a few minutes ago?"

"No, I . . ."

"So here you were, messing up my whining time, so I called you." Her face was a lopsided smile filled with apprehension. She stood back from me moving nervously from foot to foot, dancing slowly on pins and needles.

"Melanie . . ."

"Shhh, don't say anything. Hold me," she said and pulled me close again.

"I hated talking to you that way."

"I know. I love you, too, Michael."

***

Was she in love with me? I wondered. She'd had so little experience. Could she really be in love with me or just in love with love? Can you truly be in love and allow yourself to live two lives of commitment? Which one was real, which one the more important? I'm not sure I wanted to know. I didn't want to compete, and I didn't want to be the cause of hurting her more. What a miserable place to be, totally in love but afraid for her to be in love with me while still afraid for her not to be.

Later, I wasn't surprised at my weakness, how I had given in to her will. I let her talk, absorbing more of her through words. We ended up talking into the evening, and I was still bothered, but she finally drew it out of me.

"It's more than me taking you to the house, isn't it?" she said. "It's me being with Jamie, his coming over and your seeing me with him in church."

"Of course, it is," I told her. "What else could it be? Everything else is perfect. It's become too real now. He was always there before, but he wasn't real, or at least not tangibly so. I didn't have to face it before. Now, I do. Your husband is real. I've been in his house. I've seen him with you now. If there is a chance of you two getting back together, then you should pursue it."

She held my hand, looking at me patiently. "I can't change that I'm married. I am. But since you've come into my life, I know my marriage is more of a business arrangement than anything else. Today was like my daughter and I were on his list of things to do for the day."

We were quiet for a moment.

"She's beautiful, isn't she?" she said.

I grinned, thinking back to one of the pictures she'd been so proud to show me that night. "Yes, your daughter is beautiful. Don't change the subject."

"Okay, but she is." Her face lit up.

"Knowing he came to see you bothers me. I couldn't stand it. I got a vision of him curled up around you, you turning into his arms. The visual intimacy of that bothered me. It's crazy. It's not even jealousy over you two having sex. It's larger than that. Before I knew you were separated, I figured you were having sex, but this thought of intimacy beyond sex really shook me."

"But it's not like that, honey. You must know that. What you've described is you and me. I've never had that with Jamie, only with you."

I walked a few feet away and came back.

"Listen, my office called me yesterday," she said.

I looked up.

"The nurse who job-shares with me was supposed to go to a seminar in Orlando this Wednesday but can't. I'm going instead. I didn't want to go before, but now I do. Come with me. We can have the evenings together. Please, we need this time together. We need to talk."

* * *

I thought about it all later. What was the breach in her marriage that brought her to me? What about the husband? She loved him, but not in the sense that she loved me. As I learned more, I didn't think she'd ever loved him in that manner, but she did love him. He was her husband, the father of her children. She wanted for nothing material, but even without him, she would make a good living as a nurse practitioner.

I didn't understand it, the remaining bond, maybe because I'd never had the long-standing involvement that their marriage offered. All of that was foreign to me: the raising of children, resolution of day-to-day problems related to any family, the problems of enough money or the place to live, school issues, the stress of work, and making life itself work.

Did I lose something there? Probably. Did they grow apart? Did they become neglectful of one another? What was the breach? It wasn't money. Was it sex? She was naive, inexperienced, actually. And was he also? Had he not taken the time to gently explore her, to open up her sexuality? Was he not interested enough in her as a woman?

What was it in some marriages but not others that drove the partners apart? A marriage that lasted over fifty years wouldn't seem to be so different from one that lasted only twenty. Why did so many marriages fail after the children were grown and life was financially and materially better? Was there really such a thing as soul mates?

Husbands could be neglectful, but so could wives. Melanie seemed like a good partner, one who would seek a balance in life. Why, then? Were they both seeing other people? Were they each hiding behind a mask of "let's pretend"? She wasn't before I came along. I knew that. Maybe, as in the Pink Floyd song title, they had become "comfortably numb."

Did we—Jamie's new love, if he had one, and I—see and fall in love with different people from the Melanie and Jamie who had married each other? Had they become someone else or subordinated their real selves to a façade of what they thought they should be? Were they the real Melanie and Jamie, or were they now people they didn't even know? Perhaps they had individually evolved into something new, personifications developed purely for a new life outside of marriage while the sanctity and sanctuary of marriage was preserved. Could they truly continue such a game?

If so, those of us outside the traditional sphere of their marriage were surely doomed.

Chapter Twenty-Five

*A*s I drove to Orlando, I was determined to have a good time, put away the demons and false responsibility. I began to reconcile with the realities beyond my control and moved on to the other emotional piece of the relationship.

We had talked about the sexual aspect of things. I believed her when she told me that the intimacy fear I had described was not about her and her husband but the two of us. Did that mean she and her husband were having sex but there was no real intimacy in the act between them, just sex? That's what she had implied before when it had come up. It bothered me now, intimacy or not, and my blood boiled at the thought. I realized I had no respect for the man. *Do something! Get off your ass and reclaim your wife.*

Every time I considered her being free, seeking a divorce, I came up blank. I couldn't see it for some reason, so I moved on to the next question.

If she were single, would I want to marry her? The thought frightened me. Stephanie was right. Millie had left an awful imprint on me. It wasn't that long ago that I thought Stephanie and I would eventually marry, so why not marry Melanie when I knew in my heart she was the one?

Slowly, I worked it out. Analytically, I worked through the issues, arriving at a conclusion that I believed to be the truth. I loved Stephanie, and marrying her would have been natural at some time after John's passing. Until Melanie, there had been no doubt.

With Melanie, it required divorce, an action that proclaimed not only failure but more. I would be the cause, and there was that responsibility I hated. Melanie would not seek a divorce though. I was convinced of that.

I became angry at that reality, hurt about the situation even though I knew it all centered on her values. She had no idea how to back out of her marriage, how to bring that kind of pain to her family. It was foreign to her, abhorrent even. She could go through with it if he initiated it, but he hadn't and probably wouldn't for the same reasons. Both of them were trapped.

How could I be angry with her? I knew her values, and they were all a part of what I loved about her. She came to my bed, gave herself to me, a major step in her life, so how could I be angry? How could I continue to worry and be the way I'd been, allowing the guilt and frustration to falsely overwhelm me? I simply couldn't be angry with her for being who she was. I loved her. Nor could I continue to suffer great remorse for my part.

"She's yours, Jamie," I whispered upon conclusion. "She's yours, but she belongs to me. Her heart belongs to me; her soul belongs to me; her entire being belongs to me. She's materially committed to you—socially, religiously, traditionally, all that— but damn it, she belongs to me."

As I put it all in perspective, I downshifted and moved to the passing lane. I pressed the gas pedal, kicking in the turbo, and upshifted as I quickly slipped by a line of cars and back into the right lane. The Porsche felt good. It provided the exclamation point I needed as I came to an acceptable understanding of things and a new freedom in the relationship.

* * *

I picked her up at her hotel on International Drive several long blocks from the convention center where she would be attending seminars. Traffic was heavy. I'd called earlier to see if she had checked in, and she had. We met in the lobby at four o'clock that afternoon. She was beautiful. She approached with that devilish smile again, carrying a small overnight bag. She needed to get the hotel room for appearances, but everyone close to her knew to contact her on her cell.

"Hello, baby," I said.

She swung her overnight bag casually in one hand and held her purse strap to her shoulder with the other. Her eyes were on mine as she approached. Her feelings for me were in her smile and the carriage of her body. They were in her voice, too.

"Two nights," she said. "Just us."

Taking the bag, I put my arm around her and escorted her outside. Then I turned her towards me and kissed her.

"Are you tired?" I asked. "I mean, too tired to walk down the street for something to eat?"

"No, I don't have to be at the first seminar until ten in the morning, and I'm starved."

"Good, we'll put this bag away and take a walk. I can do some grocery shopping while you're working tomorrow."

"Okay," she said, "but stay away from the tuna fish aisle. That's our special place."

"It is special," I agreed with a smile. "It's where I met you."

Melanie looked around. "Where's the truck?"

"That's right, you haven't seen the car," I said, pointing out the Porsche.

She pulled up and stopped as she looked. "Wow! Bet that

impresses the girls." She walked to it, looking it over closely. "Can I drive?"

She was excited, like a child wanting to open a present.

"Sure, soon as we get you checked out in it."

"Okay," she said.

We put away her bag and walked down I-Drive holding hands. I liked that. She was taking in the glitter and activity, holding my arm tightly as I guided her to a small Italian place I frequented. I'd made a reservation there as soon as I knew we were coming to town.

Tucked away in a touristy shopping pavilion, the front doors faced a small parking lot away from I-Drive. We were seated at a table near the grand piano.

"Wine?" I asked.

"I don't know. What are you having?"

"A Manhattan."

Her eyes lit up. "Can I have a taste? I've never had one."

"Sure," I said, laughing at her enthusiasm.

"Then I'll have a house cabernet," she told the waiter, a stocky blond in his early thirties.

"Good choice," he said. "Our house is actually a fine wine."

Melanie wasn't one to put on airs and order the most expensive wine for show. She was happy with the boxed cabernet I kept on the boat. It was actually very good.

We sat back, taking in the place as we waited. Even though the middle of the week, it was crowded.

"My name is Peter," the waiter said as he set down our drinks and handed us menus. "Are there any requests for us to perform?"

"Give us a minute, Peter, and I think we'll probably have something," I said.

As the waiter left, Melanie turned to me, looking confused.

"The servers here are all Broadway-level performers," I told her. "This work allows them to make a living between other performing jobs and keep their voices active. No matter what song you come up with, they're almost certain to have someone here who can sing it."

She lit up. "Really? I love it! Do you have a request?"

Her enthusiasm was contagious. "No, baby. I think you should pick out a song since this is your first time here." I held my glass in a toast. "Here's to us and the special song you pick."

She touched her glass to mine, and we took sips.

"'Some Enchanted Evening,'" she announced. "That's what I want to hear. I always want to remember us here with that song."

Peter returned at my signal and smiled when he heard her selection.

"Nice. I'll see if I can find someone to sing it for you," he said, looking around the room.

"Oh, no, please," Melanie said. "I really want you to sing it. You're our waiter. Please. You're part of our special evening."

"But . . ." He squirmed a bit as he hesitated. "This is not my kind of music."

He looked at her for a moment. Those big eyes must have said something to him, causing a smile to chase the worried frown from his face.

"For you," he said, "I'll do it, but I'm really going to be challenging myself."

"So are we, in a way," she told him, "and you're a part of it now, part of this moment."

Peter laughed with her as though some weird bond had brought them mutual understanding. "How about I take your orders first?"

Ten minutes later, we listened to a young lady sing "Close to You," an old Karen Carpenter song.

"That girl should be singing professionally," Melanie said. "I'm amazed at her talent."

"She is a professional, honey. She just hasn't broken out yet. Tells you a lot about the talent that's out there in the world, doesn't it?"

Moments later, the pianist started playing the opening score of *South Pacific,* then segued into "Some Enchanted Evening." All else was quiet in the restaurant as diners put aside their meals and drinks to listen. The first few notes of the song had that effect. Peter had a wonderfully deep voice and performed with passion. His voice flowed through the crowd, bringing us all to our feet with applause.

"Wow, that ought to do it for memories," Melanie said softly. I noticed tears in her eyes as she leaned into me with a kiss.

She embarrassed Peter, the way she fussed over him when he brought our dinners.

"Thank you, madam," he said, bowing, "for insisting I sing that song. I have always loved it but felt it was out of my range."

"You were magnificent," she told him again. "Thank you for making this a truly enchanted evening."

As he left, she turned to me and took my hand. "Michael, I wanted that song because of us. You left me once. I want you to remember those words and never again let me go."

Then she pulled me to her in a deep kiss.

***

After dinner, we walked up and down I-Drive for a while

before driving to my condo. Pulling into the parking lot, I reached up and pressed the remote, opening the gate into the private parking garage.

"This is nice, Michael. How many stories is it?"

"Twenty, but it should have been taller. Everything around it has grown up."

"What floor are we on?" she asked.

"Twenty."

She turned to me with those big eyes. "Twenty? That's the top, the penthouse."

I laughed at her awe. "Actually, it's one of two penthouses. Ours has the better views."

"Is it yours?"

"Why would you ask me that?" I said, still laughing.

She leaned into me. "Because I know so little about you. Is it?"

"It belongs to the owner of the house I'm working on," I said honestly.

"And the Porsche?"

"Goes with the house."

Her look was skeptical. "You know I'm going to have to report all of this to Val, right?"

"Of course."

"We need to talk, honey. But not right now. I want to enjoy our couple of days," she said.

Good, I thought. I know it was weak, but I didn't want to get into my wealth right then. I took her on a short tour of the place, putting her overnight bag away as I did. I expected her to ask me more about the place, but she was strangely quiet about it. Maybe it was too early in our being back together after such an emotional period.

We stood on the balcony looking out over the city

sprawled before us. The light pollution masked the stars above us as we enjoyed a last glass of wine. Melanie inched closer to me and brought her cheek to mine. Then she whispered, "I'm so happy you came to me."

***

We were frenzied in our lovemaking that night; the need for each other drove us. We discovered ourselves in each other again. Though we had been apart for little more than a day, we were emotionally shattered. We needed this time, needed each other. This night brought the healing of oneness.

I lay there holding her afterwards. Gentle waves of thought flowed through me, softening me more, making me more resolute in the knowledge that she was the one.

Sex is good, very, very good, but sex with love is wonderful. I'm not sure it's even describable. How do you tell someone about the magic of looking into each other's eyes, breath coming fast, faces flushed, unaware of all but each other, not wanting to let go, knowing you are one, and feeling great tenderness and intimacy as urgency suddenly overwhelms you? How do you describe the intimacy of oneness with the one you love?

I loved her soft breathing against my chest. I lay very still, afraid to move that I might wake her. I understood then the depth of her emotional draining over the past few days. I felt selfish as I thought about how I'd been trying to protect myself at our expense. More now because I had wanted to tell her that I owned the penthouse, had built and owned the whole building before I sold the other condos. Why? I had shielded my wealth from her until now. Had I wanted to use it as advantage, to bring her to me more? Maybe, but she hadn't let me. She must have known. But right then, she didn't want to. Wealth wasn't the key to her love. Something more existed within her even greater than love, and that scared me. Loyalty, tradition, church, and vows would trump true love.

Before Stephanie, and now Melanie, I'd always maintained a degree of separation between women and me, close and caring but without true intimacy. There was no sharing of private parts of my life or seeking insight into theirs, no talk of dreams or the future. We just were, existing in the now, each comfortable with having someone even though it wasn't true sharing. Selfish, yes, but it worked for us. We cared for each other and enjoyed each other's company as though each were helping the other through a transitional phase. Friends and lovers, trust without intimacy.

Susan was one of those friends and lovers, and as she came to mind, I felt a terrible ache run through me. I tried to shift my thoughts, but she intruded with even more clarity. "Stubborn woman," I said aloud and realized I was smiling at the memory of her. And stubborn she was. I couldn't keep her out. I turned to look at Melanie, sleeping quietly with her head still against my chest, and thought of Susan.

Susan was a strong woman: lovely, slim, and single after a long, passionless marriage. I was barely thirty then and new to wealth, so I remained unobtrusive in my lifestyle, learning and feeling my way.

We met on a night out with friends and quickly came together through discussions on a variety of issues that first night. We danced often but always fell back into talk, mostly ignoring our friends though I'm sure they were happy for us, even hoping for more. Somehow, she consumed me, and I let her. We became lost in passionate sex, and she devoured my free time over a few months.

She thought I was an engineer, and I was at the time, applying my engineering degree while still learning. I never shared anything about my life beyond that, but she wanted me to know everything about her. She talked about her marriage, how she had tried to save it for years before finally seeking a divorce. She talked about her family and wanted me to meet them. I became uncomfortable.

One morning, I realized how much of her was in my apartment: clothing, makeup, even a coffee cup. We didn't last long after that, and she never understood. She was hurt and wouldn't talk to me afterwards. I had always been able to maintain good relations with lovers, even after it was over, until Susan. I had let her get too close.

Why couldn't I have made that work? She was great. We melded together naturally, shared the same philosophy on things, and fulfilled each other sexually. So why, I wondered, yet I knew and wouldn't go there, wouldn't examine myself again. She had been dangerous, everything I could want—except I didn't love her.

And she was single.

**

Melanie shifted and woke. It was early, too early for her to have to leave.

"Is everything all right?" I rolled over and reached for her, holding her back to my chest. She didn't answer. I wrapped my leg across her hip. "You're feeling guilty, aren't you?"

She didn't answer for a moment, and then she said, "Yes, honey, I am, but I'm dealing with it."

My heart sank at her words. "I hate your suffering like this."

"No, no, you don't understand," she said as she turned to me, wrapping her arms and legs around me, pulling me close and placing her head back on my chest.

"I am so glad we're together. You're what I've been missing all my life. I feel guilty because I still sleep with my husband. He's a good man and I love him—but not like this, never like this."

Anger boiled within me at those words. I was jealous, and jealousy had been foreign to me. I had never allowed myself to sink to the vanity of possession. Never had I allowed myself the weakness of letting anyone in deep enough to incite jealousy. I resented it as much as I resented him—and, in that moment, I resented Melanie—but I held it together. I'd always suspected she slept with her husband, so why was it bothering me now? I knew it was duty, nothing more, but why hadn't she broken away from it all—from him—before I came along? Why did I have to be the catalyst for her change?

I calmed as she continued. Everything was deeper than that, and I'd never shared the bonds of commitment as she was demonstrating. Who was I to judge?

She pushed away from me and rested on an elbow as she looked down at me. "It's not just the sex, baby, we talk, and we do things together, simple things. I've been on a certain path my whole life, and it was with the wrong person. If I had to live life over, I would only change one thing. I would live with a man before I got married. I would know, really know, the man I was going to marry, know we were right for each other. I wouldn't wait until my wedding night to have sex and discover that we were good together—but no balloons or rockets."

She became quiet for a moment, drifting to some place she'd never let herself go in the past. Or that's what I lay alongside her thinking before she continued.

"I wouldn't be satisfied to just be the good little girl and try to meet everyone else's expectations of me. I would live my life and hope that I met my soul mate. *You*, the one I should be with."

I lay there quietly, afraid to disturb this intensely personal reflection. She reached out a finger and caressed my face. "I feel guilty because I do love my husband, and I'm keeping him from finding the same happiness and fulfillment that I have with you."

She paused, looking at me, but I remained silent. She needed to get it out. "He deserves that, and maybe I'm keeping him from it."

I smoothed her hair before speaking. "Maybe he's keeping it from himself."

She began to cry softly, then kissed my chest.

"I'm so happy with you, honey," she said as tears slid down her cheeks. Then she nestled in my arms and fell back to sleep.

Later that morning, we were hungry for each other again. We made love slowly but with a need felt deep in the thrust of my hips and her arching back and pointed toes. On some level, I was aware of soft sounds of our oneness floating about the room.

Chapter Twenty-Six

I picked her up at three that afternoon outside the convention center. "How much do you get paid for these, ah . . . What is it, four-hour days with an hour's free lunch thrown in?"

"Hey," she said, "I got a couple of good things out of this morning that will help someone, plus I met some great, caring people. Can I drive now? Pull over, there's no traffic yet."

I did and looked over at her. "Have you ever driven a car like this?"

"No, but I was a Girl Scout, remember . . . and a Girl Scout leader."

"Yes, you're definitely qualified."

I got out of the car and helped her around to the driver's side.

We spent the next half hour with her getting the feel of the car on side roads. Then we took a spin on the expressway toward the coast for a few miles until I had her pull off before a tollbooth.

"No sense in paying for this ride," I said and winked.

She drove well, squealing with pleasure as she shifted through the gears smoothly, ramping up the speed quickly each time.

She turned to me for a moment, her eyes dancing with mischief. "I love it. Can I have it?"

"No, but you can have the truck if you want."

Her look soured. "I'll pass, but I hope we can drive this more."

"We'll see." I directed her through a maze of back roads, finally coming back to I-Drive. She had her bearings then and found her hotel.

"Need some things for tonight," she said as she parked.

***

We had salmon again over a green salad. I'd marinated the fish earlier in the day, and the herb-and-spice olive oil mixture had started my hunger juices even before I began to cook on the balcony grill. After dinner, we cleared the table, rinsed the dishes, and took our wine to the balcony. She tried to do the dishes, but I wouldn't let her.

"I'll take care of the housework while you're working tomorrow," I said.

Big smile. "Okay. I like that."

She continued to smile as she took in the cityscape. "I love your place," she said. "The view is fantastic." She talked about it as if she knew it was my home, surprising me.

She set down her wineglass and snuggled into me as we stood at the balcony rail. "Why did you decide to get right downtown?"

"It seemed like a good investment, and I like it downtown. This is going to be one of the real downtown revitalization success stories."

As soon as I had it out of my mouth, I knew she'd trapped me. She was interested but more, as if confirming what she thought she knew: that the condo was my home. There was little point in continuing the charade, but I chose to ignore it all for now.

"You can see how interesting it's becoming, and with the natural lakes, parks, and nearby old homes being bought and restored, it's an invigorating place to live. You can walk to great restaurants, nightclubs, anything you want."

She took my hand and pulled me into the living room.

"Who's this?" she asked, picking up a picture of a young man.

"My son."

She gasped, and those captivating green eyes went even wider with my words. "Son? I didn't know you had a son."

There were other pictures, all family, and she scanned them again as she had when we first arrived.

"Long story. Lots you don't know, honey. One day we'll talk about it all."

"One day. But not now," she said.

"Let's have our time together here first."

"I love your home, Michael, and I want to know everything when you're ready."

I nodded and eased her back to the balcony.

***

"I love this shower," Melanie said as she washed my back, reaching around every now and then to slowly stroke me, washing me erect. Four showerheads rinsed our bodies, the shower so large it didn't require a door or curtain. As the water sprayed, she sat on the built-in tile seat and turned me to her with a hand on my butt. Her other hand reached for me as she leaned in and looked up into my eyes.

"Oh, baby." I leaned back slightly, closing my eyes with the pleasure as water rained down upon me. She was excited, wanting to bring me this. I could feel it in her enthusiasm.

"You don't do this," I reminded her.

Her eyes were wide as she shrugged. "Well, I do now, and I like it."

I laughed. "Good, I love it."

We dried each other, and I pulled her towards the bedroom. "I am so beat. I need to rest before we can do any more."

She tugged at my hand and pulled me to the living room. "Oh, no, whiny Samson, it's too early. I'll give you a break for now, but no bedtime yet."

We sat there sharing another glass of wine, each of us taking small sips from the one glass as we talked.

She wanted to know more. "You mentioned that my name had special meaning to you. Was that your wife's name?"

"Once we get to know each other better, we'll talk about it." I smiled to soften the rebuke. *Where did that come from? Got to be careful around this girl.*

She was quiet and wouldn't let go of the wineglass. I laughed. Was she punishing me by holding onto it?

"No, it wasn't my wife's name. I was divorced many years ago. In fact, I was only married for a year-and-a-half. Let's talk about you."

"Oh, no, I don't know you well enough for that," she said, and quickly turned her head away as though miffed. And she still held onto the wineglass.

Then she relented. "Okay, but I'm too comfortable talking with you, so stop me when you're bored."

"Can I have a sip of wine before you start?"

"Sure." She handed me the glass and told me about her family. Everything was about her parents, kids, grandparents, but not her husband, except to say when they got married and what he did for a living.

Many things started to make sense as she spoke, and I could feel the foundation of my own beliefs about her growing as she continued. Parents married over fifty years, fifty-two in February. She went on in some detail. As she talked, filling in gaps I didn't know, I began to want her to know more about me. I felt her need to tell me, just as she had the need to take me into her home. She wanted me to know her. That need was now growing in me, too, but I let her keep talking.

I got up as she finished and poured another glass of wine. I handed it to her and sat on the carpet at her feet. "You wanted to know about the other Melanie."

She looked at me, her eyes caring, obviously pleased that I was going to share this with her. Then something I couldn't comprehend touched her eyes.

She arranged herself in a more comfortable position. "Michael, you don't have to do this. Some things are better not discussed."

"I know, but I want to now."

I took the wine from her and sipped. "I don't know if you'll understand, but I want to tell you. It's a weird story. Sure you're ready for this tonight?"

"Only if you are. I want you to be okay with it when you tell me."

I began slowly, feeling my way, wanting to tell it right but not sure I could, not sure anyone could, though it was a simple story. Simple, but significant in what it said about me. I was nervous. No one knew this but Stephanie, and she only knew it from a superficial perspective concerning my trying to protect her. Over the years, I recognized it was more.

"Well, I would describe her as strong, independent, not needing of me. She was the kind of woman I'm attracted to, but she was much more. She was my refuge, the one I called upon when others intruded. She was my sanctuary, my flight from reality, from responsibility and, most of all, from the curiosity of others."

I paused, and Melanie remained silent, waiting for me to resume. "She became a part of my life just when I needed her. I didn't mean for things to progress the way they did, but she became more and more important to me. I was dependent on her."

I looked at Melanie. She seemed to be doing okay so far.

"And then she was gone, the need for her . . ."

"Oh, my God, Michael, I am so sorry." Her actions were a blur as she moved into my lap. Her arms circled me, holding me tight, kissing my cheeks as tears ran down her face. "I am so sorry you had to suffer that, to lose your soul mate."

I was stunned. It took me a few moments to understand the meaning of her words.

"No, no, baby, it's not like that," I told her.

Melanie was choking on her sobs, her eyes so rimmed in red they were puffy. She wiped tears from them as she stammered. "She didn't . . . die?" she finally got out with a gasp. "She's still alive?"

I loved the depth of this woman, that she cared so much, that she felt things so deeply.

Softly, I explained. "Melanie only existed because I gave her life. She was my fantasy, my sanctuary. I created her, honey. She was only real to me, through me."

"What?" She dabbed tears from her eyes and looked at me. "I . . . I don't understand. She never existed? There was no real Melanie?"

"Oh, God, woman, yes! She was real to me and, more important, to others, but she didn't exist in real life.

"Here, let me help you with that." I took a tissue and

dabbed her eyes, then pulled her close to me. "I'm sorry I've confused you. I really don't know how to tell this story. It sounds so shoddy to me now."

There was more than curiosity showing in her eyes, there was trust, and I felt horrible in trying to explain to her on such a selfish philosophical level.

"I'm sorry, honey. I've misled you. I've been busy protecting myself in trying to explain and justify myself in some way instead of telling you about Melanie."

"I want to understand." Her eyes were teary, her face flushed with emotion. "I thought she died, and now there never was a Melanie? I want to understand. I can see this woman is important to you," she said softly.

She was so earnest I had to laugh, and then I couldn't stop. She stared at me, obviously bewildered. Finally, I held her away from me. "I'm not laughing at you. Let me try this again."

I paused to catch my breath.

"You know how important Stephanie is to me."

"Yes."

"Well, since my divorce many years ago, I've dated a lot of women and had a few affairs, but I never lived with anyone. Some of the women were separated, mostly in the midst of divorce but still married. The relationships just happened. I don't know why, but they developed, and it worked for us. All were wonderful women, strong, independent, and self-sufficient. All qualities I was attracted to. Then I met Stephanie, and my truly complicated relationship began. I loved her and there was the need for more discretion because of the work environment we were in at the time."

Melanie listened and watched my face intently but kept silent as I visualized the past and related it to her.

"There was an engineering intern, Amy, who worked with my group at my last job in Lakeland. She was good technically, but she had a nosy streak. Amy gets it in her head to grill me about my love life. Of course, I can't tell her about Stephanie, even though she'd never meet her.

"I was at the technical library with a couple of others around when Amy asked me if I was coming to the Christmas party. I told her yes, that I thought I would go. Then she started backing me into a corner. Question after question followed. My answers were easy at first, mostly the truth.

"Was I bringing my wife? When I told her I wasn't married, it was how about your girlfriend? Is she coming?

"No, she has her own work party that night.

"Can't you go to both? I'd love to meet her.

"I live in Orlando, I told her. It's too far since her job is north of there. Opposite directions.

"That's too bad. What's her name?

"Her probes were almost malicious. Maybe she thought I was lying and covering something up. I don't know, but she had me in a very uncomfortable position."

As I was telling this to Melanie, I paused for a moment to let things sink in. "Do you see where this is going, honey?"

She pulled me up beside her and lay back against my chest. "I think so."

"Okay, then, here we go. Ah, let's see . . . Amy asked my girlfriend's name." I paused for a moment, remembering, and then continued.

"The name Melanie came out of my mouth. It was spontaneous. I'm not sure where it came from. The only time I think I ever heard the name was in the movie *Gone with the Wind*. That was the easy part, but somehow, Melanie became more embedded in me because others heard the conversation and the nature of people took over. The next few days, people were asking and saying things like, how's Melanie, or I understand she won't be coming to the Christmas dance, and finally, what's Melanie's last name?

"Reitner, I said immediately. I still don't know where that name came from, but it must have left an imprint on me.

"A lie begets a lie and then another. So, Melanie took root as others forced me to breathe more life into her. The lie grew as the questions continued. Where does she live? The other side of Orlando. It's quite a drive but we manage."

I paused long enough to see that my Melanie was doing all right. Then I continued.

"Another question would come, and I'd fire out an answer. Oh, she's an accountant, a forensic accountant, so unfortunately, she travels a lot, which makes it difficult to get together sometimes. Gradually, Melanie took on enough life to satisfy the majority and, except for special social events that she couldn't attend because she was out of town or at her own function, the questions slowed."

I laughed suddenly, startling Melanie. She was concentrating, probably thinking it all through as I talked. Not good. There would be growing concerns.

"There were times I was tempted to pay someone to attend functions with me. A couple of times may have done it to reduce the speculation, but that was too complicated. It would require that I school someone in who Melanie was and expect that person to adjust to the complexities of supposedly knowing me intimately and remembering that her own name for the night was supposed to be Melanie.

"There was no way I was doing that. As it turned out, the nosy among us were satisfied with the persona I'd gradually presented over time. And by then, she was almost real to me."

"My God, Michael, how terrible to have locked your life up like that," Melanie said.

She had been quiet for some time as I spewed out my pitiful tale for her. I looked at her now, and her face was incredulous as she drew slightly away from me.

"What did that woman do to you to make you turn to relationships that would never grow, never open to real love, maybe even marriage again? What did she do?" she asked again.

Her insight into me was frightening, causing me to reflect on things long put away. Melanie had enough training as a nurse and had the insight and experience to believe something traumatic and dark was the foundation of my behavior. I don't know what kind of response I had expected, but it wasn't this.

I drew into myself more.

"Oh, my God, you're doing it still," she said. "With me." She buried her face in my chest, her head shaking, no doubt trying to work it out. Trying to work out the truth I had turned away from long ago.

Lifting her head to look at me, she said, "I have to know. We have to talk about this. What did she do to you?"

She was strong in her demand to know, to talk about it, and I wasn't prepared for that.

"Melanie, I'm not ready to talk about that part of my life with you."

"You have to. I have some responsibility here, too, and I care too much for you to let this go. It was your wife, wasn't it? She did something to you, hurt you. That's why you did what you did, to protect yourself. Do you realize that, Michael? Whatever she did, you've been protecting yourself ever since."

"Melanie, I . . ." She drew away as I reached for her.

"No, Michael, this is not one of my little have-to-know

curiosities. This is serious, and I'm concerned for you. Does Stephanie know? She does, doesn't she?"

"Yes. Now, slow down, honey. I'm not an axe murderer, and if I did protect myself, well, I didn't intend to hurt others."

"Of course, you didn't. You aren't a bad person. But I'm finally beginning to understand you, Michael, and this is important to us both.

"What does Stephanie say, now that you've broken up?"

She drove home the reality of intuition, coming too close and making me uncomfortable. I turned away and walked to the kitchen, but she was right with me, wrapping her arms around me, hugging me to her. "Honey, whatever it is, it's all right. You have to know by now that I'm here for you, that I love you."

I turned to her. "Maybe you won't when you hear what Stephanie says."

"No, I'll still love you, and I'm sure she does, too. You're a good man, Michael, special to me. Everyone has issues, baby."

I held her to me, not wanting her to look at me, uncomfortable, but I continued.

"Stephanie was sad that I was ending our relationship, but she was happy for me, too, when I told her about you. I hadn't been to bed with you yet at the time, but I still needed to tell her I'd met someone. You were significant to me, and so was she. I couldn't be with her anymore. She needed to understand why."

I paused for a moment, looking into Melanie's eyes, searching for something I couldn't define. Relief, maybe. "She asked me if you were married, and then everything changed. She told me I was punishing women, married women, that . . ." but I couldn't say any more.

I let her go then and moved to the sofa. There I leaned

back into the cushions, exhausted with the emotion of the whole conversation, wanting to crawl away somewhere, go to sleep, escape, die.

"Because of your first wife, that's why she said that, isn't it?" Melanie asked, interrupting my morbid desires. "She knows what happened between you, doesn't she?"

I gathered myself and turned to her. I was calm, maybe too calm. My senses had dulled.

"Melanie, that's enough for now. We all have demons. I'm not talking about this anymore. Soon maybe, but not now," I said firmly. "It's late, baby, we have to get you to another seminar tomorrow, and then we have the drive home."

I held out a hand to her, afraid that she wouldn't take it, but she did and let me lead her into the bedroom.

Chapter Twenty-Seven

I woke the way you should, to the smell of coffee. Slowly, I came to, groggy from a night of restlessness, floating on the energy promised in the aroma drifting to me. I felt for Melanie and bolted upright when she wasn't beside me. She was standing at the foot of the bed with two steaming mugs of coffee.

"Look what I have," she said, moving to my side of the bed.

"You scared me. I can't believe you got out of bed and made coffee without my waking up."

"Well, I did, and I think you needed the sleep. I was rough on you last night." She was smiling as she handed me a cup and sat beside me.

"Hold on a minute, let me get these pillows straight." I handed the cup back to her and propped up the pillows. Scrunching back into their cushioning softness, I reached for the cup, then her, helping her into the pillows beside me.

"Yeah, you were rough. Any problem making the coffee?" I asked, more to divert the subject than anything else.

She laughed. "No, this pot stops when it's done perking. I like the old percolator in the trailer and on Cay Tam better though."

"Me, too. We need to get back out on her soon."

"Okay. I have a long weekend coming up since I filled in for Andrea."

"You're kidding."

"Hey, I drive a hard bargain. She owes me."

"When?"

"Two weeks," she said. "Labor Day." Then she laughed. "Actually, we just close down for four days. You didn't really think I'd do that to Andrea did you?"

I sipped my coffee. "Yes, you'd do anything to get your way. Look at how you abused me last night."

"I'm sorry about pushing you. I really am."

"It's all right. I'm ready to talk about it. Just not now," I said, looking at the clock. "We have to get you to the seminar, then back to Jax."

She looked at me, looked into me actually, probably concerned that I wasn't really ready. "Are you sure?"

"Hey, we're good. Really," I said.

"Michael, maybe you should talk to someone else. I may not be the right one, but I know you need to talk."

"No. You're the one. You're it, baby, like it or not. It's not as bad as it seems, but for the first time, I agree. It has been an issue with me. No more married women. You're the last."

"Last *woman*," she said. Her voice was more reminiscent of a drill sergeant than my sweet Melanie. "No more women, ever again," she continued in the same manner. Then she softened back to her usual self. "There's no need. You have me."

I laughed as I pulled her to me.

"Yes," I said, "I have you."

Chapter Twenty-Eight

*T*im, my replacement in Millie's life, only lasted two years, but then along came William, and I guess it finally worked for her. She and William got married and actually stayed together. She called me once after their marriage, the only time I'd spoken to her since I went to Vietnam. I was surprised I recognized her voice.

Millie was awkward, and once I established that the boy was all right, she got to the point. Her new husband, William, wanted to adopt Robbie. That bit of reality struck me hard, and I realized I still harbored some hope of being more to my son. He was only ten then.

I asked how the boy felt about it. She said he liked that he and his mother wouldn't have different names. She set up a meeting at my request, and I flew out to Dallas to meet the boy with William at a playground. Robbie stayed by William's side the whole time. In the end, I decided the adoption was a good thing. I didn't like it, felt the failure, but too much time had passed, and Millie's influence had taken a toll.

It was the last time I ever saw my son. I shook my head at the old memory. Millie really had been a bitch about the whole thing.

***

Labor Day came and went. We weren't able to get together for the long weekend. Melanie's children decided to spend time with their mom then. I was happy for her, especially after my recent trip down memory lane regarding my own son. I should have done more about him.

Later, Melanie told me her kids were in and out of the house, seeing friends more than being with her, but that was life, too, and good.

We'd planned our sailing trip. She'd already scheduled the time off and told her family she'd be out of town with a couple of girlfriends. Three more weeks. Nothing was going to get in the way this time. Too much longer and there would be the chance of an early cold front moving south to interfere with our plans. We needed to go soon.

I asked her to come to the house when she could. As she turned into the driveway for the first time one afternoon, I waved her over to the garage where I stood talking to Nathan and Nan.

As Melanie pulled to a stop, I went to her door. "Hey, time to meet my friends."

I helped her out of the car, and she came into my arms. My lips went to hers naturally, and then I pulled her with me. She reached up and held onto one of her funky hats as I pulled her along to my friends. Introducing them was long overdue.

"Love the hat," I said over my shoulder.

She gave me that glorious smile.

"Nan, Nathan, I want you to meet Melanie," I said, releasing her hand.

"Melanie, this is Nan and Nathan, two of my best friends in the world." They beamed at her, Nan especially.

"I am so glad to meet you, honey," Nan said as she took Melanie's hand. "We were wondering if he was ever going to share you with us."

Melanie laughed. "I was wondering the same thing, especially since I know how important you are to him. It's good to finally meet you."

Nathan stepped up and took Melanie's other hand. "Do you like sweet tea, Melanie?"

"Well, yes, I do, Nathan."

"Come on then, we just made some."

We went upstairs to the garage apartment. Nan pulled Melanie along behind and took her straight to the rear balcony that overlooked the river.

"This is so beautiful," Melanie said. Then she was gushing. "I didn't realize this balcony was here." She moved around, looking out at the view as she did. "It's shielded by the oak. You can't really see it from the house or Michael's trailer."

"Yeah, Nathan planted that thing for privacy when I told him I was coming up for several months," I said. The oak was tremendous and at least a hundred years old.

Nathan made a face, some kind of bogus smile. "Michael, the funny man, ha, ha. He's funny, ain't he?" Then he smiled a real smile as he went up to Melanie and handed her a glass of tea. "Here you go. Best tea around." Then he turned to me. "You can get your own, funny man."

Nan ignored all this and smiled at Melanie, then at me.

"I'm going to pick up Hannah. I'll be right back," Nathan said, moving to the door.

"Hannah is coming over, too," Nan said.

I looked at Melanie, who was still gazing at the river.

"Good," I said with genuine pleasure. "Melanie gets to meet everyone today."

"We decided to have a barbeque, and you two are invited," Nathan said over his shoulder as he walked out.

I think Melanie made a hit with all of them. She was quiet as she felt her way but joined in more once comfortable. Nan stayed close to her all evening.

Early on, I noticed Nan looking at Melanie's ring finger. Nan had taken Melanie's hand and was looking into her eyes. I don't know what she saw then, but as we talked later that evening, she told me.

"She's delightful, Michael. I can see she's right for you, but she's got recent ring marks, honey."

Her face took on a pleading look. My heart jumped to my throat. Nan's approval meant so much to me.

"She's separated, Nan, has been for quite a while. I told you that. This just happened somehow, for both of us."

"I know, honey. We've been aware for a while now. But those rings haven't been off long. We just don't want to see you hurt."

"We're gonna be fine, my wonderful friend. Don't worry, okay?"

She smiled.

"All right," she said as I hugged her to me.

***

Melanie spent every bit of spare time that she could coming to the house and working alongside me. Early evenings we cooked together and made love before she had to go home. She began bringing flowers and small things to brighten up the trailer.

She left notes for me and started a shopping list so I could pick up things for our meals at the trailer. Somewhere on the list, there would always be a note, "Make love." I'd have to pause and smile in the store, wondering if anyone else had noticed the words as her list lay in the basket.

One afternoon, she shyly asked me if there was a place in the trailer where she could leave a few things. I cleared out a drawer in the bedroom and a space above the small closet.

She gradually filled them up until I said, "Hey, we're going to have to get a bigger place if you keep moving in."

"Okay," she said excitedly. Always, the energetic *okay.* "Let's move into the big house."

"I'm kidding."

But she wouldn't let it go now. "The smaller room on this side of the house is ready."

She was talking about the downstairs bedroom that we could see below a huge oak tree that faced the trailer. I'd left the damned light on somehow, amplifying everything in her favor.

"It just needs to be painted," she said, "and I'll do that. And the guest bathroom is working."

I loved her enthusiasm and the big smile. How could I say no?

"All right, we'll move in if you paint it." Warming to the idea as we talked through it, I told her we could go look for furniture, too.

Two days later, I pulled into the gates to find her car. No call. It wasn't a problem, just a change from the norm.

"Hi, honey. I'm home," I said as I opened the trailer door. She wasn't there. I put away the groceries and went looking. Only one thing I hadn't checked off the list, and I like to complete my lists. Sometimes I write a to-do list after the fact just so I can check everything off and throw it away. I smiled thinking about it. Gotta have that last checkmark. It was my favorite one.

I found her in the house. Nan and Hannah were there,

too, and all three of them had paint rollers and trays. The walls were going to be bright, a minty-green color, which reminded me of Melanie's sundresses or maybe a pair of her flip-flops. I liked them both.

They were laughing, having fun, so I backed out quietly and went to the other side of the house. No fun check mark today.

I was happy they were spending time together getting to know each other. They had been together before, all three of them, going shopping at a mall once, and I'd spotted Melanie's car at Hannah's one day as I got back from somewhere late in the afternoon. "Tea," she told me. At first, I was concerned Melanie would grill them about me, but she hadn't.

She came to the trailer after her tea with Hannah that day and found some flowers I'd brought for her along with a card. Her eyes became teary as she read it. She turned to me and held me tightly before putting it away in her drawer.

Turning back, she pulled me to her again. "I'll have to leave it here, honey. I can't bring it home."

I felt pangs of loss in that moment. I realized again, only more vividly this time, how contained our relationship was. She loved me, I knew, but love was not everything. Yet I had accepted the terms, rationalizing my behavior once more. Still, I had moments of bitterness.

I came to understand she was living two lives and intent on making them work. She wasn't oblivious to the pain it caused me, but she must have felt she could manage it okay. I had come to know that not to succeed wasn't within her, just as it wasn't in her for her marriage to fail. She would live the lie, complex as it was. It was several small things over time that clarified it all for me, but once I took note, everything was clear. And it scared me.

We were out dancing late one night. She looked stunning in a sexy black dress and heels, and I told her so. She did a slow turn, looking back over her shoulder as she did, and beamed with the attention my eyes gave her. *This dress is for you, only you,* that look told me.

There was more, and I was now attuned to it. Yes, she was intent on our life together being distinct and special. A CD that she had burned the night before, placed in my player, and turned on, saying, "This is our music." And "This necklace is for us," she said, referring to a cheap necklace I'd bought her at a flea market in St Augustine. Or "I only wear this perfume when I'm with you." Finally, I saw and remembered—she'd been a virgin for her husband, and she'd been one again for me.

She was a complex woman, keeping her two worlds apart, trying to find a way to exist in both. She was trying to fulfill the love with me that she wanted, needed, and felt while still holding onto the shadow of a lifetime's commitment to moral values and family responsibility. By nature, she was grounded in doing what she set out to do. But she was a hypocrite and a self-deceiver even as she bloomed for me.

Deep inside, I knew the end, but I fought it.

***

Thursday the weather was right, and we went sailing. I talked Captain Nemo into going with us so one of us could take the helm and the other could teach Melanie. Actually, I took the helm and Nemo did the teaching. I knew better than to try to teach anyone I was personally involved with. Nemo put her through it all, handling lines, trimming sail, coming about, jibing, heaving to, and more, all the basics. Even so, I was still intent on sending her to a sailing course so she could learn more.

She loved the way Cay Tam heeled over, almost putting the rail in the water as we came close to the wind before coming about on a different tack. She felt she was ready for the ocean and pressed me, telling me she had scheduled time off, and I promised to take her. Another week and we'd go.

Friday night, I decided to go over to Orlando's where Melanie and Val would be practicing their ballroom dancing. Maybe I could corrupt them with some pagan—or "sloppy" as Melanie's instructor called it—dancing later. After allowing Val to try to teach me the samba and then having Melanie lead me through a waltz, I insisted on relaxing with a drink until their practice time was over.

We stayed late and got in a lot of pagan dancing with me leading on the slow stuff. Then Melanie came home with me for some more pagan stuff. By then, I don't think either of us really cared who led.

Chapter Twenty-Nine

*L*ate to bed, early to rise. We both had things to do and time was running short. We needed to get to them. A quick breakfast, a long hug, a kiss, and we were both out the door and on our way.

I'd just gotten my mind wrapped around things when she called.

"I can't be with you today."

A call had just come in as she drove home. Her daughter was asking to spend the day with her.

"All right, things come up. Is everything okay?"

I had to ask. There was something in her voice, a little tremble, a catch. Something. Was she nervous? She'd been happy and upbeat thirty minutes before.

"Yes, I just wanted to be with you, and now I may be out of touch till tomorrow afternoon."

"It's your daughter, honey. Be with her when you can."

I turned back to the day I'd planned but couldn't concentrate. We were days away from being on board Cay Tam. Everything was working out for us to go away together for a few days. We'd be sailing to Cumberland Island, north of Jacksonville near the Florida-Georgia border. Finally, we would have four days together. Not a big deal to most folks, but we'd never had this kind of time together and I was excited at the prospect.

So, why did I feel so nervous?

***

She was back the next day. The bedroom she had painted was almost ready, and we picked out the furniture for it that afternoon. Nathan would take delivery while we were sailing, and soon we would spend our first night in the house.

"So, maybe I'll get a night or two by myself before you get back over," I said as she drove us away from the store.

Melanie's head snapped around to me at that. Her eyes quickly returned to the road ahead, but the look on her face told me I was in trouble.

"No way," she said. "You don't even have sheets for the bed, and I'm not bringing them over until I'm there."

"Hey, I'm a guy. I don't need no stinkin' sheets."

"Guess you don't have no stinkin' needs, either."

As I eased closer to her with a hand on her thigh, she looked over at me again. Her serious look and nod set me to laughing.

"Hmm, I guess I'll wait."

Later, we met with Nan and Nathan for dinner with Hannah joining us. This time it was at the trailer with me grilling steaks and potatoes for us pagans and Portobello mushrooms for Melanie. Except for occasional salmon, she was vegan. Black beans rounded out her meal over a large salad. The picnic table outside the trailer was overloaded.

The sweet potato crunch I brought out last prompted a squeal from Melanie that set everyone to laughing. Simple pleasures are best.

As we enjoyed each other and the meal, Melanie seemed to draw more and more into herself. I noticed her glancing at

Nathan and Nan a few times as they cuddled and kidded each other, then at Hannah as she talked about her late husband.

I don't know what Melanie saw, but I imagined she was seeing in Nathan and Nan what was missing in her own marriage. And as I listened to Hannah talk about her deceased husband, the thought amplified. It was obvious they had been a match: soul mates, lovers, and friends.

Later, Melanie called me as she was driving home. "Hey, baby, I'm turning into the driveway now."

"Sleep well, love. I still smell you here, your perfume. I love it, baby. I'll be wrapped around that pillow like it was you."

She laughed. "Good night, sweet prince, until the morrow."

"Hey, don't go all Nemo on me," I said with a chuckle.

"Actually, that was Ben," she corrected. "Good night, baby."

Chapter Thirty

She arrived at the marina late after working all day and was tired. We would be together the next few days, just the two of us, on Cay Tam.

I already had all but two lines removed and stowed, along with the power cables and water hose. After we got her bags on board, I moved her car off the pier to the parking area and returned to the boat. We worked together as before and eased away from the dock with daylight fading fast. Once everything was under control with Melanie at the helm, I went below, then reached a hand through the hatch and wiggled a bottle of Merlot before poking my head out.

She lit up when she saw the wine. "You must be a mind reader. I'm ready for some refreshment after this week."

I came up to the cockpit and poured two glasses before relieving her at the helm. She kissed me on the cheek, then leaned back into the cushions and sipped her drink. I was taking in the river and the navigation lights that were just coming on to mark the channel. The GPS clearly marked everything, including the navigation lights and depth. It was warm and calm, but the air was dry. The breeze we made gliding through the water provided some welcome coolness.

"Look, look," she said, pointing just above the horizon. I turned to see a crescent moon emerging behind trees on the shoreline. "Beautiful, isn't it?"

She moved closer beside me even as she continued to look behind us at the moon. Then she was between the wheel and me with her cheek resting on my shoulder.

We went a little past the Buckman Bridge for the night, easing Cay Tam well outside the navigable channel close to the Rudder Club and dropped the hook. Tugboats that passed through frequently would stay well away from us. Very little other traffic would be out on the river at night.

It was full dark as we prepared dinner. Publix had again supplied us with sushi, and Melanie prepared the wasabi sauce as I set the compact cockpit table with chopsticks, napkins, and more wine. We ate in silence, enjoying the evening, absorbing the feel of the water around us, getting used to new sounds. The wine soon proved too much for her, so we made an early night of it. It was wonderful being in each other's arms, drifting to sleep with the gentle sound of water lapping against the hull.

Awaking early, I tenderly caressed her body until she woke and turned into my arms.

"I love this, Michael. Listen to the water on the hull. Water music." She pulled me on top of her. We moved together naturally, making love slowly, until the need for each other overtook us once again.

***

The ocean was still several hours away, and the current wouldn't be with us fully until we approached downtown Jacksonville. Due to the tides and opening times of the bridge, we were moving early, before daylight. There was little river traffic at that hour and we made good time, clearing the Main Street Bridge a full half hour before it shut down for rush hour.

Just before we rounded the last bend in the river, I brought up the mainsail and trimmed it tight fore and aft amidships. We still had a couple of miles to go before we started through the mounded rock jetties that formed the breakwater into the inlet.

I waited, and finally Melanie turned to me, her eyes wide. "Is that the ocean I feel?"

The ocean had been with us for a short time now, gently pulsing as it rose and fell against the river beneath us.

"Close your eyes and feel it," I said.

She did for a few moments before her eyes snapped open. "I can't. I have the wheel."

I stood behind her and took the helm, holding her captive between my arms. She swayed against me provocatively, then released the wheel and swayed with the ocean swells. "It's building," she said with her eyes closed. "I can hear it now." She opened her eyes as we rounded the last turn to find the inlet in front of us. "It's magnificent, Michael. Alive."

"It is alive, honey. All life springs from it. And it's ours for the next couple of days."

I watched her, feeling what she was feeling. As we drew closer, the swells increased to long, slow rollers several seconds apart. The current was running hard with us, and we surfed through the jetties towards the sea. She squealed with delight at the discovery of it, the life of it as the waves built, rising and gently surging, so different from the flow of the river, the ocean ever powerful even on a calm day. As we rose and fell with the surf, she cried out again, "Look! Look how green it is! This is so beautiful."

She looked around more, surveying the ocean surrounding us before whipping off her top, bringing her sweet breasts out into the light, free and wonderfully innocent. Little goose bumps rose across her breasts with the fresh coolness upon them. Her nipples reached for the sun. I held the wheel with my knee and released my hands to cup her breasts in my palms, slowly rolling the nipples with my fingers. I loved the hardness they immediately took on. It was another good moment. I punched on the autopilot as I pulled off my shirt so I could feel her against me. As I turned her towards me, her eyes pulled me in, telling me how special this was for her.

Abruptly, she pulled away and went below, her eyes beginning to tear. I don't think she wanted me to see, but I did. Soon she came back topside. She stood behind me, pressing her naked breasts into my back, her arms around me. I turned and held her, feeling her breasts against my chest for a moment before I went on deck.

She took the helm as I pulled out the headsail. Then she brought us on course to the next inlet. For once, the wind was from a direction that let us sail to our destination.

We trimmed sail on the new heading, and I had just cut the engine when Melanie squealed again with excitement. "I love that sound!" she said to the exquisite silence of just the wind and ocean and us moving effortlessly through the water.

Then that damn ring came through the open hatch from below, the one that meant voicemail. Hers. We hadn't heard the ring above the noise of the engine running. There was a message, and I could see something in her eyes, just a flicker. I thought it might be embarrassment. She was going to answer it.

"I guess I need to check it. Sorry, honey, I should have turned it off. Just too tired last night, I guess." She went below to retrieve the phone.

She came back up, listening to the message, and I could see in her face that she had to return the call. She leaned back into the cockpit cushions and continued to listen.

"I'll go see about something to eat while you tend to your messages," I said as I pulled on a pair of shorts after stripping off the workout pants I'd started the morning in.

"I need to return this one." Her eyes were pleading.

I leaned down and kissed her.

Checking the autopilot, I moved to the hatch, hoping there was nothing seriously wrong, worried for her but sure it was the husband again. He wasn't going to let us have this time together after all. "The autopilot will hold it. I'll be below."

Returning ten minutes later, I entered the cockpit quietly and found her still on the phone. I eased back below, closing the hatch as she looked down at me. It was the husband.

I leaned back into the cushions in the salon, thinking. She had told me about their conversation the previous Saturday. She was honest, telling me that she hated lying to me by telling me her daughter had wanted to spend the day with her when it was really her husband, and she was bound to see him. She just didn't know how to tell me at the time. Then, she went on to talk about what he'd said and how he'd brought things up, questioning her, interrogating her actually. They had dinner and talked again Monday. I hadn't questioned her, just listened as she worked through her marriage.

I knew then the husband knew about me. Not me, personally, but that she was involved. He sensed the nature of things between her and another man, and now, with this phone call, I knew more. What I couldn't figure out was why, if he thought something was going on, didn't he do something more to stop this weekend? Maybe he'd planned this call for now.

I'd know more soon, but for sure, I knew something already at that moment. I was losing her, and a quiet calmness came over me. *Never again, damn it, never again.* Married, separated, recently divorced? Never! No more women filled with the baggage of a recent relationship.

I needed to get away and not on Cay Tam. Melanie was too much a part of the boat now. She was everywhere. The scent of her, her perfume, the one she had discovered after we met—the perfume she wore only for me. A bottle of it was in the forward head. A pair of socks she'd left behind waited in the aft cabin. What else? Oh, yes, a couple of notes I'd come across, notes that she'd scribbled on one of the pads I kept here and in the trailer. Then she'd placed them in a location on the boat where I would eventually find them. I had fanned the pad on the table before she arrived the previous night and found two still in the binder. What else was there of her here or in the trailer? Serious as it all was to me, I couldn't help smiling. They were small things, but they were of her, signs of my importance to her and so damn meaningful to me. The essence of her was everywhere around me.

I went quietly to the hatch and listened a moment. She was still talking, so I went forward and sat in the salon again.

Melanie didn't know that I'd had Jamie checked out when I realized how deeply involved I was. My attorney in Orlando made some calls and gave me a recommendation for a discreet investigator. She was good. Within days, she discovered Melanie's husband was all but living with another woman.

That was enough for me, so I called off the investigation. But by then the investigator had informed me that Jamie was in the club one of the nights Melanie and I were dancing. It had to be the night his new interest in her emerged.

I would never tell Melanie any of this, but I wasn't ashamed. I'd been determined to leave her at the time if her husband was deserving of her. He wasn't. Regardless, I had no right being where I was or interfering with her marriage. I had to let her work through it without my influencing her decision.

The call lasted almost half an hour. We were doomed.

The hatch opened, and she smiled down at me. "Hey, you're missing a beautiful day."

Up I went, and she was there for me, looking into my eyes, pulling me to her.

"It's all right," she said, her words muffled by my shoulder. "He talked a lot, but in the end it was just to ask me to see him next Saturday."

She said it all too casually. I could feel a new apprehension in her, and it was spreading to me.

* * *

We got that day of sailing in, then had the night together. She was bare breasted, wearing only a sexy sarong around her hips the entire day. As we turned into the wind and brought the sails down, she stayed at the helm.

Just as we motored into St. Marys inlet, a sportfisherman came roaring up behind us and passed on the port side. An air horn blared, and we turned to see three guys hugging the starboard side of their vessel, yelling something and waving.

Melanie raised a hand to wave as the big smile on her face abruptly turned to horror. "Oh, my God! I don't have my top on!" she yelled. I laughed as she scurried below.

Such innocence. I loved it. I hoped she never lost it. I was feeling up again, positive. Maybe I'd throw her damn phone overboard when she wasn't looking.

We grilled out that night, anchored near Cumberland Island. Two other boats were already there, and we kept our distance for privacy. When I brought out the rather large, raw ribeye, she made a face. "Yuck, did you just kill that?"

I put it on the grill to her horror and went back below. I raised a large overflowing salad bowl through the hatch and got a "nice" from her. When I came back up with a couple of Portobello mushrooms dripping from the marinade, she drooled.

We split the grill and cooked.

"Don't expect this all the time," I warned her. "I'm a meat eater."

"I knew that from your pagan dancing."

Then she smiled and offered me a slice of the Portobello. It was juicy and delicious.

"Hmm, good. I did a good job marinating that thing, didn't I?"

She laughed and closed her eyes as she took a bite of mushroom. Her long neck extended, and her head fell gently back as she savored it. "Sooo good, and it has protein, too."

I took another bite of steak and admired her naked breasts. She couldn't resist losing the clothes once we were away from other eyes again. Her nipples were hard, and I saw a little shiver. The sea breeze had picked up, and it was getting cool.

"Brrr," she said with another shiver.

"I'll get you something to put on," I said

"Please."

I ducked below and came back topside with one of my blue cotton button-up shirts.

"Nemo shirt," she said.

Cap'n Nemo had an endless supply of faded blue shirts he always wore. If you didn't know him, you'd think he never changed clothes.

I laughed as I held the shirt open for her and she eased

into it. Then I caressed her hard nipples with the palms of my hands again. "These don't need to go away so fast."

She smiled, and we sat there with our drinks, talking quietly. The moon rose behind the island, casting a soft glow over the water. We watched all but the anchor lights go out in the other two boats, and Melanie thought it was late. It wasn't. It was just life on the water. Early to bed, early to rise. It had been a long day for sure.

We made love in the cockpit, slowly, allowing waves of pleasure to build and wash over us. She held onto the wheel while I stood behind and pushed into her with slow, forceful circles of my hips. I nibbled her neck and ears, almost drowning in the delight of her scent and feel of her body.

Then, I reached around and found her sensitive nub and felt her go with a rush of breath. "Oh, baby!" she cried out, letting it all out this time, not holding back as I stroked with my fingers and thrust slowly with my hips. I was with her then, thrusting harder as she rode through the pleasure.

Something bolted from my throat as raw ecstasy overtook me. I don't know what I said. I was only aware of pounding with my hips, slapping her buttocks as she held onto the wheel. On some level I knew I was claiming her, taking her, and punishing her husband for being between me and my woman. My disgust for him and love for her merged into a terrible dance of love, hate, and punishment that scared me.

Still, I held on, holding her to me, one hand on a hip, the other on the opposite shoulder as I drove into her. I pulled her to me with uncontrolled urgency, my thrusts frantically pushing her away as my hands pulled her back for more. She held the wheel tightly, leaning against it, pushing back to me.

"Come for me baby, come for me," she cried out. And I did, pulse after pulse draining me as I held onto her.

Finally, still holding onto the wheel, she turned her head towards me, giggling. "Hey, gone to sleep back there?"

It had been a long day, an emotional one for sure, and my woman had just claimed all that energy. I eased us back onto the cushion behind the helm, still one with her but going soft. My head returned to that sweet resting spot on her shoulder.

A little later, she stirred me. "Come to bed, Samson. Come on, baby." And she guided me below as she might have a child.

I remember curving around her, pulling her against me as she spoke soft words I could feel but couldn't touch.

***

The next morning, Melanie checked her messages. She listened to one message, then another as she glanced at me and worked the buttons on her phone. She gave me an odd look. There was more.

"Michael, I'm sorry," she said, coming to me and wrapping her arms around me. I remained silent.

"Something is wrong, very wrong. There are more messages to listen to, and then I need to make a call."

"It's him, of course?"

"Yes," she said and went below.

"Damn it," I said quietly, then got busy. In a flash, I knew she would be going to him. He was up to something. Jamie didn't call her twice a month sometimes, and now it's several times in two days. Yes, something was going on.

Why, damn it? Why?

But I knew why. Of course, I did. He was scared to death she was with another man, and he couldn't stand it. The asshole moved out and was almost living with another woman, but when he saw Melanie with me, saw something between us, something in him must have snapped. No, he didn't like it, and I knew Melanie. She would go to him.

I got busy on deck, quietly moving about, preparing to get under way. My mind immediately jumped to solving the logistics of getting her back. It provided diversion from the reality, kept me from going mad.

When she came back up almost an hour later, I was emotionally prepared—or thought I was. Cay Tam was ready to go once we pulled anchor. I knew she had to go to him. I could see that even before she started apologizing for taking so long.

Her husband had lost control. Mister Selfish had wanted some space. Told Melanie they needed to revitalize their marriage that way and promised more quality time together. None of it happened, and now he sensed losing her. Now he was interested.

"He's not used to my not answering his calls or returning them right away. He thinks I'm having an affair."

"You are."

"I know, honey. I know, but, well . . . He's been talking to an old friend who just went through a nasty divorce." She turned away from me then, just slightly, but my heart sank.

"He's been up all night going through our financial things and checking my cell phone records."

I could only listen helplessly. It was hard for her, but I couldn't help.

"He's seen the record of calls between us, the 407 area code. I guess we talk a lot," she said with a weak smile. "I'm sorry, honey. I never thought about the cell phone, never thought he'd care enough to check. It just never occurred to me. I have to go to him, sort this out."

"Okay," I said as calmly as I could.

"Tomorrow. I told him I'd be there tomorrow. He wanted

to come to Orlando, but I told him I was with my girlfriends and not to embarrass me."

"Call him back. Leave today. We'll only be miserable if you don't."

"No, no," she said. She came to me and held me tightly. "We need this time together, and I'm not leaving until we decide when we can be together again."

I held her for a moment more. Her heart beat as rapidly as my own, each of us caught up in our own personal turmoil at the turn of events. Gently, I backed away.

"Melanie, take the helm, please, and start the engine. Let's get the anchor up, and then we'll talk about it."

"Okay," she said, suddenly smiling. Her enthusiasm took me off balance for a moment before I realized we were not thinking the same thing.

She was revitalized, thinking we were going sailing again. I took the helm and headed for the marina in the city of Fernandina Beach.

"Michael?"

I turned to find confusion in her eyes and gathered her to me. "It's no good, honey. He'll just keep calling."

She started crying and sat down. "I don't care. I'll turn the phone off. Please, don't do this."

I had made two calls in the hour she was below. A rental car would be waiting for us, and the marina was ready to take our lines and tie Cay Tam to their main dock for the rest of the day. It was less than a two-hour drive from there back to her car.

She cried much of the way to Fools Cove until I finally pulled over in a rest area. I held her, talking to her softly, and told her it would be all right, that I understood her need to go.

We drove back the rest of the way in silence. There just

wasn't anything else to say. I was empty inside.

As we approached her car, she turned to me. "Michael, I want to see you tomorrow. I'll call as soon as I can."

I put her luggage in the trunk and helped her into the car, buckling her belt for her.

"Keep this for us. I bought it for you, for us tonight," she said, handing me a small package. "I love you, Michael. You know that, and you love me. We'll work this out."

It was too much for me, my emotions barely contained. All the time I was thinking how I loved this woman. More than that, I needed her. She was part of me now, but I knew I couldn't compete with her husband over basic values she'd held for a lifetime.

I held her shoulders briefly. "I'm going. You'll be all right now."

The look on her face killed me, a look imploring me to understand, that she would work through this. But I knew it was over, that she would yield to his promise of things being different. He'd apologize for not spending more time with her in the past and tell her he now knew how much he loved her. Right now, his ego was hurting. Selfish bastard.

I leaned through the window and gave her a kiss, then walked to the rental car.

As I drove back to Fernandina, pent-up emotion washed over me. I had continually denied the reality I knew to be true. The reality of her commitment to marriage, the influence of tradition and pride to stay together until death do they part. Blessed by the church and bound to it though her heart and soul remained with me. *Come on, God. You can do better than that!*

I couldn't blame her. I'd known better but didn't have

the moral courage to walk away. I'd been powerless to do that even though I did make a few token tries. *"Go home, Mrs. Langstrom. Go home to your husband."* It hadn't worked then, but it would now.

It was never about her leaving him. No, he would have to leave her, and he wouldn't, especially now. Not when he thought someone else prized her, wanted her. Now she had attained the rightful place of all marriage partners, above all others, where she should have been all along. Where she had put him until he'd made her vulnerable—and I showed up.

Now he wanted her, but for the wrong reasons, and was reduced to shameless begging to get his way. I reflected sarcastically on what poor Jamie might be saying. *Oh, how could you do this to me, Melanie, after all the sacrifices I've made for us? Don't I give you everything you want? Think about how the kids are going to feel about this. Think of your parents, our friends.*

"Bullshit!" I said aloud, shocking myself as I finally got angry with the self-serving son of a bitch. Angry with her, too, for buying into the short-term emotional fix he was prepared to make. It was all about him, and if she would stop and think, she would see that.

Back on Cay Tam, a dockhand threw me the lines, and I was once more under way. It was early afternoon with plenty of light left, but I was emotionally beat. I went to anchor near the inlet, staging for an early start well before dawn the next morning. Once I got out to the ocean, it was only about eighteen nautical miles to Mayport, the entrance of the St. Johns River. I kept busy organizing for the long day ahead, which kept my mind away from the reality I'd soon have to face.

The moon was waning; a smaller crescent would be

breaking the horizon later that night. It would provide enough light to make my way out of the inlet before the sun broke the horizon. The weather forecast was for good wind and mostly sunny skies. And the tide was right.

Why was God so good to me in some ways and so . . . I laughed out loud at my ridiculousness. "God gets the credit and blame for everything." Saying it out loud reminded me of how easy it was to blame God for my foolishness. I had a lot of penance to do.

I could make good time, especially since I should be able to ride the tide into the St. Johns River at Mayport. That should carry me through downtown Jax, so I might even make the marina early enough to tie up before dark. Maybe.

Hours later, I settled in with a Dewar's in the cockpit. It was just growing dark. The leftover steak sat on a platter in the galley. One bite had been enough, just like this one drink would be enough, maybe even too much tonight. There was nothing more to do but wait on sleep and a call from Melanie.

Two hours later, when neither came, I took one of those aspirin PM pills to help me sleep. It helped, but I still had a miserable night.

***

I brought the anchor in around five the next morning. It was still dark, but the moon lit the way through the inlet with the GPS keeping me on track. The tide was at ebb, and an hour later, Cay Tam and I were making good time. As miserable as I was, it was good to feel the wind and water working together, taking me home. I closed my eyes to relish the sensation of physical harmony and found myself riding a winged dragon, Cay Tam carrying me back to—what?

Later in the morning, she called.

"Things have settled down, but he's still very upset. He's gone through our bank accounts and charge cards to see if anything would show up."

I really didn't give a shit about him by then.

"So, he had a rough couple of days," I said.

She skipped right through my sarcasm. "Yes, he did, and I still don't know what caused this except he has that friend who recently got divorced."

"What about my phone calls?"

"I told him you were a friend from the gym who was working up here for a while."

Well, what did I expect? There's no loyalty when you get involved in a domestic issue. Hey, the sex was good, I told myself, feeling like shit.

"Maybe you should have just admitted you were seeing me." I was done, angry at it all, tired of the games, and tired of denial.

There was a long pause, and I could tell she was struggling over my words. She hadn't seen this side of me, and I let it out. I'd always been patient, understanding. It was time she knew my pain.

"Michael, I know you're hurting. I am, too. Please understand just a little longer. I only have a few minutes, honey. He's just gone to the store for something. I need to see you, feel your arms around me."

"So, he spent the night?"

"Yes, but . . ."

"Forget I said that."

"I . . . I . . . Where are you?"

"On Cay Tam, just approaching the St. Johns Inlet."

"You know I want to be with you, sharing that. I loved

being on the ocean with you."

"I did, too, baby. Maybe we can do it another time." I knew there'd never be another time but said it anyhow, the way we frail humans do.

"I'll call you tomorrow," she said, then hung up.

I turned off my phone. *"I only have a few minutes, honey. He's just gone to the store for something. I need to see you, feel your arms around me . . ."*

Her words rang in my head as I sailed towards Jacksonville. The words said it all. All was right in the Langstrom household today because Jamie had been placated once more and, surely, God was happy.

Melanie had subordinated herself to him and probably fucked him, too. Maybe I should have asked her that straight out. I regretted the thought immediately. Yes, all was right in the world for Jamie. The shit husband wins.

Suddenly, the energy drained out of me. I was tired. To hell with all this. I was weary of it and angry that I couldn't release it. Damn, this must be what it's like to be bipolar, joy and distress in the extreme.

I needed a damn pill or a shot or something. I couldn't keep going this way, and neither could poor Melanie. I only confused the issue for her.

Chapter Thirty-One

*D*istracted as I was, Cay Tam and I were one, working together and making good time. The tide whisked us into the inlet aided by only the headsail. Normally, I would take real joy in the feel of the big genoa pulling the boat through the water at hull speed. Today, I was just getting her to the dock as soon as possible. I made decisions along with some phone calls. Arrangements had to be made.

A fast six hours after entering the inlet, I tied the lines to the dock at Fools Cove with the aid of Cap'n Nemo and a newcomer whose name I can't remember. I knew I would have to answer some questions with Nemo, but I was comfortable with that. I thanked Nemo's helper, and the guy walked on down the pier.

"Are you okay, Michael?" Nemo asked. He'd seen me drive in with Melanie the day before, and now I was returning without her.

"He wants her back it seems, so I brought her home."

Nemo studied me, not saying another word, and I continued.

"Breaking my heart, Cap'n, but that's the way it is."

"Did you give her a choice?"

The question pissed me off. He didn't relent under my gaze.

"Not really, but she was coming back today to see him anyhow. It would have been a miserable time for both of us if

I'd let her stay. He's fucking with her head."

Nemo nodded. "Go away, Michael. Just go away. We'll take care of Cay Tam. You and that girl belong together. I saw it immediately, but just go away a while. Let it all work itself out. It will if it's right, and I believe it is. Put it behind you for now. Don't do or say anything you're going to regret. Just tell her you're going away, and do it."

"Thanks, Nemo."

"Michael, go be somebody else for a while. It can be nice actually. Hell, be Mick for once. That's it, just be Mick again for a time."

I walked to the truck and stood there a moment, then looked over at my friend. "Love ya, Nemo."

To my surprise, I laughed. *Yeah, I'll go be Mick for a while. Let Michael dwell on this pain.*

With a glance over my shoulder and a wave to Nemo, I drove away.

***

Hannah was one of the people I'd called on the way back with Cay Tam; the other was Joe, the carpenter. He was meeting me at the house the next afternoon. He was surprised at my request that he take over coordinating the last of the work on the house for me, but we had come to a tentative agreement. He would schedule and coordinate the rest of the work. His approval would be required before Hannah signed any checks. We'd work out the details the next day.

Hannah always took care of my travel. I had asked her to book me on a flight to Italy and make reservations for a couple of nights at a little hotel I knew of in Montecatini Terme, a little town I'd discovered and liked in the foothills between Florence and Pisa.

Pisa.

"For how many, Michael? I may need more information."

"Just one, Hannah, just me. Make it for a week, please."

Just me.

"You don't sound right. Is everything all right?"

May as well get it out of the way. Like Nan and Nathan, Hannah knew me too well. I couldn't brush her off or avoid telling her the truth. Besides, I didn't want to; she was too important to me. And she could set the stage with Nathan and Nan. I'd made my decision. They all needed to know. "I'm all right, Hannah, but it's not working out with Melanie. I need to get away for a while."

"I'm sorry, honey. I don't know what to say. I . . ."

"Don't, Hannah. It's all right. Everything will be fine."

I told her I would explain everything to them in the morning. I could tell she hung up the phone reluctantly. She hadn't intruded but was concerned, and I knew she would already be on the phone to Nan by now. All the better. They would be prepared for something, but what could I tell them beyond what I'd already said to Hannah?

They were my friends—not just Christmas-card acquaintances but real friends, family, damn it, and I would be truthful with them. I just needed some space and hoped they would understand. Nemo was right about that.

Now, as I drove away from the marina, Hannah called back. She had me on an early morning flight two days from now. She hadn't asked any more questions, but when it came to making the reservations, she hadn't rushed it, either. Plenty of time for me to talk or change my mind, I guess. I should have been on a plane the next night at the latest. Women! She thought she was looking out for me. She wasn't.

I needed to leave now.

Chapter Thirty-Two

*I*t was late, and I'd had a long day sailing with too little
sleep but decided to stop at Harvey's for a drink. I needed
one now before crawling into bed. I went in and sat at the bar.
It was a quiet night, and I realized it was Sunday.

"Hi, Michael. Haven't seen you in a while," Becky said from
the other end of the bar.

"Hi, Becky."

She brought a Dewar's and splash of water over ice.

"What's up? Anything special going on?"

"All is great, Becky. In fact, I'm going to Europe for a
while."

"Are you really?" She paused, and I was aware of it but
just wanted to have a drink and leave. If she wanted to say
something, she would.

"Where are you going?"

"Italy." I took a sip of my drink and looked around. "Hey,
where's Jigger tonight? I've never been here when she wasn't
around."

"Funny you should ask," she said with a big smile. "She left
for Europe Friday. Gonna be there a couple of weeks."

A moment later it sank in. "That's great, glad they did it.
Maybe I'll run into them. Where are they?"

"Italy. You should get in touch."

I laughed. "That's easier said than done. I'll need more

information than that. Do you know the city and maybe hotel or even the travel agency they might have used?"

"How about a phone number?" she said with the lift of an eyebrow.

"Well, sure."

I must have looked confused. Becky giggled.

"Sorry," she said, "just having fun. Jigger had her cell activated for over there so she can check in on me."

"So, you're in charge, the responsible one."

"Of course. You know Jigger is just a figurehead around here. I do everything." She sighed and gently collapsed her head on the bar. "Ev – re – thing," she slowly drew out. Theatrics over, she lifted her head and smiled, and I laughed until she joined in. I needed this release. I was glad I'd stopped in.

She handed me one of Jigger's cards with her cell phone number on it. "Those numbers penciled in are for calling from the States. I don't know how you do it from there."

"I can figure it out." I pushed my glass towards her. "One more for the road, Becky."

As she took my glass, I thought I'd call for sure. It would be good to see Jigger and her husband. Maybe spend a little time sightseeing with them. "Becky, I'm embarrassed to ask, but what is Jigger's husband's name? I've never met him."

Her frown held me as she gave a small shake to her head. "I thought you knew. His name was Drew. He passed away a couple of years ago."

It took a moment for that to get to my frazzled brain. Dead? I couldn't even picture the man.

"No," I said, "I didn't know. I'm mostly in Orlando. Sorry, Becky, I didn't know."

My time next to Jigger on the treadmill came back to me. Martinis and how she liked them, my telling her to have her husband make her one and . . . No wonder she'd looked saddened by my recommendation. Damn.

"It was hard on her," Becky said. "They'd been married since they were teens. And they loved each other, Michael. You know how it is when you see a long-time married couple married for fifty years and you can see how close and in love they still are."

I nodded.

"Well, that was them, except they only got thirty years together instead of fifty."

"I didn't know." For the first time in days, I couldn't feel sorry for myself. I put money on the bar and told Becky goodnight. I didn't want the other drink anymore. "I'll call her."

"She'd like that. Say hello to her for me, and tell her I said to have a good time."

"I will."

"Michael," she said, stopping me. I turned back as she came around the end of the bar and pulled me aside. "Maybe I shouldn't say this but . . . she likes you."

I searched her for meaning and saw panic overcome her face. "She'd kill me if she knew I told you that."

Why couldn't I just grieve for Jigger? Why did I have to know this other information? *She likes you.* "I'll just call and say hello then."

"That may be best," Becky said. "She's my friend, Michael. I wasn't thinking clearly when I told you the other."

"She's safe with me, Becky. We'll let Jigger work through life the best way she sees fit."

"Thank you, Michael."

***

I tossed in bed for half an hour that night before I got up

and pulled on shorts and a pullover shirt. Stepping outside, I slipped into my old boat shoes. Too much was going on in my mind to sleep. I sat in one of the chairs under the awning. The air was cooler, summer was over, and the night air felt good. The sky was clear with just a trace of moon showing, an even smaller crescent now. I love crescent moons.

I pulled my chair from under the awning and another one close to put my feet up. Relaxed, I turned my eyes to the sliver of moon.

I let myself go where I hadn't before, to reality, and I was cruel to both Melanie and me. There was a selfishness about Melanie she wasn't aware of. Ultimately, our relationship was messing up three lives, maybe more, but definitely three. She and her husband weren't committed to one another except in a selfish, material sense. There was no oneness of real love, yet they had each opened themselves to it with another with no real commitment there, either.

Of course, they weren't committed to each other, and I knew her husband had been seeing someone else. How could either of them be satisfied to live such a superficial relationship, continuing to grow in different directions that involved others?

I couldn't understand it, especially how they could selfishly use someone outside the marriage without getting divorced. Because with Melanie, it had to be about love, not sex. She loved me. I knew that, and only the breach in her marriage allowed the weakness of awareness and attraction to let me in. But it was love that allowed us to grow to sex. The sex was good but incidental. Only love allowed it. With her husband, the sex was incidental to the vows of marriage, expected. They were selfishly destroying others, me anyhow, destroying others' abilities to find true commitment with someone else, someone who might fill their lives with constant and true love. But, of course, I was no innocent here, and the acceptance of that hung over me.

I was the pot calling the kettle black, and I knew everything went back to my wife, Millie. Maybe she'd thought she was in love back then, too, like Melanie and I were now. I don't know how long I sat there with that realization, but as I came back from some deep, dark place of long ago, I knew I had been wrong for decades. I had been the problem all along, not Millie.

I looked back at me and questioned who was using whom. I'd always felt I was using them, the married and separated women I became involved with, but it was for companionship and sex, not love, in my mind. I'd been selfish, too, rationalizing that I was consoling them, being there for them while they sorted out their lives. Champion of the forlorn? Maybe, but ridiculous. I was a user, nothing more. Could they have found that lifetime relationship had I not been involved with them? I didn't know, but I knew I had used them. I had always known. Was I punishing them? Were Stephanie and Melanie right about that, too?

Could I be monogamous with Melanie? Of course, I could. I felt that strongly about her, I told myself, even as I realized my thoughts and emotions were rambling dangerously. Love without commitment was what I had while Jamie had commitment without love—or at least, without passionate, all-consuming love. I should have been happy with that, I told myself, but I didn't mean it. I wanted all of it.

Remember that you only live the good times, I told myself. *You don't have the day-to-day responsibilities.*

There's an important distinction between having an affair and being in love versus the reality of a day-to-day marital relationship. I recognized that distinction even though I'd never had the long marriage, one that could change over the years, could allow people to grow apart. So, how could I judge?

How do some do it? Melanie's folks had; Nathan and Nan had; Hannah and her husband, and Jigger and hers. It wasn't unheard of, and it sounded wonderful to me. Could I have been happy with Melanie? Yes!

Why couldn't we just let it be the way it was? I drifted again, remembering her hair tickling my nose, smelling her perfume and shampoo. Perfume and shampoo brought out only when we were to be together, holding herself special for me even in that small way.

How could I be so selfish and mean in my thoughts of her now? I knew better. She was always about commitment. It even existed in the complexity of the unconscious separation of the two lives she was living. Which one was real? I was sure it was the one we shared, but it didn't matter.

I went inside and made a drink, a strong scotch, then stepped back outside. Nathan and Nan's place was dark now. They'd been up earlier, probably waiting for me to get home after a call from Hannah. I smiled at that. Yes, Hannah would have called them after getting off the phone with me that afternoon. They would be worried.

I stood looking at the moon for a minute, remembering how beautiful Melanie thought it was, then sat back down. I propped my feet up and drifted, floating on the night air, sipping my drink.

Alone with only the drink and the moon, emotions overtook me. I felt sorry for myself, then angry at others, but finally I had to face reality, and I suppose that's what it's all about. The responsibility came then, and I hate responsibility, but you're always accountable to someone—ultimately, yourself.

I'd gone down the same path for years, but this time I'd embraced that which could not be. I hadn't been seduced; I'd surrendered and wholeheartedly opened myself for the first time in years to another. I still clung to my own protection, but Melanie was in me now, a part of me, just as essential as any vital organ in my body.

Yes, I saw it clearly: I was in need. I needed her. Not just wanted her, damn it, but needed her like I needed my own heart.

This love stuff sucked. Reality was a bitch. I didn't like it, didn't want it, and wished it to go away. If I could have torn it from my body, I would have.

The pain and sadness enveloped me and took me down, way down with the absolute realization that I couldn't have her. Oh, yes, I'd already accepted it many times over but not for real. I'd still been in the "let's pretend" world.

Sex is easy, but I was finding love to be hard and unfamiliar. And damn it, love hurts. Never before had I known anything like the heights of joy I'd found with the woman I now knew I was in love with. And after falling hard and fast for her, I'd now leapt from those heights in an act of hopeless chivalry and feared I might never achieve them again. With anyone.

Chivalry? Or was I just slipping into a protective suit of armor again?

I had told Melanie before that the relationship was ultimately up to me, that as long as I could reconcile the realities, we would be fine. She would listen patiently and not respond, just sit quietly until I finished my indirect ultimatum. I was a gray-area person, despised the absoluteness of black-and-white mentalities, but this was more than simple gray.

I felt she was determined to have it all her way, and I was angry about that. I wanted all of her, absolutely, black and white, mine. *"We can make this work, Michael. We can. We love each other."* The words kept coming back to me.

She was wrong. We couldn't make it work. I'd always be second best to the lie of her marriage though she would forever deny it. I was the outside man. I was nothing in the end, the equivalent of a mistress, expendable when it came to the deeper roots of sharing children, religion, and parents who had been married for over half a century.

My heart beat wildly as my mind raced. Thoughts ran together as resentment, anger, and self-pity reduced me.

She could move on, a difficult situation reconciled through the newfound interest of the husband scrambling to make things right. Doting on the woman he now saw with new eyes, the eyes of another. One who found her to be all those things her husband had failed to see. Or probably had just forgotten.

My eyes—the bastard loved her through *my* eyes.

I was disgusted with myself for being so easily discarded. *"I told him you were a friend from the gym, working up here for a while."* I don't know what I expected, but that clearly said I was unimportant. I thought I was more, much more to her. But was I when it counted? She was there for him, not for me.

It all came rushing back again. Stephanie was right. I still had old issues, but who was punishing whom? Seems I was the one getting hurt.

"Sorry, that number has been disconnected. Do you want to try another?" Well, fuck no. That one hurt. No, I don't want to try another, thank you.

If only the outside man had the ability to step away from the real involvement and look on this relationship as a positive thing, like a counselor, then he could realize some satisfaction.

I mean, what the hell? The pussy was good. Be happy you had that for a while. But, damn it, if it was just about sex, it would be easy, wouldn't it?

I hated being a part of this age-old story of the mistress being repeated in the outside man. Same old story, except he wasn't left with any financial compensation. So much for equality. Stupid thought, ridiculous, yet I rambled on.

I was mixed up, not making any sense to myself anymore. I just knew Melanie had chosen her husband over me. Or had she? I didn't know because I hadn't had the strength to open the emails she'd sent me or listen to the voicemails she'd left. I couldn't bring myself to erase them, either, but I was afraid to find out I was right. I couldn't take it again. This way, I was in control. It worked.

Finally, I made my way back to bed. Checking the time, I was surprised to see it was after three in the morning. I had to get some sleep, so I took one of those damn PM pills again. Just one, but it must have been enough with the emotional drain and lack of sleep I'd had the last two nights.

Love hurts, but sleep helps. At least until you wake up again.

Chapter Thirty-Three

I woke to pounding on the trailer door and Nathan's voice calling me. "Michael, are you all right?" More pounding. "Michael! Michael, are you there?"

The voice brought me around quickly. Nathan never got excited, but his voice was filled with alarm. I was sluggish with the long night of emotion and the sleeping pill, but I still bolted to the door.

"I'm all right, Nathan. What's wrong?"

"You're wrong. What's going on?"

"I'm okay, Nathan, really. What's wrong?"

"It's after noon, Michael, and you're not all right, damn it."

I gave him a blank stare.

"And," he added in an even gruffer voice, "you look like hell."

"Hey, watch your language." Somehow, I managed to smile, and it seemed to bring him relief. I felt better that the only thing wrong was me.

"Sorry, Michael," he said a little sheepishly. Then he launched all of his worry on me again before telling me, "You've got one hour to clean up and get up to the apartment. Don't make me come back and get you. Nan and Hannah are worried sick about you. I'm mad with you for worrying them. It's not like you."

I smiled at him again. "I'm sorry, Nathan. I apologize. I took a sleeping pill when I couldn't get to sleep. Tell them things are all right. I'll be up as soon as I clean up some."

"Are you sure?"

"Yes. I'll be up shortly."

"We'll get some breakfast going for you," he said. "Then we talk."

I needed to get a handle on it. I'd never seen Nathan so concerned or adamant. Time to put my big-boy pants on and get back to being me again.

I put a pot of coffee on, stumbling and bumping into everything that was so familiar to me that normally I just naturally ducked going through the low doorways of the trailer. Not this time, and my head hurt enough without the new bump. Somehow, I managed to make it into the tiny bathroom for a shower. I was still exhausted from everything, including the pills I'd taken two nights in a row. I wasn't used to them.

Refreshed as I came out of the shower, I had a cup of coffee and organized my thoughts. Finally, I checked the phone and found several messages from Melanie, all asking me to call and to please leave a message if she couldn't answer.

If she couldn't answer. That said all I needed to know. I found the same thing in her emails and with more details. She was trying to explain everything to me and asked me to understand a little longer. After looking at the most recent one, I quit. No sense in reading the rest.

I couldn't stall any longer. Waiting for me were people I cared about and who cared about me. I walked up to the apartment to talk to my family. I tried to explain everything, but they still seemed a little bewildered and unsure of things. They wanted to talk. I didn't.

"I love her. She's a good woman," I said. "She should be with her husband."

Nan was shaking her head. "Do you men think we women

don't talk? Michael! How dare you make it so simple! It's not that easy a thing for either of you." She looked at the other two.

Nathan didn't say anything. Smart man. I was stoic.

"You shouldn't make rash decisions, Michael. It's too important," Hannah said. "Go away, but don't decide anything. You're just trying to escape the pain of it. Melanie's going through her own hell, too."

I looked up at that. She'd struck a nerve, and I didn't want to hear it. Hannah held her ground, her face determined and challenging.

"Hannah's right," Nan said. Nathan backed them both up.

"Okay, then, it's settled." I smiled as I stood and gave them each a hug. "She is going through a lot. Thank you. See you in a few weeks."

They stood there, mutely. Nathan wanted to take me to the airport. I told him no and went to the door. Then I turned back.

"I want you all to know that I've been living with a problem since my wife left me years ago. That's what all of this is about. Not Melanie, not the two of us, it's me. I never should have been with her, never should have disrupted her life. You all know that. I'm just finally facing it. What you don't know is that, in some way, I've been punishing other women for my wife's abandoning me years ago. Stephanie knew it. She told me so, and now Melanie has, too. They're right. I'm going to get myself straight."

***

Two days before, when I took Melanie to her car, I knew how it would end. God, was that just two days ago? I shook my head in disbelief. It seemed so long ago when we'd last held each other.

The crisis for me ended when I left Nathan, Nan, and

Hannah upstairs. My therapy had just begun. Accepting the right path, finally, was only the beginning of pain. A terrible journey lay ahead, and I wasn't sure I was prepared for it.

I thought of drug addicts and alcoholics, about the misery one goes through in kicking a habit and the aftermath of sustaining one's self. It's a joyous thing, intending to move down the path to righteousness. It's another to do it.

Melanie wasn't a habit; she was everything. I was thankful for how she had enriched me, made my heart and soul soar with the wonder of her and of us. We were magic, but I couldn't bear not having all of her. In that way, I was selfish. Maybe I could have chosen to continue leading two separate lives, but she'd shown me what I could be with a soul mate, and I no longer wanted to compromise. For the first time in decades, I was ready to open my life to someone, to allow someone in. I wanted to share life. I wanted a partner, but more than anything, I needed to heal, and part of that healing lay in Pisa. Hardly the most romantic of places, but that's where the overwhelming need to share my life had sprung up. Venice would still have to wait.

I thought of what I could offer Melanie. There was nothing, at least not materially, for she didn't want for anything. She had money, security, a wonderful home and family. Everything! Except the husband, who might get it right now. Then there were the parents who formed the model of her being, a model that she could not break or diminish. The only thing I could offer her was protection, protection from the exposure of us, our relationship, to her family, the protection and trust of someone who loved her. One more email was necessary to tell her that and that I admired the values that had brought her to the struggle she was now going through.

I punched out the email. It was short and encouraging.

But I couldn't hit the send button. Instead I reached for my phone and made a reservation at an airport hotel. Then I called a cab and asked for a pickup in two hours. It would take me that long to pack a bag and settle the trailer for a couple of weeks.

A little before the two hours ended, I had everything ready. I just needed to pack the computer. Picking it up, I reread my message to Melanie. I started to delete it but hit send instead.

With that done I packed the computer in its own case and swung it to my shoulder as I picked up my bag. Minutes later I stood in the late afternoon sun, just outside a back gate that was mostly concealed in the bamboo stand. The bamboo stalks were still now, barely a breeze stirring the air. I stood there waiting, trying to suppress some crazy emotional shit about Hannah driving around the corner catching me sneaking out of my own property. Her house was around the corner of the street I was on. She would drive that way upon leaving Nathan and Nan's if she hadn't already. Ten minutes later my ride pulled up.

**

Checking with the airline, I discovered the early flight Hannah had booked for me was not due to start boarding before ten the next morning. I knew I had to eat, so it was bar food at the hotel with a strong scotch.

Two drinks were enough. I settled into my room and let the last few days drain from me. I didn't want to relive it all another hundred times. I felt good for the first time in a long while. I had finally made the right decisions.

And that was the essence of what I had told her in that last email. That I loved her and that she would always be special. That we were special and that no matter how bad a day, she had sanctuary, a place to go inside herself to feel loved and nurtured. That we had existed for a time, and that I had truly loved her.

***

I was floating with dragonflies again, enjoying the peace of discovery as we moved among each other. New views came alive before us as we climbed and dove amid life in a sun-speckled forest.

Something from far away drew me back to silence around me. I was so at peace, wanting to return to the dragonflies. Daylight filtered through a seam in the heavy curtains that covered the hotel-room window.

There was a quiet knock at my door as a piece of paper was slipped underneath. I yawned. How long had it been since I'd had a good night's sleep?

I walked over to pick up the paper. The bill, I supposed. As I picked it up, an envelope remained on the carpet. I picked it up and turned it over.

Montecatini Terme. Do not open before.

I was disoriented for a moment. Then I felt a smile coming as my heart beat crazily. After all those love notes, Melanie's handwriting was now touching me again.

Maybe Venice would be on my itinerary after all.

About the Author

Ran Register retired early and went sailing. Stuck at anchor during frequent winter fronts moving through the Caribbean, he began to dabble with writing. Porch People, his debut novel that introduces The Outside Man's main character, was born in the Turks and Caicos Islands. Now married, he and his wife live in coastal Florida where he continues to write.